The Longer Bodies

A Mrs. Bradley mystery by
Gladys Mitchell

Rue Morgue Press
Lyons / Boulder

First published in Great Britain in 1930
First U.S. Edition 2009

Copyright 1930 © by the Executors of the Estate of Gladys Mitchell
New Material Copyright © 2009 by The Rue Morgue Press

978-1-60187-034-6

Rue Morgue Press
87 Lone Tree Lane
Lyons CO 80540
www.ruemorguepress.com

Printed by Johnson Printing
Boulder, Colorado

PRINTED IN THE UNITED STATES OF AMERICA

The Longer Bodies

CHAPTER I

Vagaries of a Rich Relation

I

Great-aunt Puddequet was reputed to be enormously wealthy. It was also a tradition in the family that she was extraordinarily mean.

"The only thing she seems inclined to give away without stint," said her nephew Godfrey on his wedding day, "is unasked-for advice."

He eyed her wedding present, the plated silver teapot and cream jug to match, with unaffected disgust. The unstinted advice she had seen fit to bestow upon him on this important occasion had been a solemn recommendation to marry Money instead of his chosen bride, the meek and gentle Elizabeth Tully, daughter of a country clergyman and a nursery governess in her own right, and Godfrey had replied briefly and suitably to the suggestion. For three years aunt and nephew neither met nor corresponded.

"And now," Godfrey remarked to the unassuming Elizabeth three days after the birth of their first child, "it's up to us to buck things up all round. The old girl shan't have the satisfaction of seeing my son grow up a poor man. She says she's sending him a christening mug."

There is nothing more conducive to success than a definite aim. By the time his fourth child, also a boy, was of an age to attend a preparatory school, Godfrey Yeomond was a prosperous man.

It took Matilda Puddequet exactly thirty-two years to forget the cause of her quarrel with her nephew. At the end of that time she summoned her paid companion, an angular, romantically minded, unmarried woman who had spent twelve years of self-abnegation in the old lady's service, and observed, without preamble of any kind:

"Companion Caddick, I am growing old."

"Yes, Mrs. Puddequet?" replied Miss Caddick hopefully. She had read in the paper only the day before of a housekeeper-companion to an aged gentlewoman who had been left a fortune of fifteen thousand pounds on the de-

mise of her employer, and Miss Caddick, who was of a mathematical turn of mind, had put down, in the form of a proportion sum at the back of her diary, her own hopes and expectations, thus:

> "Housekeeper-companion receives £15,000 out of net personalty of £161,512 after ten years" continuous service. Companion-secretary receives £x out of net personalty of £y after twelve years" (minus three days for Cousin Aggie's funeral) continuous service, taking gross fortune of employer to be £500,000.
> "N.B.—Or it might be a little more."

She had worked out the answer by using various approximate amounts in the place of £y, and had then found the average of the results. The sum of twenty-five thousand pounds, which evolved from these complicated proceedings, frightened her, so she scribbled all over it to hide it from view.

"Just in case ..." she murmured to herself, thinking of eyes other than her own which might read the astounding answer to the sum.

Like a murderer who has hidden the corpse in the wardrobe, however, she knew that it was there. Twenty-five thousand pounds! Twenty-five thousand!

Old Mrs. Puddequet regarded her companion-secretary with suspicion. She was a very old lady, parrot-beaked, shrill-voiced, and imperious.

"What do you mean by agreeing with me in that tone?" she squealed. "Why did I quarrel with Godfrey?"

Immediately and intelligently perceiving that if any possible beneficiary was in her employer's mind it was one of the several relatives whose names were so seldom mentioned in the house, Miss Caddick relinquished her dreams of the twenty-five thousand pounds, screwed up her pale eyes, wrinkled her pointed nose, and adopted an expression of agonized mental stress. She had learned by experience that it did not pay to remember things which her employer had forgotten; therefore, after a period of facial contortion lasting perhaps fifteen seconds, she shook her severely neat head, pursed her thin lips, frowned again in stern concentration of thought, and finally shook her head again.

"I am really very much afraid, Mrs. Puddequet—" she began.

"You're a fool, Companion Caddick," squealed old Mrs. Puddequet viciously. "Order the bathchair, and send for the cook."

The cook was Scottish, unafraid of her employer, strong, capable, and a woman of one remark which she produced, apparently from the pit of her stomach, on all domestic occasions. It was short, and to the point, and consisted of the words, "I'll see masel' drooned first." She came into old Mrs. Puddequet's room on receipt of the summons from Miss Caddick, gazed dourly on her employer, and listened in scornful silence whilst Great-aunt

Puddequet outlined the meals for the day. Then she spoke.

"Is it the hash ye'll hae for lunch? I'll see masel' drooned first!"

"And why cannot we have the hash for lunch?" screamed old Mrs. Puddequet, who, by a daily encounter with this redoubtable foe, had kept herself alive and healthy for the past ten years.

"And why will ye no be hae'ing the hash? Forbye, ye puir body, there'll no be mair than a quatter o' a poond o' the beef remaining since Mr. Timon was feeding his beasties wi' it the morn."

"Oh," squealed Great-aunt Puddequet, "he was, was he? Well, cook, suggest something yourself, and don't be a fool!"

"Ou, ay!" retorted Mrs. Macbrae. "Is it me to be daeing your wark for ye? I'll see masel' drooned first! Cook the guid meat I will, but fash aboot thinkin' it oot I winna! Ye ken me. *I'm* no' the leddy o' the hoose!"

"Promptly at one you will send a well-cooked, well-served lunch to table, and no more nonsense!" squealed Great-aunt Puddequet, "and I don't care whether you see yourself drowned or not!"

The cook went away, and old Mrs. Puddequet turned again to Miss Caddick. The passage-at-arms had restored her good humor. She lowered her cracked old voice and spoke kindly.

"You will find Godfrey Yeomond's address at the back of my bureau," she said. "Write to him, Companion, and say that I am going to visit him on Thursday. I want to have a look at his children."

Godfrey Yeomond guffawed when he read the letter.

"She wants to see the children before she dies," pronounced his wife. "Poor thing. I expect she's very lonely and unhappy right out there in the country. Write back quickly, dear, and tell her how very welcome she is."

"I'd better tip the boys the wink to be civil to her," said Godfrey, pursuing a different train of thought. "Her money's got to be left somewhere, and she was never one to be fond of cats."

He paused.

"I don't see why she shouldn't take a fancy to the boys or Priscilla," he went on. "They're nice kids though I say it. But, of course, there are the Brown-Jenkins lot and the Cowes, besides that Anthony family she married into. I'll drop the boys a hint to mind where they put their feet while she's here. They'll have their work cut out to be civil, though, if she's the same vinegar-tongued old hag she used to be."

Although Godfrey Yeomond's affairs were in a flourishing condition, he suffered occasional twinges of conscience at the thought that, because of some bitter remarks made thirty years before, his children's chances of inheriting Great-aunt Puddequet's thousands were extremely slender. He spent considerable thought, therefore, on the remarks he proposed making to his

family on the subject of their aged relative's visit, and decided on the Sentimental Appeal as being best suited to their youth and mentality.

At dinner on the Wednesday evening preceding Great-aunt Puddequet's
arrival in their midst, he brought off a neat speech.

"The First P.M. was in form tonight," said Francis Yeomond later to his
brother Malpas.

"Yes, deuced good," replied Malpas, critically examining his cigar. "I suppose he gets these at wholesale prices?" he added, lighting it cautiously.

"I wonder how long she'll stay?" said Priscilla Yeomond. "Shall we have
to push the bathchair?"

"The P.M. says she can get about without it," said Hilary, the youngest
boy.

"I shall arrange to get my leave canceled if it proves too fierce," said Malpas. "Old lady's a bit of a pussy."

"I'm taking ten boys to Switzerland on the eighteenth, thank God," said
Francis, the second son.

"I shall write to old Shoesmith to ask me over to his place if I can't stick it
here," said Hilary.

"You're a beastly selfish lot," said Priscilla hotly. "Poor old lady!"

"Poor old you, you mean," said Hilary, with brotherly candor, "to be left
holding the baby while we push off. Cheer up, duckie, and Frank will send
you some picture postcards, won't you, brother?"

"Understand," said Priscilla, eyeing them steadily, "that, if you do slink
off, I let her know why. And you know it's her cash the P.M.'s after. So
there!"

"But, my *dear* kid—" said three scandalized male voices in chorus.

Great-aunt Puddequet, however, proved a good deal less trying than they
had expected. For one thing, as the sensitive nineteen-year-old Hilary expressed it, she looked all right when you took her out. She certainly had a
pretty awful voice, they agreed, but fortunately considered London air bad
for her throat. Parentally forewarned, the Yeomonds walked delicately. They
endured even classical concerts without audible protest; they accompanied
their great-aunt to the two or three London theaters which were showing
pieces suitable to her age and experience, and on the second Saturday of her
stay they escorted her to the White City ground to witness an international
athletics match between Sweden and England. She had seen it advertised on
the station platforms, had asked about it, and had demanded that she should
be taken to see it.

"Companion Caddick won't want to go," she added.

The newly released Caddick, therefore, on the appointed day, with beating
heart and secret ecstasy, stole away from the high, plain-fronted Georgian
house to the nearest fare-stage for the buses. Armed with her spectacles and

a packet of bulls'-eyes, she set off for the unknown. She was out to bag her first talkie. Her pale eyes glittered with a new light. She grasped the bulls'-eyes firmly.

"But why can't they?" demanded old Mrs. Puddequet.

Her grandnephew Hilary surveyed the White City ground resignedly from a front seat in the center stand. Having lost all the field events to the United States athletes in June, the English hopes were as consistently losing them to the Swedish athletes in August. Amsterdam had told the same tale; South Africa had testified to its truth. England might point to her hurdlers, her sprinters, and her long-distance men with equanimity and even pride, but at the jumps, the vault, the shot, the discus, the javelin—where, oh, where was she?

"Down among the dead men." The military band on the left supplied a ready if somewhat tactless answer.

Hilary Yeomond sighed.

"It's the public schools," he said briefly.

"But I thought, Grandnephew, that the public schools—" His great-aunt's tones were piercing. She had heard much in praise of the public schools.

"Oh, rot!" Francis Yeomond—watching, through field-glasses, the super-human efforts of a yellow-thatched child of twenty or so to break the record for the ground over the pole vault—spoke peevishly.

"It's nothing to do with the schools. Can't train *kids* to do the pole vault and put the weight."

As junior languages master at one of the schools in question, and the chosen first string of his college (beaten) in the hundred yards at the University sports, he spoke as one having authority.

"Of course you can train them." Malpas Yeomond leaned back and clapped his hands perfunctorily as the yellow-haired Swede, amid vociferous applause, cleared the bar and fell gracefully to earth on the farther side of it.

"It's the style does it," he continued to the old lady. "Style and constant practice. You needn't let boys try for great height at first over the pole vault, and you needn't let them use a twelve-pound shot for the put until they've sufficient bodily development—but you can get correct style, and you can make them practice regularly."

"Piffle," said Francis concisely.

Malpas shrugged his shoulders, consulted his program, and made feverish hieroglyphics with a gold pencil as the megaphone boomed out the order of running in the last race.

"We shall take this all right," he announced confidently. "Better represented than the Swedes. Their Amsterdam winner isn't here, and that chap who always turns out in horn-rimmed glasses—what's the fellow's name?—I saw him in Paris last year—"

"By Jove! There's a fellow with a trowel digging down to Australia!" said a boy; and from farther off a rough, good-humored voice shouted loudly:

"Hi! Give it up, boy! The Test's over!"

A burst of hearty laughter greeted the sally. The young Swede finished digging the holes for his starting position, and then looked up and waved his trowel happily at the broadly grinning crowd. It is doubtful whether he had caught the words or understood their application, but there was no mistaking the genuine good-fellowship of the waves of laughter.

"On your marks!" The red-coated starter was raising the gun.

"Get set!" The two runners raised the back knee from the track and leaned forward with the weight of their bodies resting on the front foot and the hands. Steadily they gazed at the surface of the track ahead of them.

The pistol cracked sharply, and they were off.

"There you are, you see, Aunt." Malpas Yeomond turned to the old lady as the first man home breasted the flimsy tape. "England wins. We can run all right, but, all the same, we've lost the match. Look, Aunt. They took the shot, the discus, and the two jumps. We haven't a chap on the ground today who can touch twenty-four feet for the long jump. Another two inches on our aggregate total would have given us the high jump, but we couldn't produce them. Then there's the pole vault—a perfect gift to them. And we lost the first sprint event through poor changing of the baton. Still, on actual pace we were sound. No, it's the field events that do it—and they always *will* do it until something pretty drastic is done about training boys early enough for them. As long as men with a twenty-one-foot long jump or a six-foot high jump or a forty-foot shot, and chaps doing eleven-six over the pole vault, are in the championship class in England, our case is hopeless. By the way, we'd better shift. We're blocking the traffic by remaining here."

The drive home was short, and Great-aunt Puddequet spoke little. She sat in a corner of the big car, busy with sports program and Malpas's gold pencil. The brothers discussed the events one by one. Dinner followed almost immediately upon their return to the house, and, to the general amazement, for she was in the habit of retiring to rest at about nine o'clock after a very light repast, the old lady, resplendent with diamonds, was pushed in her bath-chair up to the dinner table. Clutched in her left hand was the program of events she had bought on the sports ground. She laid it beside her plate, and said not a word throughout the meal except to squeal venomously at Timkins the butler for offering her wine.

When the meal was drawing to its conclusion, she put down the apple she had begun to peel, and looked meaningly round the table.

"What did you tell me they call that plate thing they throw about the field, Grandnephew?" she demanded, looking at Hilary.

"The discus, Aunt," he returned, with a promptness which did credit to his

intelligence. "But England didn't—"

"I know they didn't. Do you know how to throw it, Grandnephew?"

"Well," replied Hilary cautiously, "I've seen it done, of course, and I know the theory of throwing it, but I've never actually had the thing in my hands."

"You could learn to do it." Mrs. Puddequet nodded her gray head decidedly, and disregarded her youngest nephew's dissenting voice.

"And what about you, Grandnephew?" she continued, turning her yellowish eyes upon Malpas Yeomond.

"High jump," said Priscilla, from the other side of the table. "Used to win it at his private school. He's ever so good at it."

"Oh, rot, Priscilla," said Malpas, grinning. "You're thinking of a chap called—er—called Smuggins."

"She is thinking of a chap called Yeomond, Grandnephew," screamed old Mrs. Puddequet furiously.

"Answering to the name of Malpas," said Francis solemnly. "He's a liar, Aunt. Take no notice of him. I saw him win it in about the year 1920. Did three-ten and a half at Tenby House School, with the matron and old Squarebags at the stands to see fair play. I always swear the matron shoved her end down two inches for him, but that's neither here nor there. He won. You know you did," he concluded, kicking his elder brother vigorously.

"And he did three feet—nearly four feet," said Great-aunt Puddequet thoughtfully. Her eyes brightened. "Very promising. And at the White City next year he will do nearly eight feet—or perhaps a little more."

"Eh?" said Godfrey Yeomond, startled. "But, my dear Aunt, the world's record figures for the high jump are—"

"Six eight and a half, pater," interpolated Hilary promptly. "H.M. Osborne of the United States holds the record, and it was clocked at Urbana in May 1924. Excuse me, Aunt. It's printed here, I believe."

He turned to the end of his great-aunt's program.

"Here we are."

"Well," screamed the old lady indomitably, "it's a very poor record, in my opinion!"

Her nephew and his sons gasped.

"Blasphemy," said Francis, under his breath, kicking Malpas with great joy.

"Do you mean to tell me," Great-aunt Puddequet went on in her raucous, cracked, high-pitched old voice, "that grown men cannot jump twice as high as a little boy of ten at a private school? Rubbish, Grandnephews! I don't know what the world's coming to nowadays!"

Malpas took up the cudgels.

"It isn't quite a case of jumping twice as high, Aunt. You see—"

"Take the force of gravity, for example," broke in Francis, trying, in spite

of his amusement, to do his bit towards clearing the great names of the world's champions from an undeserved slight.

"And the law of what-do-you-call-it," said Hilary helpfully.

"And, of course, the binomial theorem of radio-electricity," interpolated Priscilla, keeping both eyes fixed demurely on the tablecloth.

"You may all be silent," said Great-aunt Puddequet, with sudden decisiveness, "and listen to me. I am going home at the end of this week. Immediately I arrive I shall summon Queslake to draw up my will." She glanced around the table in order to observe the effect of her words. The assembled company gazed back at her. At the sight of their facial expressions, Priscilla was compelled to check a desire to giggle.

"To draw up my will," repeated Great-aunt Puddequet, staring deliberately at each of the family in turn. "The bulk of the property and almost the whole of my private fortune I intend to leave to one of my grandnephews."

She paused.

"Which one?" asked Francis, unable to think of anything adequate, but feeling that in order to retain the high dramatic tension something ought to be said by someone other than Great-aunt Puddequet herself.

Great-aunt Puddequet regarded the interrupter malevolently.

"The one who is first chosen to represent England in one of these field events you have all talked so much about," she said. "I ought to mention that the three girls—"

"Three?" enquired Hilary.

"Certainly. Your sister Priscilla, Celia Brown-Jenkins, and Amaris Cowes."

"Oh, Celia and Amaris, yes," said Malpas. "I seem to remember them vaguely. Celia was a pretty little kid, I believe, and Amaris rather a piece of frightfulness in looks. Glasses and things."

"Your creed appears simple, but is fundamentally sound, Grandnephew," retorted Great-aunt Puddequet tartly. "Perhaps I may be allowed to continue without interruption. The three girls will each receive one hundred pounds, irrespective of their attainments"—she glanced contemptuously at the mildly pretty and faded face of Elizabeth Yeomond, whose marriage to Godfrey she had strongly opposed, and which opposition, vitriolic in expression, had called forth an (at the time) unforgivable retort from the bridegroom-elect—"their manners"—she glanced at the averted face of Priscilla, who was laughing— "or their conduct." She shut her lips tightly together. They all knew that the reference to conduct had been called forth by the recollection of Amaris Cowes, who, at the age of twenty-two, had run from the Welwyn Garden City, where all is peace and joy and light, to sordid Bloomsbury. There, in defiance of the family minor prophets, including Great-aunt Puddequet herself, she continued to enjoy life among the artists in an altogether brazen, and, so far as her nearest and (presumably) dearest were concerned, an ex-

ceptionally irritating and successful manner.

"One hundred pounds?" said Priscilla, who had overcome her risible faculties by a strong effort. "That is very kind of you, Aunt. I shall buy——"

"Two new dinner frocks and a *thé dansant*," said her unregenerate brother Hilary, grinning behind his hand. "Cheer up, sister!" he added, *sotto voce.* "Mean old cat!"

His great-aunt regarded him with disfavor. Her hearing was inconveniently acute at times.

"Of course, should you find yourself heir to my property and fortune, Grand-nephew," she remarked, in a tone which indicated that she considered such an event extremely unlikely, "you will be at perfect liberty to give any or all of the inheritance to your sister. Far be it from me to comment upon your implicit generosity!"

Propelled by the stalwart Godfrey Yeomond, the bathchair containing the rich relation then left the dining room. Mrs. Yeomond, smiling her unvarying, faded smile, went after it.

The family dropped its jaw. Malpas spoke.

"Well, I'm damned!" said he. The others nodded gloomily.

"Senile dementia," said Francis, shaking his head. "Poor old girl."

"Of course, she can't be serious," said Hilary. "International champions! My God!"

Priscilla began to laugh again.

"Who's holding the baby now?" she enquired, with sisterly chivalry.

CHAPTER II

The Gathering of the Clan

I

MALPAS YEOMOND reread Great-aunt Puddequet's letter for the fourth time.

"She's certainly worked the thing out rather well," he said. "Me the high jump, Frank the long, H. the discus, her grandson chap the javelin, Brown-Jenkins the pole, and Cowes the weight."

"What do we do about it?" asked Hilary.

"Might as well go down there as she suggests, and find out what the idea is," said Francis. "The Brown-Jenkins people and the Cowes will go, I expect."

"I can't think what possessed Mary to marry a fellow with a name like Brown-Jenkins," said Godfrey Yeomond. The family were at dinner on the first Tuesday in April. He frowned into his wineglass. "Why on earth couldn't he have stuck like a man to the Jenkins, and left the Brown alone?"

The gentle Mrs. Yeomond, who was the only person present at table to take any particular notice of her husband's remarks, shook her head hopelessly.

"Or, of course, he could have dropped the Jenkins, and put an 'e' on the Brown, dear," she observed timidly.

"I wish, Pater, you'd write to both the relations and see what they're going to do about it," said Francis. "We really don't want to go down into Hampshire and sweat about and look fools if the Brown-Jenkins and the Cowes are not bothering."

"Ought to put the old girl in a home," muttered Malpas darkly.

"I believe I'll go and see them," said Godfrey, deciding at length that the port was nonpoisonous. "Always better to see people. I'll run down tomorrow. Far more satisfactory. They live less than twenty miles apart, and Jenkins's place is just over thirty from here, so I can manage them both on the same day I should think, if I don't hang about at either house too long."

"I suppose," said Malpas slowly, "that, if these other people fall for the damned silly scheme, we must have a stab at it too."

"Please yourself, my boy," said his father. "It's merely a question as to which branch of the family shall inherit about half a million pounds."

"I don't know that I hanker after the cash," said Francis thoughtfully. "It

isn't that. But I should hate to stand down in favor of Dick Cowes. Remember him as a fearful worm. Had the cheek at school to bend me over for six when he was head of the house. Beastly weed he was, too!"

"And the Brown-Jenkins tribe are bounders," said Hilary, in round, handsome terms. "After all, why shouldn't we have a cut? Jolly decent holiday down there. Take our motorbikes, and walk sometimes, and I dare say there would be some quite decent cricket if one knew where to look for it. Wonder how long we shall stay?"

"I shall come too," said Priscilla unexpectedly. "I shall be company for Great-aunt Puddequet. Besides, the Digots live quite near, and there will be some quite decent tennis on their courts. I was at school with Margaret Digot, and Rex Digot is ever such a nice kid."

"Yes, I should certainly go, if I were in your place," said Godfrey to his sons. "At the worst, you'll get plenty of fresh air and exercise. At the best— well, if your great-aunt *should* take a fancy to one of you!—Of course, the idea itself is absurd, but then, what are the old for, if not to impose their absurd ideas on the young?"

"The hon. member," said Priscilla wickedly, "then resumed his seat amid tumultuous applause."

II

"Look here," said Clive Brown-Jenkins with spirit, "when I say valve-rubber do I mean inner-tubing?"

"You should run about after yourself, then," said his sister Celia with finality. She stuck both hands into her jumper pockets and walked into the house.

Clive stood up and wiped a hand covered with lubricating oil across an already grease-stained countenance. He grunted discontentedly and spun the front wheel of his upturned bicycle. He was a big, squarely built boy of twenty, with an untidy thatch of hair and perpetually grease-stained hands. His father had put him into the office of his own works, but Clive was a born mechanic, and invariably looked like it. He was strong and hardy, and resembled a rough cob; his face was good humor itself when he smiled, but in repose it wore a determinedly bulldog expression and showed the hard line of an obstinate jaw. He had big hands and feet, big strong teeth, and appraising gray eyes. His was a fighter's face. He was continuously at loggerheads with his father, from whom he inherited his temperament, and each had a secret respect and affection for the other.

He put his hard hand down on the whizzing wheel and arrested its gyrations. Then he rubbed the ball of his strong, dirty thumb over a suspiciously rough place on the tire.

A moment later Celia reappeared.

"Do you mean this wormy-squirmy stuff?" she enquired, proffering a tin box.

"Thanks," grunted Clive. He worked away in silence for about twenty-five minutes. Celia stood and watched him.

"Going far tomorrow?" she asked at last.

Clive screwed the nozzle of the hand pump on to the top of the valve of the back wheel and pumped steadily for several seconds. When he had disconnected the pump and tested the tire with thumb and forefinger, he stood the bicycle upright against the side of the house and replied tersely:

"Brighton. Club test. By the way, did my white sweater get washed last week?"

"How should I know?" said Celia. "I don't look after your things. Better go and ask Mum. Anyway, the laundry hasn't come home this week yet, because I wanted my organdy frock for this afternoon, and I can't have it."

"Your sweater is quite clean and nicely aired, dear," said a woman's voice from inside the house. "I *never* send woolen garments to the laundry. They are really *too* bad with them. When do you want it?"

"Tomorrow at five in the morning," replied Clive. "Hang on; I'll come and get it now. I shall be back to dinner."

"Lunch, dear."

"Oh, all right, lunch."

"It will be ready by one-thirty, dear, so you won't be late, will you?"

Clive grunted and went into the house.

"Oh, there you are," said his father from the dining room. "Come here, I want you."

Clive followed his mother up the stairs, obtained possession of his sweater, put it neatly with the rest of his kit, stopped at the bathroom for a wash, and then went downstairs to his father.

Brown-Jenkins Senior lowered his stockinged feet from the arm of the settee to the carpet, and observed:

"Now, then. Are you going down into Hampshire, or aren't you?"

"No," replied Clive.

"Then you're a damned fool," said his father, picking up the newspaper. "Half a million. That's more than I've got to give you, by a damn sight. I've done damn well, but I 'aven't—haven't—done as well as that. Now don't be a B.F. Your Uncle Godfrey was here an hour ago. His boys are going down to Hampshire next week. What about it?"

"I shan't go," said Clive. "Cranky old girl!"

"Well, she is, but there's nothing cranky about her money, my lad, so don't you forget it. Thought you'd got your head screwed on tighter than that. Still, if you don't trouble about it, no more shall I. Get out."

Clive returned to his bicycle and Celia. His mother was standing there talking.

"But I don't think you are invited, dear," said Mary Brown-Jenkins. She was the feminine counterpart of Godfrey, her brother, but had worn not quite so well.

"I don't care whether I'm invited," said Celia. "If that Yeomond girl can go—and Uncle Godfrey said she had made up her mind about it—then I can go. Besides, you know what an awful ass Clive is when he's left to look after himself. And he *will* go in to meals with oily dirt under his nails if he isn't watched. The Yeomonds would get up and leave the table, and then what would you feel like?"

Clive's grunt behind them terminated that portion of the conversation.

"You needn't worry yourselves," said he coldly. "I'm not going."

"Not going?" cried Celia. "Oh, but you *must* go! Look what a chance it is for us to get to know some nice people. Priscilla Yeomond knows people down there and everything. Uncle said so. And if you don't go, Cliff, *I* can't. You might be a sport. Besides, think of the will! *I* wouldn't say no to all that money!"

"Now, look here, young Celia," said Clive, setting his jaw, "once and for all! If any of you people think that a cranky old girl of ninety is going to jockey me into turning myself into a monkey on a stick for the sake of her rotten cash, you're wrong! I'm not breaking my neck over that pole jump to please anybody, and if Dad thinks differently—"

"But, Clive, it isn't altogether the money. Think what a score for Uncle Godfrey if one of his boys got the house and property, and you didn't! He'd never get over it. You know how they look down on us because Dad started as a hand and worked his way up, and because I haven't been 'finished' and you haven't been educated at Oxford like the Yeomonds."

"Yes," said Clive, "that's all very well! And it's all very well for you to talk, young sis! Hang it all! Nobody's asking *you* to trot a great pole up to a bally hole and heave your beastly carcass over the moon on it! It's easy to talk! Let the Yeomonds do it, and I'll have a cut at the javelin or the discus, or even the weight. I bet I'd put it farther than that ass Dick Cowes."

"Well," said Celia, "there's no point in grousing. You might just as well have a try at it! After all, poor old lady, she's awfully old! And surely you can go in and knock spots off the Yeomonds! I mean, just look at your cycling! Club champion two years running! I bet the Yeomonds couldn't get to Brighton and back in seven hours! *Nor* win the gold medal on the track."

Clive grinned.

"Oh, well—" he said modestly.

"Oh, well, there it is, anyway," said Celia, with sisterly spirit. "And if you *did* beat them, you could afford to start the Club Cycle Stores instead of

mugging away at the office. Great-aunt Puddequet's money—"

Clive looked at his sister.

"There's something in that," he admitted, "but it's chewing a tough egg, old thing. Still, I don't mind going down to the house and seeing what's what. After all, we needn't stay there. And now—"

"There's a good boy," said his mother. "I knew you would like to please your father."

Clive turned and regarded her with deep distrust.

"Oh, so you're keen on it too, Mum, are you? What's the idea?" he said.

Mrs. Brown-Jenkins smiled, and walked into the house.

"She'd just hate Uncle Godfrey's boys to get something you couldn't," said Celia, in a low voice. "People of that age are awfully funny, you know."

III

Richard Cowes rang up his sister's studio.

Amaris Cowes, holding a piece of bread and treacle in her left hand, reached for the receiver with her right, and invited her brother to unburden his mind.

"Going to stay with Great-aunt Puddequet?" she repeated after him. "Well, I've no objection. Do they know at home? ... Oh, really? But why worry? You can't possibly do it can you? ... Yes, of course there is that. You don't think she'd care to sit for her portrait, do you? ... Oh, I don't know. Most old people are vain, I think ... Yes, I'll come down and see you if you like. All the best. ... What? Can't hear you. ... S.P.P.I.? What's that? Primitive impulses? I haven't any; and as for pandering to them! ... Good-bye."

IV

It was obvious that Great-aunt Puddequet had spent a great deal of money. More than ten thousand square yards of what had been rough pasturage less than a year before had been dug up, leveled, drained, and laid with turf. A fine sports ground with a splendid oval running-track four hundred and forty yards long; with a long-jump pit and cinder lane and permanent takeoff; with a recognized place for the high jump and another for the pole vault—these wonders had taken the place of a dank and marshy meadow which at one time had bordered Great-aunt Puddequet's domain. The piece of waste land had proved wide enough from east to west for the required purpose, but not sufficiently so from north to south, and Great-aunt Puddequet had furnished proof of her enthusiasm for the new scheme by sacrificing a stretch of beautiful garden to the needs of the athletics ground. Where her lawn had de-

scended in gentle undulation to the hawthorn hedge which had separated her property from the adjacent water-meadow, a small sunk garden was in process of completion, and a flight of a dozen stone steps, dividing the sunk garden into two equal parts, led down to a wooden door in a high brick wall which formed the barrier between the house and garden and the new sports field. This sunk garden, from being a hideous necessity about which she had screamed furiously every day to the patient and long-suffering Miss Caddick, had suddenly become the apple of Great-aunt Puddequet's eye. She herself designed its decorative effects, and an eminent firm of landscape gardeners was dealing with her instructions as tactfully as possible.

There were to be two round waterlily-goldfish ponds. There was to be crazy paving. There were to be alcoves, stone garden seats, statues of fauns and mermaids, and a seated stone figure of Poseidon. There were to be small, unexpected stone steps. There was to be a small maze. There was to be a sundial. …

The expert in sunk gardens smiled noncommittally and wrote copious notes.

So far the main flight of steps was completed, and two concrete basins, each of ten feet in diameter, one still covered modestly with a large tarpaulin, were the main indications that Great-aunt Puddequet's designs for the sunk garden were in process of being carried out. The statuary consisted of a stone mermaid with a very curly tail and a life-size, slightly ironic rendering of a Roman gladiator in bronze.

The hawthorn hedge, which had once upon a time divided the desert from the sown, had been removed. So had another which separated water-meadow the first from water-meadow the second—another stretch of unhappy land which sloped down to a sad-looking mere of considerable size, into which a slow-flowing, reedy stream meandered.

This second meadow Great-aunt Puddequet had also acquired for the use of the athletes. The mere had been deepened and cleaned out, and its sagging, oozy banks had been cunningly shored up. At one end a high diving-board had been erected. A low wooden shelter had been put up to accommodate those wishing to bathe. A clump or two of writhing thorn-trees and some scattered pollard willows gave melancholy attractiveness to an otherwise dispiriting scene.

Dinner was over, and Priscilla Yeomond, who, "as threatened"—Hilary's words—had accompanied her brothers on their journey to Great-aunt Puddequet's house, put on a wrap and came out on to the top of the stone steps for air. A peculiarity of all the downstairs rooms in Great-aunt Puddequet's house seemed to be an atmosphere of oppressive stuffiness. Entranced by the beauty of the evening and attracted by the unusual character of her surroundings, Priscilla, who entirely failed to recognize the environs of the house for those she had known from her father's descriptions and

stories, walked down the steps, through the wooden doorway, and on to the sports ground. She pursued her way upon the turf which bordered the cinder track for about fifty yards until she came to an open gate. She passed through this, and found herself facing one of the huts which old Mrs. Puddequet had caused to be erected for the housing of the athletes while they were in training.

A slight sound behind her caused her to look round. A light-haired, weedy young man in a flannel suit was standing in the gateway leading into the sports ground. It was Great-aunt Puddequet's adopted grandson, Timon Anthony.

"Go indoors! Go indoors!" he said urgently.

Priscilla gazed in amazement.

"I mean it," said the light-haired young man. "And get those brothers of yours back to London."

"I don't understand you," said Priscilla frigidly. "What do you mean?"

The young man waved his hand expressively.

"All this low-lying land is most unhealthy," he informed her. "All the infections that the sun sucks up from bogs, fens, flats—"

Priscilla laughed.

The young man shook his head at her. "I really don't think the night air here does anybody any good, so come along indoors," he said.

He took her by the left elbow and piloted her back by the way she had come. At the top of the stone steps he released her arm and walked away without a word.

"Well," said Priscilla, as she leaned on the balustrade and looked at his retreating figure.

At the bottom of the stone steps he turned and waved to her.

Priscilla knitted her brows. He seemed a queer boy, she thought. She wondered how much he liked the idea of a group of his patron's relatives coming along to wrest from him the inheritance he had been brought up to believe would be his own.

"It's jolly unfair of Great-aunt Puddequet," though Priscilla, as she stepped inside the great outer door of the house. "And he looks as though he's taking it very well."

She put a question to the old lady next day.

"Timon Anthony?" squealed Great-aunt Puddequet venomously. "No, Grandniece! No! The puppy wants to go on the stage! On the stage, I say! I won't leave him a penny-piece, and so I've told him!"

"But won't he have a chance of—of running and jumping with the other boys?" asked Priscilla, whose sense of fairness was up in arms.

"Run?" squealed Great-aunt Puddequet. "Yes, he can run from his creditors when he's run through his allowance! That's the amount of running he'll do!"

And she refused to hear or to say another word.

CHAPTER III

Rabbit and Javelin

I

"IT's a funny thing," said Joseph Herring meditatively. He went from hutch to hutch and counted again.

"There's three Belgian 'ares and two white Angoras—that's all right on that side. But them young Flemish Giants—blowed if I don't think there was three in each 'utch! But there's only two in 'ere."

He counted again to make certain, and then scratched his jaw.

"It's a bloomin' rum go, that is! I'll 'ave to see into it. The old girl won't 'arf say 'er prayers if she gets to know anythink about it being gorn."

II

It was the beautiful morning of Friday, April 18th, and the athletes had been in training for eleven days. As the day was so fine and warm, Great-aunt Puddequet, having emerged triumphant from her diurnal battle with the cook, signified her intention of going to watch the lads at practice on the sports field.

The first person she and her escort encountered was the trainer Kost, a fair-haired, stocky, determined-looking fellow, clean-shaven, blue-eyed, handsome in a clean, hard, Scandinavian fashion, and clad in flannel trousers and a heavy woolen sweater. He looked warm and angry, and was for the fifth day in succession engaged in initiating Clive Brown-Jenkins into the mysteries of the pole vault.

"And it's no use, perhaps, to be timid, Mr. Brown," he said contemptuously. "I can't instruct cowards. No."

Clive Brown-Jenkins dropped the pole on the ground, pulled his sweater over his head, dropped the garment beside the pole, and walked deliberately up to the trainer. His jaw was set hard, and his gray eyes gleamed.

"You can't instruct what?" he said, with a quiet but ugly pugnacity. Kost stared back at him.

"Fools, perhaps," he said, with a grin. "What's the matter with your temper, perhaps?"

Clive turned on his heel and picked up the pole again.

Great-aunt Puddequet nodded approvingly. The trainer was earning his pay. She gave the word, and her equipage rolled along the cinder track to the long-jump pitch.

"You want to jump higher," said Hilary Yeomond to his brother Francis as old Mrs. Puddequet came up behind them.

"Nonsense, Grandnephew!" she squealed. "He wants to jump a long way along, not a long way up!"

"Pardon me, Madam," said the voice of the trainer behind her, "but Mr. Yeomond there is quite right, perhaps."

He stepped in front of the bathchair, and quickly and neatly stretched a piece of white worsted across the long-jump pit between two four-feet high sticks which had apparently been placed there previously for the purpose.

"Now, Mr. Yeomond two," he said, stepping back a pace, "right over without breaking the thread, perhaps."

Francis paced the required distance, and commenced his run.

"Faster, faster! Lazy you are! Lazy!" yelled Kost, dancing in agony on the verdant pasture as Francis burst the flimsy wool and fell forward on to his face.

Francis picked himself up and smiled slightly.

"You must better go back and teach yourself to walk holding the seats of the chairs," said Kost unpleasantly. Francis's smile deepened. Unruffled, he paced out the number of strides again.

"What a difference," murmured the angular Miss Caddick to her employer, "from the attitude adopted by Mr. Brown-Jenkins."

"What?" said Great-aunt Puddequet, clicking her tongue, as, for the third time in succession, Richard Cowes lost control of the shot in making a spasmodic leap across the seven-foot putting-circle, and dropped the heavy weight with a dull thud almost on to his own foot. The eagle eye of the trainer chanced to fall on him.

"You are the animated clockwork grasshopper, perhaps!" he roared. "Sure, you have contracted the housemaid's knee, isn't it!" He left the docile Francis to his own devices and dashed across to Richard, who had retrieved the twelve-pound shot and seemed undecided whether to hurl it at the trainer or to burst into tears.

"Most noticeable," continued Miss Caddick brightly.

"Don't be a fool, Companion Caddick!" screamed the old lady.

"Oh, but I'm not, dear Mrs. Puddequet," said Miss Caddick, blinking her pale eyes earnestly. "It *is* most noticeable! The beautiful, the *gentlemanly* behavior of Mr. Malpas, and Mr. Francis, and Mr. Hilary when they are taken to task by our dear trainer! And the morose, the boorish, the almost *resentful* way in which Mr. Richard and Mr. Clive receive his well-intentioned comments."

At this moment the wheel of the bathchair jolted uncomfortably over something on the grass, for Joseph, in response to a snapping of his employer's fingers, had pushed onwards towards the center of the ground. Here, looking, even in his shorts and singlet, more like a fifth-century Greek than the fifth-century Greeks themselves, Hilary Yeomond was in the act of throwing the discus.

The obstruction over which the wheel of the bathchair had passed proved to be a javelin of the kind that is used in athletics. The bathchair halted. Its occupant and her satellite investigated. The Scrounger, always thankful for any respite from his duties, stood back and let his eyes rove over the now familiar scene. Hilary Yeomond, having finished his throw, and being disinclined to walk after the discus and retrieve it, strolled across to his elderly relative and bent to see what was lying half-hidden in the grass by the wheel of her chariot.

"Pick it up, boy! Pick it up!" squealed old Mrs. Puddequet, leaning forward in the bathchair and dealing him a swipe across the legs with her umbrella.

It was the angular Miss Caddick, however, who stooped and gingerly raised the long shaft of the javelin from the ground. She held it out so that its discolored point came within ten inches of Great-aunt Puddequet's face.

"Blood," said Miss Caddick, with great pleasure. She licked her thin lips hungrily, and touched the stained end of the spear delicately with her fingertips.

"Repulsive," said old Mrs. Puddequet. "Prod the attendant."

Miss Caddick, however, discovered a more tactful method of attracting Joseph's attention. She walked forward until she blocked his line of vision, and then spoke. Joe, who was preparing to expectorate, less from necessity than as an expression of opinion on Malpas Yeomond's performance over the high jump, which he had been watching in growing disgust during the past moment or so, recollected himself hastily and stood to attention.

"Mam?" said he, turning smartly towards Great-aunt Puddequet.

"Remove this implement."

"This 'ere javelin, mam?"

"Certainly."

"Where to, mam?"

"Attendant," said Great-aunt Puddequet irritably, "don't be a fool!" She clicked her tongue in annoyance as Malpas Yeomond failed for the third time to clear five feet eleven inches.

"Up, Grandnephew, up!" she squawked angrily. Malpas replaced the high-jump bar and smiled at her.

Joseph Herring took the javelin which Miss Caddick handed him and walked away in the direction of the house.

"And, attendant," screamed Great-aunt Puddequet at his retreating back, "discover, if possible, how it came to be lying there on the grass."

Joe lifted his left eyebrow comically, and observed:

"Beg pardon, mam, but I expect it was left on the grass be one of the young gents after practice yesterday and 'as gorn rusty. Steel what is left on the damp grass, mam, 'as an 'abit of going rusty."

He wheeled smartly, and, pursued by a screamed objurgation to which he paid no attention whatsoever, skirted one of the huts and made his way round to the kitchen garden.

Great-aunt Puddequet raised her field-glasses and watched another abortive attempt by Clive Brown-Jenkins to clear the bar of the pole vault.

"Very poor, Grandnephew," screamed his elderly relative unnecessarily. Clive, who had fallen awkwardly with his leg doubled under him, looked round. Then, slowly, he stood up and came limping towards her.

"What did you say?" he enquired.

Great-aunt Puddequet ignored him. She snapped her fingers and motioned Miss Caddick to take up the duties of the absent Joseph. Clive picked up his pole, and prepared to try again, while Great-aunt Puddequet looked grimly on.

At this moment the fair-haired trainer, Kost, came up to Clive.

"You'll never do yourself justice, Mr. Jenkins, while you hold the pole so low," he remonstrated briefly. "Look here, perhaps. Now watch me."

"Blasted acrobat," said Clive Brown-Jenkins pithily, as the trainer concluded a finished exhibition.

"It is not a case of acrobatics, Mr. Jenkins," observed Miss Caddick, before Great-aunt Puddequet could deliver a broadside. "I believe the correct development of the abdominal muscles plays some part in the proper performance of the exercise, and the lift of the legs, forward and upward, together with a certain measure of confidence in one's own ability—"

"Abstain from quotation, companion," said Great-aunt Puddequet querulously. "Quotation is the last refuge of the little-minded. If you have no thought of your own on the subject of success in the pole vault, remain silent. Grandnephew, you should develop the arm and shoulder muscles. You appear to me flabby and spineless. You lack biceps and determination, Grandnephew. Remedy these things. A slow-motion film will be shown in the village schoolroom this evening. Trainer!"

Kost came trotting towards her.

"A creditable performance, trainer. The Home Cinematograph, operated by Grandson Anthony, will now record your method. Repeat."

Kost bowed, walked back to his starting place, and picked up the pole. Great-aunt Puddequet produced and blew a small silver whistle. From the sunk garden appeared Timon Anthony with the cine-camera.

"Trainer Kost will demonstrate the pole vault," she said. "Record his performance."

Timon Anthony grinned and nodded. The rest of the practicing athletes came up to watch.

"The chap shows style," observed Francis to Malpas, as Kost cleared the bar and made a faultless landing.

"So do I, over ten feet," retorted his elder brother. "Put that bar up a foot and a half, and there would be a different tale to tell. Everybody is the same. I look like a world-beater when I'm doing four feet six over the high jump. I always take great care to be doing about that height when Aunt appears. She told me yesterday how nicely I was getting on. Kost has bunged it into her head that style is everything, you see. Unfortunately, she saw me sit down on five-eleven this afternoon, so I'm no longer the blue-eyed boy."

"Well, style *is* everything, to a certain extent," said Hilary. "Look at batting, for instance."

"Yes, but the prettiest style gets you nowhere unless you've got the guts to back it up with," contributed Clive Brown-Jenkins. "What's the time?"

"Half-past twelve, thank God. Time for a bath and some lunch. Come on. The bloke's putting on his sweater, so *he's* finished for the morning."

III

"What's the matter?" asked Celia. She was walking round the sports field with her brother before the afternoon's work began.

"Thought I kicked something," replied Clive. "Yes, I did, too."

He bent and picked up a javelin from the long grass where it had lain hidden from view.

"That's rather queer," he said. "There was one lying there this morning. Aunt sent Joe away with it. I wonder who left it here again? We had better take it in. It will get spoilt."

They were about to put their suggestion into practice when Great-aunt Puddequet's bathchair emerged from the central gateway and was propelled swiftly towards them. Clive and Celia walked up to it.

"What is this?" said the old lady, pointing to the javelin with her umbrella. Clive held it out.

"Attendant," squealed Great-aunt Puddequet, "take the implement to the trainer. Desire him to restore it to its rightful place, and ask him how it is that he leaves the tools of his trade about the field so that they become damp, mildewed, and rusty."

"Very good, mam," replied Joe.

He took the javelin and glanced at it curiously.

"Beg pardon, mam, but this is the same javelin you give me this morning

to take away, and I took and stood it in a corner of the kitchen to get dry, and then I cleans the rust off the end, and then I up and takes it over to the gymnasium and puts it beside the other two there, and 'ere it is again."

He looked dubiously at it, as though it were the rod of Moses and might turn into a serpent at any moment.

"Attendant," screamed Great-aunt Puddequet, tapping the shaft of the javelin irritably with the ferrule of her umbrella, "be off! Be off! And don't be a fool!"

Joe grinned, and retired. He found the trainer engaged in putting a new battery into a powerful electric torch. He smiled when he saw Joe, and put the torch down.

"I suppose I'm to come and start work, perhaps," he said. "Is the boss there?"

"She is," said Joe.

Kost laughed.

"You know anything about electricity, boy?" he asked, looking at the torch.

Joe smiled sadly and wagged his head.

"Just enough to lose me money at the White City when I goes 'ome to see me poor old mother," he said. "Why?"

"No reason in particular," said Kost. "What's this?" And he pointed to the bloodstained javelin.

Joe shook his head.

"Know anything about this 'ere?" he enquired, pointing to the tip of the javelin.

Kost did not appear to understand the import of the question.

"I should say so, perhaps," he said, taking the long shaft from Joe's hand. "A Swede named Lundqvist holds the record for the last Olympic Games. Two hundred and eighteen feet and a bit. Come outside."

Joe complied with the request.

"Now, then, I bet you can't throw it as far as that clump of meadowsweet. This is the action, perhaps. Look."

"Nothing doing," said Joe, arresting the movement with a touch of his hand on the trainer's arm. "I been sent to ask you whether you chucked it at the old lady just now."

"Me?" Kost grinned and lowered the javelin. "Sure I didn't! Why should I?"

Joe lowered his voice.

"Look 'ere," he said. "It's a damn funny thing. This morning she finds this 'ere javelin in the grass, and she cusses some and sends me away with it. That there Miss Caddick points to the end of it—this 'ere tin part—and talks about blood. I thinks it's rust. But when I comes to clean it, blowed if it ain't blood after all. What do you make of that?"

"Nothing," said Kost. He took the javelin and looked attentively at the point. "Except that, unless I'm mistaken, there's blood on it again. Did you clean it all off properly, perhaps?"

"I did, mate."

Joe squinted down at the dark discoloration and then touched it gingerly with the tip of his forefinger.

"Well, come on to the old lady," he said, "and tell 'er what you think."

Kost, however, declined to do anything of the kind until the afternoon's work was over.

"I will do what I am to be paid for, perhaps," said he. "And that is not to run after silly old ladies—no! It is to teach the leap, the put, the throw, perhaps. I will go later."

"Trainer," said Great-aunt Puddequet, as Kost drew near the bathchair at the conclusion of the short afternoon's practicing and instruction, "attend to me." She indicated the javelin, which was propped against the brick wall which divided the sunk garden from the sports ground. "What do you mean by mislaying this implement? Slackness, trainer, slackness!"

"Madam," replied Kost, drawing himself up and looking her straight in the eye, "I don't know what you are talking about, perhaps. Since it was decided—wasn't it?—that Mr. Anthony should not participate in the training, perhaps, the javelins, to my knowledge, have not been used by any of the gentlemen, and I disclaim responsibility for them—yes, sure."

Great-aunt Puddequet laughed.

"Creditably proclaimed, trainer," she observed. "Attendant!"

Joe stood to attention.

"Take the implement to the nearest police station."

"Very good, mam!"

"And get the inspector to find out the nature of that dullish substance on the point."

"Blood," said Miss Caddick again, with the same intense pleasure she had shown on the preceding occasion.

"Nonsense, companion!" squealed old Mrs. Puddequet. "How can it be blood? Attendant, off with you!"

"But, if you are certain it is not blood, Great-aunt," said Hilary, "why send it to the police?"

"You're a fool, Grandnephew!" screamed the old lady, switching round in the bathchair so suddenly that she almost precipitated herself and it through the doorway into the sunk garden. Malpas put a steadying hand on the conveyance, and said soothingly:

"Never mind him, Aunt. What about tea? It's half-past four."

Great-aunt Puddequet looked at her gold watch.

"Time. Quite time," she said. "Grandnephew Malpas, take me in. I sup-

pose you will all look sulky if I ask you to come out and practice again later this afternoon, but I am compelled to state, Grandnephews, that you make little progress. Be earnest! Show grit! Be determined. Rome was not built in a day! But it *was* built! Build it, Grandnephews! Build it!" And she thumped on the ground with her umbrella to lend emphasis to her words.

"I'll see masel' drooned first," said Hilary under his breath.

Miss Caddick, startled by hearing that dire quotation thus heretically burlesqued, gave a quaint little snort of laughter.

"You're an ass, Companion Caddick," whispered Hilary, working his eyebrows up and down as old Mrs. Puddequet did when she was in a rage.

"Mr. Hilary, you really must behave yourself," said the angular lady, bridling coquettishly, and holding her lace handkerchief to her lips. "You young gentlemen are too *humorous!*"

"Seriously, sister Caddick," said Hilary in a low voice, as the two of them dropped to the rear of Great-aunt Puddequet's bathchair, "if something doesn't happen soon, I'm going home. This *is* a hole. However do you stick it?"

"It's my living," responded Miss Caddick, "and Mrs. Puddequet is not a hard employer. Not hard at all. And *always* goes to bed at just after nine."

"Always?" asked Hilary. "Oh, that's not so bad."

"Yes, *always*," replied Miss Caddick. She glanced hastily about her, and then dropped her voice. "But I *would* like to know, Mr. Hilary, who it was took her bathchair out in the wet last night?"

"How do you mean?"

"Well," said Miss Caddick, "it *was* taken out. And that's all I know. At nine o'clock last night she went to bed, and at eight o'clock this morning Joe asked to see me. Mr. Hilary, that bathchair was soaking wet. We had an awful job to dry it in the kitchen without her knowing. It may *still* be damp for all I know. And if it *is* still damp, and she has the rheumatism, whatever shall I feel like? But I *dared* not tell her, Mr. Hilary, because I made *sure*, and so did Joe, that some of you young gentlemen had been playing about with it! But if so, Mr. Hilary, I do *please* wish you would not do it! I should get into such *dreadful* trouble if she found out! I might even be dismissed from my *post*! And I have certain expectations, Mr. Hilary, you see. Not *'Great Expectations'*—she giggled girlishly—"but still expectations. And if I were to be dismissed—"

"Yes, yes, of course," said Hilary hastily. "Quite. Well, I didn't take the bathchair out last night, and I don't know who did. Does that satisfy you? I suppose it doesn't."

"Well, it *was* out," said Miss Caddick, "because it got soaked with the rain, and there *was* no rain, Mr. Hilary, until after ten last night. And a bathchair *may* run downhill by itself, but *not* out of the door of a lockup shed that *is* locked up, Mr. Hilary! So there it is! And then that javelin—I don't like it. If

you gentlemen *must* have your joke with the old lady, I *wish* you would be a little less *ghoulish*. Please, Mr. Hilary!"

Hilary looked at her and sadly shook his head.

"I suppose it's a waste of breath to inform you, sister Caddick, that I didn't so much as know that there were any condemned javelins about the place," he said. "Still, for what it is worth, I pass the information on. Neither is it my idea of a joke to attempt to scare an old woman of ninety."

He sighed.

"And to think that in you, sister Caddick, I fancied I had discovered a twin soul," he added sorrowfully.

At twelve o'clock that night there were once more three young Flemish Giants in each hutch; and in the outer scullery, to which he had gained admission by methods peculiarly his own, Scrounger Joseph Herring was cleaning some yellowish clay off his boots.

CHAPTER IV

Friday Night and Saturday Morning

I

PRISCILLA YEOMOND removed her evening frock and hung it up in the wardrobe. She closed the wardrobe door, picked up the candle from the dressing-
table, and walked over to a long Venetian mirror on a writhing wrought-iron
stand, and, holding the candle aloft, stood for a moment studying her very
pleasing reflection in the glass. At last, with a little sigh, half of satisfaction,
half of amusement at knowing herself satisfied, she replaced the candle on
the dressing-table and began to brush her shining, short, dark hair.

It was nearly one o'clock. She had intended coming to bed earlier, but
when Great-aunt Puddequet retired at nine o'clock they had put on the gramophone and there had been dancing. Then at half-past eleven she had accompanied Celia up the stairs, but had lingered in the girl's room, talking,
and had only just wished her good night. She liked Celia. She wondered
what Amaris Cowes was like. Dick Cowes was queer. Perhaps Amaris was a
freak. She was a plucky freak, anyway. She had cut loose from her family
and had struck out on her own. It was sink or swim, thought Priscilla. There
was Celia, too. She was only eighteen, and yet she had work to do and earned
money. Mentally she reviewed her own life. It seemed a trifle feeble and inad-
equate compared with the comings and goings of these Amazonian cousins.

A sharp crack at the window caused her to start violently. For a full thirty
seconds she stood there, her heart thudding. Recovering herself, but still
trembling, she went to the casement, drew aside the curtains, and peered out.
Even in the darkness, she thought, it was possible to make out a darker shadow
below. She pushed open the window and called softly, but in a voice sharp
with nervous tension.

"Who's there?"

There was no reply. Straining her eyes, she realized that the dark shadow
was the new cypress tree which Great-aunt Puddequet had caused to be planted
in the sunk garden that morning.

The candle behind her flickered and sputtered in the draught from the
open window. Priscilla was about to withdraw her head when the moon
struggled out and showed with astonishing clearness a strange sight. Someone was pushing Great-aunt Puddequet's bathchair round the cinder track at

a fair running pace, and, so far as Priscilla could make out, Great-aunt Pud-dequet was in it! At one o'clock in the morning! …

Suddenly the candle gave up the unequal contest and went out. At the same moment, in the enveloping darkness immediately behind Priscilla, some-one coughed.

Priscilla shut the window with trembling hands and swung round.

"Who—who's there?" she called. Her own high-pitched voice surprised her.

There was no answer or sound of any kind.

Priscilla suddenly realized that she was looking straight at the luminous dial of an alarm clock which stood on top of a small cupboard on the landing opposite her bedroom door.

The door was open, then. Somebody had come in!

Priscilla gave a wild glance round the darkened room. A feeling of panic came over her. With shaking hand she relighted the candle and by its light gathered up the things she required for the night. Go to the window she would not. Stay by herself she could not.

"I'm sorry to be a nuisance to you," she observed, walking into Celia's bedroom, armed with nightdress, dressing gown, and brush and comb, "but I'm not going to sleep alone."

Celia looked round in surprise. She finished dabbing night-cream on to her face and then smiled happily.

"Three cheers for the company," she announced.

"Before we go to bed I propose we lock the door," said Priscilla. "I'd feel ever so much safer. I don't want to frighten you, but someone came into my room just now in a sort of queer way—I can't explain it quite—and I *know* I saw Great-aunt's bathchair careering round the sports field at twenty miles an hour."

Celia giggled, unimpressed, and, bending down and groping under the large four-poster bed, she produced the leg of a chair. It was made of solid mahogany, was beautifully turned and polished, and made a weighty, well-balanced weapon. She grasped it in both hands and wagged it playfully at Priscilla.

"Anybody who comes in here will wish he hadn't," she observed with spirit. "I vote we fix a notice on the door: Visitors Enter at Their Own Risk. What about it?"

Priscilla laughed.

"I know you think I'm an idiot," she said, "but I don't care. And I've brought a box of chocolates, so you needn't say you don't want me, because I've made up my mind to stay."

Half an hour later Celia was still awake. A vision came to her of Great-aunt Puddequet taking the air in the bathchair round the cinder track, and she began to chuckle softly. An insane desire to go and see whether she was still

at it took hold of her. She slid out of bed.

The moon was full now. The sky was clear. Every object in the room was clearly to be seen.

"Lovely night for a record-breaking run," thought the sister of a champion cyclist, giggling to herself.

She crept to the door and turned the key. Priscilla stirred in her sleep, responsive to the slight sound of the moving lock, but she did not wake. Celia took her dressing gown off a chair, and slipped out of the room. The thick carpets everywhere gave grateful warmth to her bare feet. She passed up the long passage to Priscilla's room and peeped in at the open door.

A figure was bending over the bed.

Celia Brown-Jenkins drew in her breath sharply. Then she said, very distinctly:

"Hands up!"

The figure swung round to face the sound of her voice.

"Shut up, you little idiot," he hissed.

"Oh, Clive, it's you!" said Celia helplessly. "Whatever are you doing?"

Clive stepped to the door and laid his hand on her arm.

"Get back to bed," he said quietly. "There's something funny going on, and I'm out to know what it is. Whose room is this?"

"It's Priscilla's. But she's in my room now," said Celia. "Clive, go to bed."

Clive drew her on to the landing and softly closed the door of Priscilla's room.

"I can't get back to my hut tonight," he whispered. "Door's locked between the sunk garden and the sports field. And the kitchen regions are all locked up too. I should make an awful row getting out. I shall go down to the dining room and sleep on the settee."

"I'll give you an eiderdown," whispered Celia. "Come with me."

She led the way to her room, went in, and immediately returned with the eiderdown, which she thrust into his arms.

"Good night," she whispered. "I wish I knew what you mean. What's queer about the house tonight?"

"It's all right," muttered Clive. "Tell you more in the morning. Good night. Keep your door locked."

He turned and walked away. Celia stood at her bedroom door listening intently. Suddenly she heard a cry and a crash.

"Silly ass," she thought, running towards the head of the stairs. "He's tripped on the corner of the eiderdown and fallen downstairs."

Candles and electric torches soon lighted up the scene. They issued from every bedroom door except that of Great-aunt Puddequet. Priscilla, awakened by the noise and finding Celia gone, came running out to the head of the stairs.

Clive lay at the foot of them. He was completely entangled in a thick and

handsome eiderdown quilt of a rich shade of orange. It had broken his fall. Save for a bump on the head and a bruised shin, he was none the worse. He had a strange tale to tell. As he had trodden on the first stair to descend to the hall, someone had given him a hearty push in the small of the back. Burdened with the eiderdown quilt, he had been unable to offer any resistance to the unexpected pressure from behind, and had rolled from top to bottom of the staircase.

"It's all very well for you fellows to look like that," he concluded, when he had told the tale to the other athletes in the gymnasium before breakfast next morning, "but some very funny things went on in the house last night. To begin with, somebody frightened Priscilla out of her room. I stayed in the library reading until after half-past twelve last night. I'd forgotten that the gate between the sunk garden and the sports ground is locked at half-past eleven, so that I couldn't get back to my hut without a lot of trouble, so I let myself out by the front door (which of course I had to unbolt first) and shut it behind me. It was not until I had walked down the steps that I remembered about the gate. Still, it struck me I could probably climb over, but, just as I got to the bottom of the steps and was making my way to the gate, I was just in time to see a jolly queer bit of business. Somebody came out of the front door. Couldn't see me because of the darkness of the sunk garden under the shadow of the wall, but I could spot him because he showed up like Indian ink in the moonlight against the white wall of the house. He walked along the terrace and began coming down the steps. All at once, just as I was going to hail him, for of course I recognized his walk, something struck me as being rather queer. For a second I couldn't quite work out what was wrong. Then I knew. The chap was coming down those stone steps without a sound.

"He stopped when he was about halfway down and turned round. In the bedroom immediately above the steps a candle was burning. I saw his arm go up and I heard the crack of a stone hitting a window. No sooner had he flung the stone than he bolted up the steps again as fast as ever he could go. At the same instant the window opened and a girl's voice called out:

" 'Who's there?'

"At the same minute, or pretty nearly so, the candle went out. Too much draft, I suppose. Well, I thought it was a funny thing to do, to go heaving bricks at girls" bedroom windows at about one o'clock in the morning and scaring them to death, but, still, I didn't see what I could do except chase the fellow and point out what a poor sort of fool I thought he was. So I was just going to hop it up the steps when I'm blowed if there wasn't a sound of wheels on the cinder track just outside the garden door where I was standing, and, do you know, it sounded for all the world like the old lady's bathchair doing a record sprint round the ground. Couldn't have been, I suppose, but it gave me quite a jar.

"Anyway, I took to the steps and mounted into the house. Opened the door with my latchkey, of course. Luckily the other fellow hadn't shot the bolts. Couldn't find him, though. Tried all the downstairs rooms. Searched quietly but well for about half an hour. Quite a sporting way of getting through a dull night. By rotten luck my torch gave out then, but, as it did so, I passed an open bedroom door. Thinking my bird might possibly have gone to ground in a spare bedroom, I toddled in. The moonlight was lovely. I soon found that the room was empty. I stepped to the window, and was rather surprised to find that this was the very room the lout must have aimed the brick at. The girl occupant, however, had obviously tazzed off. I stepped up to the bed to take a cautious squint and find out whether this really was so, when my young sister at the door nearly frightened me to death by suddenly yelling, 'Hands up!' Though I say it, that kid's got sand. It isn't every girl who'd have yelled 'Hands up!' at a fellow she had every reason to believe was a burglar or something. It seems the other girl was Priscilla, and she had legged it into Celia's room for the rest of the night. Then Celia gave me an eiderdown so that I could camp out on the dining-room settee, and, as I say, I'm blowed if someone didn't jolly well shove me down the stairs. I suppose it was the stone-throwing effort who did it, but I can't think where he was in hiding."

"But who was the chap?" asked Malpas Yeomond. "You said you recognized him."

"Yes, so I did. It was that blighter Kost, of course. I'd know that walk of his anywhere."

"Kost?" repeated Francis Yeomond in surprise.

"Impossible," said Richard Cowes firmly, biting the head off a young spring onion.

"Shouldn't think it could be Kost," said Malpas. "You see, he's never up at the house. Sleeps in his own hut. No reason for him to be up at the house. Besides, the idea of Kost playing foolish tricks like throwing stones at bedroom windows and shoving people down the stairs doesn't fit in with what we know of him. I don't care for the man, I must say, but he isn't that sort of fool."

"Well," said Clive deliberately, "I may be wrong. It was night. I didn't see his face. He came out of the house, and went back into it. But it was Kost's walk and run to the life. I'd swear to it anywhere. Where's your young brother, by the way?"

"Gone for a swim," replied Malpas. "Too jolly cold for me. In fact, this whole place about does me in. I'm tired or making a fool of myself. Championship class! We shall never be anywhere near the championship class in these field events. Honestly, I'm wondering whether I won't tell Aunt that I'm sick of it, and push off home tomorrow. I mean, we've all given the thing a trial, haven't we? And we're none of us any good. Besides"—he waved his

arm towards the southern end of the sports ground and at the horizon beyond—"I ask you! Did you ever see such a hagridden hell of desolation in all your life? I never did. What do you say, Frank?"

"Term begins in a week's time," said Francis Yeomond, dancing up and down on his toes and tying his sweater more closely about his neck, for the morning air was golden, but inclined to be cold.

"Personally," said Richard Cowes, "I find myself longing for a real bed once more."

"And H., I know, is fed up with it here," said Malpas. He looked expectantly at Clive Brown-Jenkins. "So how do we go?" he asked.

Clive Brown-Jenkins eyed him very deliberately.

"I take it, you mean that because you chaps don't stand an earthly chance of getting a place in the next international athletics team, you want me to give up my chance of collecting the old lady's money to keep you company," he said. "Well, you can take it that I've no intention of standing down. If you want to chuck up the sponge, do it. I'm staying here."

He set his obstinate jaw.

Francis grinned.

"The old girl ought to be in a home," he said. "The whole thing's a lot of rot. Still, if Brown-Jenkins is going to stick it out, so am I. Although if that fellow Kost doesn't alter the tone of his remarks, the next jump I make is going to be on his fat face. The man's a swine. I mean to say, one has sat in a boat and endured a certain number of quietly insulting epithets, but the man Kost is offensive. Still, if we're here for the duration"—he made a gesture of resignation—"we're here."

Richard Cowes, who was now consuming a lengthy stick of rhubarb, waved the twelve inches of it which remained with a sweeping gesture.

"For my own part," he said, "I agree with Cousin Brown." He turned to Francis Yeomond. "I confess, too, that at present, every time I attempt to put this weight I am told, unkindly, by the person surnamed Kost, that I am putting it at the wrong angle or with the wrong hand or on the wrong wormcast. However," he bit a succulent two inches off the stick of rhubarb and chewed them defiantly, "the brave man faces scorn and calumny with a light heart and an undaunted demeanor. Besides, my sister's coming down here any day now, so I must stick it out until then."

Malpas Yeomond looked at first one and then another of them thoughtfully. At last he said with bitter emphasis, "Any of you ever heard of a play called *Wurzel-Flummery*?"

"Don't be harsh, Yeomond, my dear fellow," said Richard Cowes soothingly. "What about a little breakfast? The laws of the S.P.P.I. demand that I shall be fed."

CHAPTER V

Abrupt Termination of an Inglorious Career

I

"I TELL you for the ninth time," said Priscilla heatedly, "that a man walked into my room at about one o'clock this morning and distinctly coughed."

Her brothers hooted her down.

"And I tell you for the nineteenth time," said Clive, helping himself liberally to the marmalade, "that just as I was coming downstairs at about one-thirty this morning, some blighter put both hands into the small of my back and shoved me a mighty good shove. I bounced off every stair separately. Stand by my yarn, Priscilla, and I stand by yours," he concluded handsomely.

Priscilla's face clouded.

"I do believe you, Clive," she stated, glaring defiantly at her brothers. "Some nasty things happened in this house last night."

" 'There is something terrible about this house,' " quoted Malpas solemnly. He winked at Francis.

"It isn't funny," said Priscilla. She poured out a second cup of coffee for herself and dropped in a lump of sugar like a full stop. It appeared that the subject was closed. Timon Anthony reopened it.

"Well, I tell you all for the twenty-ninth time that it was real blood on the tips of those two javelins—or, as Joe Herring will have it—on that one javelin which made positively two appearances. Blood, children, blood!"

He smacked his lips and looked wickedly across the table at the angular Miss Caddick.

"And one of the poor little bunnies was missing yesterday," day," he added pointedly. "I believe the cannibal Kost ate it, having first dipped the javelin in its ber-lud."

"There's another funny thing, if you really want to know," said Clive Brown-Jenkins. "And that's the tale of the old iron pot, or, in this case, of Great-aunt's bathchair. Which of you girls was taking it out for a walk at about ten minutes to one this morning? It passed the wooden door of the sunk garden at, roughly, one o'clock."

Before anyone else could reply, Priscilla Yeomond broke in.

"You needn't laugh at him," she said. "He heard it. I saw it."

"*Saw* it?" said Miss Caddick, interested. All eyes turned upon the thin,

angular, upright woman. "Did you, really?"

"Yes," replied Priscilla. "The moon came out and I saw it quite clearly. Someone was in it, and someone—a man, I think—was pushing it. It was going along ever so fast. The man behind was running."

"I knew it went out at nights," said Miss Caddick, with a little shudder. She turned to Hilary. "I said so, you remember."

"No longer ago than yesterday, sister Caddick," replied the young man. "I disbelieved you. I apologize. Sweet coz, forgive me."

"No I didn't mean that. I mean, corroboration," said Miss Caddick vaguely. She glanced into her cup, drank what remained of its contents, glanced at her watch, and rose from the table.

"You must please excuse me," she said. "Mrs. Puddequet will wish to interview the cook, and I must go along and help her to dress first."

"I'll tell you another rum thing," said Hilary slowly, when Miss Caddick had gone. "I went for a swim this morning." He held up his hand to stem the tide of brotherly comment which this simple statement immediately invoked. "No, I'm not calling you stinkers," he protested. "Let me get on. Well, I dived a bit deep and my fingers touched something clammy."

"Mud," said Francis helpfully.

"Couldn't have been mud," said Timon Anthony. "Old lady had it all cleaned out and decoded—I mean deodorized, and the bottom nicely sanded with the best materials only—you should have been here when it was all being done! There's no mud within a hundred feet of the diving-boards, I know."

"Well," continued Hilary, "it felt like somebody's face! You know when you play water polo, and you push a chap's face with your foot—"

"What sort of water polo do *you* play, for heaven's sake?" asked Richard Cowes.

"Oh, shut up, Dick," said Priscilla. "Go on, H."

"Yes, well, it felt like a face on the end of your foot, only it was my hands that grabbed it," explained Hilary. "I expect really it was a fish."

"Oh, yes. A fish would stop there at the bottom of the water while your great paws grabbed hold of it," said Celia Brown-Jenkins with fine scorn. "I am surprised that a boy like you should be such a little liar."

The approval of the Yeomond family at this frank expression of their own sentiments was only quelled by the entrance of old Mrs. Puddequet in her bathchair. She seemed annoyed. Miss Caddick, who was pushing the bathchair, was finishing a sentence as they came through the doorway.

"And so, of course, I sent him away," she said.

"I should think so too," squealed Great-aunt Puddequet. "But that is no reason for leaving me to be dressed by Amaris Cowes and the cook, particularly as the cook is greatly incensed at the loss of her privately owned and almost new clothesline!"

"Amaris?" cried Richard. "You didn't say Amaris, did you, Aunt?"

Old Mrs. Puddequet turned her yellowish eyes upon him.

"I have never been told that my articulation is indistinct, Grandnephew," she retorted. "You will find your sister in the sunk garden. I offered her breakfast. She refused it. I asked her for explanations. She laughed at me. It appears that at just after three o'clock this morning she arrived on a milk train at Market Longer Station and walked to the house. She says that she did not expect to gain admission to the house, so she strolled about until she found an open door to one of the erections in the grounds, and there"— Great-aunt Puddequet's scandalized tones rose higher and higher in her indignation—"she slept. Slept! With the door wide open!"

"That was for reasons of health, Great-aunt," said Amaris Cowes from the doorway.

She sauntered in, both hands in the pockets of her knitted suit, large walking-shoes on her feet, and a cap of closely cropped black hair crowning her well-poised head. Her face was large, clever, and ugly; her dark-blue eyes deep-set and austere. She had a prizefighter's jowl, and, when she took them out of her pockets to accept and light the cigarette which her brother immediately proffered, exceedingly slender and beautiful hands.

"Thanks, Dick," she said, as he returned the case to his pocket. She grinned, and nodded to the others. Malpas Yeomond offered her his chair. Celia poured out coffee. Clive rang the bell for hot food. Timon Anthony tilted back his chair and regarded her with intense interest. At length he restored the chair to its normal position on four legs and observed negligently, "The New Woman."

"As a matter of fact," said Amaris Cowes, taking careful stock of him, "I regard myself as the direct reincarnation of Lilith, the legendary wife of our great forefather."

"Irreverent," squealed Great-aunt Puddequet, who objected to becoming part of the background to this exceedingly vital figure. Amaris Cowes stared at her.

"Great-aunt," she said slowly, "after breakfast I want to see the sunk garden again. I've been looking at it for half an hour, and I want to look at it again in company with somebody who knows it really well. And tell me— who *is* the ancient Roman complete with sword? Not Horatius keeping the bridge, surely?"

She paused. Great-aunt Puddequet said nothing. Her yellowish eyes glowered suspiciously upon this ugly duckling who was so obviously something of a swan.

"That sunk garden," Amaris Cowes went on, taking the cigarette from between her lips and making a graceful and expressive gesture with her left arm, "that sunk garden has a soul, Great-aunt."

She replaced the cigarette, took a plate of kidneys and bacon from the maid, and accepted a piece of bread from a plate proffered by Hilary.

"Throw that thing away and get your breakfast, do," said Celia. "You must be starving."

Amaris Cowes took out the cigarette, glanced at it, and then tossed it through the open window. She grinned at Celia and picked up her knife and fork.

"I am," she said.

It is always interesting to watch other people eat. The Yeomonds, the two Brown-Jenkins, her brother Richard, even Great-aunt Puddequet and her companion followed the movements of Amaris as she ate a hearty meal.

Just as she had refused a fourth cup of coffee, a maid entered and conferred with Miss Caddick.

"Dear me," the angular lady remarked. "Ask him into the library."

"Who?" demanded Great-aunt Puddequet peevishly.

"Jane says it is the sergeant from Market Longer Police Station," replied Miss Caddick. "They seem to have lost a man called Jacob Hobson. At least, his wife has. So awkward, of course, to lose one's husband at the weekend."

"*Lost him?*" squealed Great-aunt Puddequet. "Well, do they suppose I've found him? Go along at once, companion, and send the sergeant away. What nonsense to come here after every drunk and disorderly ruffian in the village! What was Constable Copple thinking about, to allow such a man to get lost?"

"I don't know, Mrs. Puddequet. I'll go and ask," said Miss Caddick obediently.

"Send the sergeant to me. I'll talk to him," squealed the old lady, slapping the arm of the bathchair with rage. "How dare he come chasing his ridiculous ne'er-do-wells into my house!"

In a short time Miss Caddick returned with the sergeant in tow. He was red and warm, for he had just cycled too rapidly, and too soon after breakfast, up a fairly steep hill.

"Now, sergeant," snapped Great-aunt Puddequet.

"Well, mam," replied the sergeant, wiping his face, "it's like this. Police Constable Copple of this village rung us up an hour ago to say a certain Jacob Hobson, also of this village, has never been home since tea last night, and they can't find him anywhere."

"But what—" began Great-aunt Puddequet.

The sergeant held up a large, red, soothing hand.

"One minute, mam. We have evidence to show that this Hobson was at the pub—public house in the village until about a quarter-past nine last night. He then announced 'is intention of coming here to complain about the state of the roof of his cottage, it being on your land and him hoping you would do something to have it repaired, and he was seen by reliable witnesses to start

off in this direction. He was pretty well drunk, mam, according to the same witnesses, and the idea of his wife is that he may have fallen in your lake."

"Fallen into the mere?" squealed Great-aunt Puddequet with tremendous vigor. "Then she can think herself lucky if he has! A drunken, poaching, graceless, wife-beating ruffian if ever there was one."

"And do *you* think he has fallen into the mere, sergeant?" enquired Timon Anthony.

"Well, sir, it's no odds to me what he's done, but his wife seemed certain that's what must have happened, so Constable Copple asked if we'd come over with the apparatus and get permission to drag the lake. I suppose you've no objection, mam?" he added, turning to Great-aunt Puddequet. "You see," he added tactfully, "if he *has* fell in the lake, he'll have to be got out some time, so it may as well be now."

"I have every objection!" shrieked the old lady. "But get on! Get on! Amaris Cowes, come out and see the sunk garden!"

"Let in the clutch, Companion Caddick," whispered Hilary to the motive power of the bathchair. Miss Caddick, looking very pale, started at hearing herself addressed, and hastily ran the bathchair out on to the terrace.

Malpas turned to the sergeant.

"No need to go to all that bother unless you like, sergeant, you know," he said, good-naturedly. "At least, not at first. One of us will go on to the high diving-board and look down into the water. Then, unless he's caught up among the weeds downstream, we ought to spot him easily enough if he's there. But wouldn't a body—Hullo! What the devil's up with you?" He broke off at sight of his young brother's face.

"He's there! He's there! He's drowned all right!" stuttered Hilary, with cheeks like chalk. "I—I dived right on to him before breakfast! I knew it was a face! Couldn't have been anything else. A dead man! Ugh!"

II

With rubber-soled shoes on his feet, a sweater pulled over his running vest, a light-colored knapsack slung on his back, and watched by a small crowd of interested spectators—which included the sergeant from Market Longer, Constables White and Willis, also from Market Longer, Constable Copple, the lugubrious village policeman, the Yeomond family, with Celia and Clive Brown-Jenkins, Richard Cowes, Timon Anthony, Kost the trainer, Joseph Herring, the knife-and-boot boy, Miss Caddick and the undergardener, Malpas climbed up to the high diving-board.

Steadying himself by the back rail, he tested the spring of the board, then

walked out to its extreme end, and gazed earnestly into the water.

"I see him!" he shouted. "Flat on the bottom!"

At the same instant a cry from the sports field attracted attention, and Amaris Cowes came bursting out of the lower gate and ran towards the edge of the mere.

"Sergeant," she cried, coming up to the director of the operations, "you are to find the statue of the mermaid. It has been stolen from the sunk garden. My great-aunt is worried to death about it."

"One thing at a time, mam, one thing at a time, if *you* please," said the sergeant testily. "We're looking for a body at present. We can't tackle more than one thing at a time."

He looked up at Malpas, who was now seated on the end of the board with his legs dangling into space.

"Throw them in, sir!" he cried.

Malpas pulled some pieces of white stone, residue of Great-aunt Puddequet's crazy paving in the sunk garden, from the knapsack he wore, and, taking careful aim, tossed them down into the water. Then he returned to earth, went into the bathing hut, where he was immediately joined by the trainer Kost, and in a very few moments they emerged, clad in bathing-costumes, and took up a position at a spot indicated by the sergeant.

"There he is, sir, said he. "Spot him? I saw him at once when you started chucking in the bricks."

Malpas nodded, glanced at the trainer, and, at a given but, to the watchers, an imperceptible signal, the two magnificent swimmers dived into the icy waters. In a second or so, their heads rose above the surface.

"Found the missing statue, I think," grunted Malpas. He took a deep breath, and dived to the bottom again with a strong knife which the sergeant had handed to him.

"Having to cut him free of something that's been used to weigh down the body," explained Timon Anthony to the girls. "Hadn't you two better cut off? You don't want to see him brought to the surface. It won't be a bit nice."

Before Priscilla or Celia could reply—before, in fact, they had realized the sinister purport of Timon's opening sentence—the sergeant abruptly suggested that everyone belonging to the houseparty except Timon Anthony himself should be going about their business. He wound up this curt appeal with some obscure remarks about a song and dance and a poppy-show. Anthony he retained first as representing Mrs. Puddequet, the owner of the house, and secondly as a person who could identify the body if it proved to be that of Hobson.

The little crowd dispersed, and were just in time to intercept Great-aunt Puddequet's bathchair, which was propelled this time by Amaris Cowes. They persuaded the old lady, much against her will, to return to the house.

"And *is* it Hobson?" demanded Great-aunt Puddequet.

It was undoubtedly Hobson. Both Constable Copple and Timon Anthony identified the corpse unhesitatingly.

"Not much doubt as to how he came by his death," said the sergeant shortly, as the two swimmers, cold and exhausted, disappeared into the bathing hut to dress. "Turn him over, Willis."

Constables White and Willis stooped and turned the sodden, ugly, pitiful thing on to its face. The top of the skull had been fractured by a heavy blow.

"But what beats me—" said the sergeant, frowning. Then he stopped and looked at Timon Anthony.

"Am I in the way? Sorry," said the young man. "I'll go. Any message for Auntie?"

"You can tell her the truth if you like," replied the sergeant, recognizing that the apparent flippancy of the young man's last remark was due to excess and not lack of feeling. "Break it easy, sir. She's a goodish age, remember. Lucky it isn't anybody in the family. Still, it's never nice to have a murder about the place."

He looked down at the body.

"He was one that could be spared easy, I reckon. Copple, when you've sent a message through to the station for me, perhaps you'll let his wife know what's happened. She'll be glad to have the uncertainty out of her mind."

"She'll be gladder of more things than that," replied the village policeman, with prophetic gloom.

The sergeant gazed glumly down at the corpse. "And *I'd* be glad to know how you came by that cosh on the nut, mister," he said to himself, "for, speaking without previous experience of a murder case, I don't seem to call to mind any instrument that would make quite *that* sort of a mess of the top of a chap's head, blowed if I do! But we'll see what the M.O.'s got to say."

CHAPTER VI

Great-aunt Puddequet is Happy

Mrs. Hobson received the news of her husband's death without visible emotion. She was a poor, thin, haunted-looking creature, who, having listened in silence to all the sensational details of the crime from Constable Copple, merely observed at the end in an oddly weary tone:

"Well, Mr. Copple, you know as well as anyone the way it's been with me. What's the sense of making out I be sorry? I bean't sorry. I be glad."

The constable shook his head sympathetically. At the last moment of departure he turned, twirling his helmet awkwardly between his large red hands.

"Look here, Janey," he said, "don't 'ee take it amiss what I be saying, but I wudden be too free with trollopsing round the place telling folks you be glad Jacob's been took. And mind what 'ee say and how 'ee say it when the inspector and the sergeant from Market Longer come to see 'ee. Happen I see 'em down the street now."

He had barely taken his leave after this friendly warning when the inspector and the sergeant thundered at the door. She let them in, dusted two chairs, and stood meekly before them, both work-roughened hands rolled up in her apron, while the two police officers seated themselves.

"Sit down, please, Mrs. Hobson," said the inspector. "This is a bad business, and we'll get over this part of it as quickly as we can. You must answer my questions as promptly as possible, and please be very careful what you say."

With this kindly preface he elicited for the second time that day all she knew of the events which led to the murder of her husband. At the end, the inspector read to her what she had stated.

"Now, Mrs. Hobson," he said, "do you know of anyone who had a grudge against your husband?"

She could think of no one.

"I suppose I be about the only one, sir," she stated calmly. "Jacob was a merry, loud-laughin' sort of chap with his mates, they tell me. He was free with his money, too. *I* never see very much of it. Friday was his kind of royal day at the public house. He was paid on a Friday, you see."

"Did he seem to have anything on his mind at all? He came home to tea, you said."

"He talked a rare lot about the roof. What a disgrace it was, and how he'd take pewmonia with it, and what he'd say to old Mrs. Puddequet up at the

45

House when he went to talk to she about it, and how he reckoned he'd go to her there and then, but afterwards he reckoned he'd have a drink first because he didn't see why her should waste his evening' and do him out of his drop of beer; and then a deal about the honest working man that some chap as ought to know better had talked about over in Market Longer where Jacob abeen on a job these two months painting the new houses there; and so on and on, till his rant fair head-ached me."

"I see. And that gave you the idea that he might have staggered into old Mrs. Puddequet's pond?"

"Ay, sir, it did that. When the clock struck twelve and no sign of him, drunk or sober, thinks I that Jacob have been run in by Mr. Copple for bad behavior, or he's slipped into the ditch, or else that he did go up to the House and maybe he's walked into the lake. But I didden do much hoping. I reckoned it would be a big lake would drown *my* sorrows."

The inspector grunted. After a pause for rumination, he suddenly barked: "Can you swim, woman?"

"Oh, no, sir!" said Mrs. Hobson, mildly scandalized.

The inspector grunted again, made an entry in his notebook, snapped it shut, and informed her that she would be wanted at the inquest. Then, followed by the sergeant, he left the cottage.

"Ought to be her, without a doubt," he said moodily, as they strode down the village street, "but, of course, she couldn't have done it."

"I don't know. She's got no alibi; you noticed that, sir, I suppose?"

"Alibi? What's a woman like that want with an alibi?" grunted the inspector. "She's got alibi written all over her."

"She never went to Copple's cottage until after twelve o'clock, sir," the sergeant argued, stoutly maintaining his position, "and that was two hours after the doctor thinks Hobson was killed. It wants thinking about, that does, to my mind. Alibi she may or may not 'ave had—perhaps, as you say, it doesn't matter—but she had motive for ten! Used to knock her about something cruel, 'e did! I had it from Copple—*and* others."

The inspector grunted again.

"I suppose," he said sarcastically, "that you think the woman we've just spoken to—height about five feet four, weight about seven stone eight—hit the man Hobson on the head hard enough to crack his skull like you'd crack the top of an egg with the bowl of a teaspoon! If she *had* made up her mind to bash him one for luck she'd have picked up the poker and sloshed him as he sat in a chair. But a woman like that would more probably have tripped him up on the stairs, or jabbed him in the ribs with a table-knife, or, better still, poisoned his grub. You can't really see that woman following him up to Longer and waiting until he got right under the windows of the house before socking him on the head with—we don't yet know what, but something pretty

heavy and, according to the doctor, quite blunt—rounded in fact. Don't forget that he was about six or seven inches taller than herself; it isn't the easiest thing in the world to bring off a really juicy clout on a head that's higher than your own. Then, again, how could a woman of her physique lug a man weighing every bit of twelve stone across that sports ground and over two fields to the lake? It's impossible. But, more than anything else, think of the body in the water. She can't swim, so I suppose she picked up the dead Hobson and tossed him lightly through the air for a distance of twelve yards ten inches! Then she skipped back to the sunk garden for the statue of the little mermaid, which weighs exactly seventy-six pounds seven and three-quarter ounces, and tossed it in on top of the body? Further, as she *can't* swim, she made a magic spell which bound the statue and the body together with seven yards of strong twine. I hope also that you noticed one of the gymnasium ropes is missing. I expect she swallowed that—and then she woke up!"

The sergeant grinned good-humoredly.

"I see what you mean, sir," he said. "I only meant she had the motive. That's all. And no alibi, sir."

II

"Reporters," said Great-aunt Puddequet, "this is the sports ground. The object on your left is the long-jump pitch, and the figure in the foreground is my grandnephew Francis Yeomond. The idea of the sports ground, reporters—" She broke off, and, leaning forward in the bathchair, reached out with her umbrella, from which she would seldom allow herself to be parted, and prodded the reporter on her right with swift and decided jabs of the pointed ferrule.

Miss Caddick gasped, and, hastily reversing gear, drew the bathchair a couple of yards backwards. To her mind, the persons of representatives of the press were sacrosanct. She said as much, meekly, but with complete assurance.

"Companion," squealed old Mrs. Puddequet, justly incensed at being deprived of her legitimate prey, "don't be a fool! The boy on the right is not attending!"

"No, Mrs. Puddequet," responded Miss Caddick soothingly, "but we must think of habeas corpus! And now you are a little fatigued. Will you not return to the house and rest awhile?"

Great-aunt Puddequet snorted with contempt at this eminently reasonable proposal.

"The inspector and the sergeant will be here again this afternoon. The inquest is on Monday. I have sent Mrs. Hobson five pounds. The statue of the little mermaid was retrieved from the deep by Grandnephew Malpas Yeomond this morning. I love my love with an M because he was murdered. Pippa Passes," she observed, with startling emphasis and great satisfaction. Miss Caddick, a serious student of what she herself always termed English Literature, not knowing what to make of this surprising *te deum*, compromised with her intelligence by smiling with vague pleasure and nodding her neat head to indicate that she recognized the title of the mentioned poem; then, taking firm hold of her courage, she turned the bathchair in the direction of the house, while the reporters made swift tracks for what they were already calling the Fatal Mere.

It was Great-aunt Puddequet's custom when something caused her particular pleasure to murmur in reverent tones, "God's in His Heaven. All's right with the world." When her conscience informed her, however, that her joy was ill-founded or was the result of envy, hatred, malice or any other of the virile human emotions which her generation classed among the seven deadly sins, she was in the habit of remarking in a loud and cheerful voice, "Pippa Passes."

This meant the same thing as the quotation, was a code rendering of a great spiritual truth, and possessed, in common with most other codes, the inestimable advantage of being uninterpretable by the chance hearer.

Having delivered her mistress over to the company of Amaris Cowes, who had promised to teach her a new version of the game of Patience, Miss Caddick went in search of Joseph Herring.

The Scrounger was cleaning out the rabbit-hutches. Old Mrs. Puddequet's pets were nibbling some early spring greens at his feet. The new arrival, previous name unknown, seemed to have settled down without trouble, and, like his companions, was making brisk headway with the succulent provender.

"Oh, Herring," said Miss Caddick, "you are to go up to the house and put away the bathchair. Mrs. Puddequet will not require it again until after lunch. You will please go at once."

Joe regarded her sourly.

"Ho?" he observed truculently. "I will, will I? And what about the b— rabbits? Am I to give over cleanin' of 'em out? You know best, of course."

He readdressed himself to the good work, and whistled insolently.

"Herring," replied Miss Caddick, "you know how Mrs. Puddequet dislikes the sight of the bathchair when it is not in use. I am only repeating her orders."

She turned and walked away. Joe scooped up a shovelful of sawdust and scattered it liberally about the hutch he had been cleaning. Then he took a

handful of straw and proceeded to wipe his hands on it.

Miss Caddick, at the gate of the kitchen garden, looked back at him. Joe caught her eye, and, avoiding it again, bent and picked up the rabbits, which he gently replaced in the hutches.

Then he looked up again, but Miss Caddick had disappeared.

"Ho! So you've spotted the noo one, have you?" he remarked savagely to himself. He glared defiantly at the currant bushes, and then spat with great accuracy into the half-coconut which his enemy had hung for a bird bowl on the low branch of a neighboring apple tree.

III

"The only thing is," said old Mrs. Puddequet shrilly, "that you must keep them off the flower-beds. Oh, and don't give them any assistance whatsoever. I do not wish this murderer to be caught."

"But I believe, Aunt, that you will find it is a punishable offense to refuse information to the police."

Richard Cowes, concealing the spring onions and the young carrots which he had coaxed from the kitchen garden and clandestinely imported into his great-aunt's drawing room, spoke seriously.

"Rubbish, Grandnephew," screamed old Mrs. Puddequet. "You misunderstand me! We have no information to give. If we have no information to give, we are refusing nothing. Get on with your training, Grandnephew. How far do you put the weight."

Richard looked nonplussed.

"To be accurate," he replied gloomily, "I put it on my own toe the last time I tried. Painful, Aunt."

Francis Yeomond joined in the conversation.

"Without wishing to appear at variance with your opinions, Aunt," he observed in his best classroom manner, "I think it right to point out that a crime against society has been committed in these grounds, and that it is our duty as citizens to bring the perpetrator of the outrage to justice."

"To justice, yes," said old Mrs. Puddequet decidedly. "To the maw of the law, no. I tell you all, Grandnephews, Grandnieces, you, Timon Anthony, and you, Companion Caddick, that, did I know the identity of the person who laid low the man Hobson, I would send all the rest of you home to your mothers and fathers, and I would make the murderer my heir. A person of sound religious views and good bodily fitness, Grandnephews."

"Go on! Own up, you hellhound," said Timon Anthony in the ear of Hilary Yeomond. "I'd own up myself, only she'd never believe me."

Suddenly the face of the sergeant appeared at the window. Malpas opened the casement wide, and the sergeant, removing his uniform cap, stepped over the low sill into the room.

"I beg pardon, mam, if I intrude," he said deferentially to old Mrs. Puddequet, "but we've got a man on duty in the sunk garden, and the inspector's compliments and he'd be glad if any person passing out of the house that way would keep strictly to the main path not to disturb clues."

"Clues," said Celia Brown-Jenkins ecstatically. "How thrilling! Is there any blood, sergeant?"

"And the inspector would be glad, mam, if a room could be placed at his disposal for 'im to question—er—interrogate certain members of the household and some of the servants about the 'appenings of Friday night," continued the sergeant, stolidly disregarding what he considered an unnecessarily flippant question.

"Sergeant," said old Mrs. Puddequet, "the inspector shall have whichever room he pleases."

"Then, if convenient, he'd like this one we're in now, mam. That is, if *quite* convenient," said the sergeant. "It overlooks the scene of the crime, you see."

The inspector's first victim was Clive Brown-Jenkins. His second was Priscilla Yeomond. The two cousins repeated their respective stories, and answered clearly, intelligently, and without hesitation all the questions asked by Bloxham.

Satisfied that their tales were unshakable, he heard what Celia Brown-Jenkins had to tell, and then sent for Hilary Yeomond.

"Now, Mr. Yeomond," said Bloxham encouragingly, "I want an account of your movements on the night of the crime. Just a simple statement, please. Must find out where everybody was and what everybody did, and then we can get to work."

Hilary considered.

"Well," he said, "we had dinner at the usual time, and then I remained here, and we put the gramophone on and danced. That's all, I think. I left the house at twenty past eleven with my brothers."

"Why are you definite about the time you left, Mr. Yeomond?"

"Well, we were intending to carry on a bit longer, but Frank pointed out that the gate leading from the sunk garden to the sports ground would be locked at half-past eleven, and that is the only way out now, unless one chases through the kitchen regions, you see. I checked my watch against his, and we decided we had better be off."

"I see. That's all for the present, then, Mr. Yeomond. I should like to see Mr. Francis Yeomond next, and perhaps you wouldn't mind asking Mr. Malpas if he'll hold himself in readiness to follow Mr. Francis."

The stories told by Francis and Malpas were similar to that told by Hilary. All three brothers had left the house by way of the terrace and the sunk garden, and none had seen or heard anything of a suspicious nature as he proceeded to his hut. Malpas had found Richard Cowes peacefully reading—his book open upon his knees. Francis had been somewhat surprised at the nonappearance of Clive Brown-Jenkins all night, but concluded that he had probably gone to the greyhound racing with Timon Anthony, and that the two of them were spending the night at a hotel. He himself had gone to bed almost immediately upon his return to the hut, and had closed but not locked or bolted the door. In reply to a question he answered that they did not lock or bolt the door at night: for one thing there was nothing valuable in the hut; and, for another, as the only method of lighting up the place was by means of an oil-lamp, they had decided there was some danger of the wooden structure catching fire, and wished to preserve an easy means of egress in case of danger.

Clive Brown-Jenkins was requested to return to the scene of inquisition. The inspector looked at him suspiciously, and demanded brusquely why he had chosen to conceal the fact that he had accompanied Anthony to the greyhound racing.

"I haven't concealed anything," protested Clive angrily. "I didn't go to the greyhound racing with Anthony. I never had any intention of going. He wanted to slip off sharp after dinner without attracting Mrs. Puddequet's attention, because she's down on the dogs, so he asked me whether I would just run him up to the station at Market Longer on the step of my bike. Of course I agreed, and at twenty to nine we made some excuse to slip off."

"Dinner over, Mr. Jenkins?"

"Oh, yes. Just about. People messing about with nuts and things, that's all. It was easy enough to get away."

"And you two went to Market Longer station on your bicycle? How long did it take you?"

"Oh, he wanted to catch the nine-ten. We managed it easily. Got there with six minutes to spare. Then I tooled home on the bike and went back to the house. I've told you everything that happened after that."

"Yes, but why didn't you tell me about the bicycle business? It may be important. Don't you see that it means we can't put our finger on Anthony at the time the crime was committed? I'd like to see him next."

Anthony entered with a narcissus in his buttonhole. He was humming a gay little tune.

"Well, inspector," said he. "Got the handcuffs ready?"

"Not just yet, Mr. Anthony," replied Bloxham, sizing up his man. "But we shan't be long now, I hope."

"Do you know what I think?" said Anthony, seating himself and then half-

rising to hitch his chair a little nearer that of the inspector. He lowered his voice to a confidential undertone. "I believe the old lady did it herself."

The inspector blinked twice, but said nothing.

"Well, anyway," said Anthony defensively, seeing that the jest had missed fire, "she's jolly keen not to have the murderer discovered. She's going to leave her money to him."

"Mr. Anthony" said Bloxham, looking him straight in the eye, "how was it that White Lady beat Star Stay? A funny thing, that."

Anthony's eyes left the inspector's face for the fraction of a second. He laughed in a slightly unnatural tone.

"You don't catch me out like that," he said uneasily. "You know jolly well no dogs of those names ran on Friday night."

"Didn't they, Mr. Anthony?" said the inspector softly. "Are you sure? Which ground did you go to on Friday night?"

"White City," said Anthony thickly.

"Really and truly?" said the inspector, with simple wonder. "Well, I never! I should think you got there just as they shut the gates for the night, didn't you?"

"I only got there right at the end of the show, if that's what you're getting at," replied Anthony. He pulled the narcissus out of his coat and tossed it through the open window. "At the very end. I didn't really see anything of what went on. So really I don't know the name of one dog from another."

"And what train did you come home by?" enquired the inspector.

"Got into Market Longer at two-sixteen," said Anthony glibly. "Of course I had to walk from the station to the house, so I suppose I actually arrived home at about three in the morning."

"How did you get back into the house?"

"I didn't. I slept in the gym."

"Oh, did you? Who pinched the second long rope, Mr. Anthony?"

"I don't think I understand."

"Did you have a light in the gymnasium, Mr. Anthony?"

"A light? No. No, I didn't have a light. Of course I didn't."

"Oh? All right. Thank you, Mr. Anthony. You won't leave the house yet, will you? I think I'll have to talk to you again later. And then perhaps you'll tell me what you really did do between the hours of nine-four, when Mr. Jenkins left you at the station, and three a.m., when you say you arrived home. Do you think'—he stood up and glared into the wretched Anthony's eyes—"do you really think I'm a fool? At any rate, I'm not such a fool as all that. I know you didn't go to London on the nine-ten on Friday night. I know you reached the house long before three in the morning. And I know that some time between the hours you've mentioned a murder was committed in the sunk garden out there."

"In the sunk garden?" said Anthony dully. His brave air and his lilting tune were gone as irrevocably as his buttonhole, the discarded narcissus. The inspector stepped to his side, placed a compelling hand on his shoulder, and urged him to the window.

"A blow such as that which killed Jacob Hobson," he said, "produces a certain amount of bleeding. Come and look."

He drew the reluctant young man on to the terrace and down the stone steps. At the foot of them he turned aside, Anthony following, until they stood on the crazy paving which surrounded the unfinished goldfish pond. Involuntarily Anthony glanced across the geometrically planned garden at the other pond. Once more in the center of it stood the little mermaid. She was wearing a smile comparable to that of the Mona Lisa. Anthony shuddered. She had seen a human creature done to death. He averted his eyes, and realized that the inspector was addressing him, and that the stalwart constable who had been placed on duty in the sun garden was standing at his shoulder. The man's attitude was the reverse of aggressive, and yet, for some indefinable reason, Anthony felt as much affronted by his proximity as though the man had laid the hand of the law on his shoulder.

"Now, Mr. Anthony," the inspector was saying, "what do you make of this?"

He bent and lifted a corner of the heavy tarpaulin which covered the unfinished pond. The white cement bottom of the dry basin was patched and stained with great dark blotches.

"Blood, Mr. Anthony, from the head of the corpse," said the inspector solemnly. With great care and precision he replaced the heavy cover.

"Now, what should you make of that?" he asked. "I'm serious, Mr. Anthony. In my place, for instance"—they walked side by side to the stone steps and mounted them slowly—"what would you say that pretty picture indicated?"

Anthony frowned.

"I should say it was the work of somebody who knew the house pretty well, and knew that the pond was there and was unfinished and was covered over and—"

"Might have been the work of one of the gardeners Mrs. Puddequet employs—the Bucks firm's people, I mean," said the inspector thoughtfully. "Is that your idea?"

"Of course," said Anthony, fastening on to the suggestion immediately. "And they know more about the sunk garden than anybody, I suppose, don't they, when one thinks it out?"

"All the less reason for them choosing it as the place to commit the murder, Mr. Anthony," said the inspector, stepping over the drawing-room windowsill into the room. "A man who is always tinkering about with tarpaulins

and cement basins and who knows this sunk garden as well as he knows his own room at home, we'll say, wouldn't imagine for a moment that I shouldn't look under that heavy cover for traces of crime. He'd know *I* would, because he'd know *he* would. See? The human mind is a very funny thing, Mr. Anthony. And now"—he waited until Anthony rejoined him inside the room— "you'll be sensible and polite and tell me where you were and what you were doing between nine-four on Friday night and one-thirty a.m. on Saturday, won't you?"

"No," replied Anthony, nervously clearing his throat. "I'll admit I didn't go to the greyhound racing. I'll admit I didn't go further afield than Market Longer station. And I'll admit that I intended to deceive Brown-Jenkins, and that I intended to deceive you. But what I actually did after Brown-Jenkins left me at the station is my own business if I choose to make it so."

The inspector looked at him thoughtfully.

"Very well, Mr. Anthony," he said at last. "Ver-rey well. It's a free country—to a certain limited extent."

CHAPTER VII

But Inspector Bloxham is Not

I

"I DON'T like it," repeated Bloxham to the sergeant.

"No, sir." The sergeant eyed the ground sympathetically and then the tree-tops intelligently. He cleared his throat, and then observed with great and discerning candor:

"The Chief Constable always gets shouting for the Yard before we've 'ardly 'ad time to get a smell at a murder, sir. What about Kost, Mr. Bloxham?"

"Yes," said the inspector thoughtfully, while the little crease of annoyance which a mention of Scotland Yard always called to his otherwise unfurrowed brow gradually faded out—"yes, there is certainly Kost to be considered."

They made their way to his hut in order to consider him.

"And then," said the sergeant helpfully, as they crossed the southwestern corner of the sports ground and negotiated the long-jump pit to save going farther round, "there's that there Miss Cowes."

"Miss Cowes?" The inspector walked through the gate on to the lower field, and then looked with astonishment at his companion. "How do you mean?"

"Well, sir, what was she up to, arriving on a milk train at that hour in the morning?"

"Well, that's the time milk trains run, I suppose," said the inspector mildly. "Besides, the young woman's a freak. Chelsea art student and all that sort of thing."

"Immoral," said the sergeant, shaking his head. "A bad lot, them art students, sir. You mark my words. I'm a Battersea man myself, and know a thing or two about them. No idea of what's right and what's wrong. That's my experience."

"Of course," said the inspector, ignoring these remarks, "there's the chance she may have seen or heard something as she came across the grounds. But, if the murder was committed round about ten o'clock, you see, well, I mean, between three and four o'clock next morning you can't say there's much doing, can you? Still, as you say, we might as well see what she's got to say."

Kost was sitting in front of his hut with his legs stretched in front of him and his arms behind his head; he was staring up at the sky, which was col-

55

ored with the mild blue of April. At his feet a small cat was playing with the laces of his boots, which were unfastened. He took no notice of the police when they approached, but continued to stare heavenwards. The inspector addressed him.

"Finished work for the day, Mr. Kost?" he enquired politely.

Kost grinned good-naturedly.

"I've never finished work in this place," he said. "Can I do something for you, perhaps?"

"You can tell us what you were doing up at the house at about one o'clock in the morning last Saturday," said the inspector, grimly regarding him.

Kost leapt to his feet and sent the chair reeling back against the wooden side of the hut.

"What do you mean?" he shouted. "You are not believing I had any connection with this murder, perhaps?"

"Steady, Mr. Kost," said the inspector coolly. "I haven't mentioned the murder, so far as I know. Will you answer my question?"

"I am not inclined to answer any questions," grumbled the fair-haired trainer, restraining his excitement and lowering his voice to its normal tone. "I know nothing. I have seen nothing. As for being up at the house on Friday night or Saturday morning either—no, I was not there. Do you wish me to swear it, perhaps?"

"You were not there? But supposing someone actually saw you?" The inspector's tone was gentle, but he watched the man's face closely. It did not change, except for a slight tightening of the skin over the jaw.

"Saw nothing." Kost's tone was at once resentful and contemptuous. "You should send them to buy some spectacles, perhaps. I was not there."

"Where were you?"

"I was here."

"At nine o'clock?"

"So."

"At ten o'clock?"

"I was not here at ten o'clock."

"Ah! Where were you at ten o'clock?"

"I was drinking a glass of stout—oatmeal stout—at the inn. That was at half-past nine, about. I finish my drink—good stuff, that!—and I return. I return at a quarter or twenty past ten. There is a noise in the sunk garden as I come in at the gate to the grounds over there. I go to look. It is the man who is dead. I call to him to go home or he will be locked up. He tells me to go to the devil. I take him by the neck and run him back to the gate and push him into the road. I shut the gate. I listen. No sound. I think he has fallen into the ditch, perhaps. Right place for a drunken man who beats his wife. I hope the ditch is nice and wet. I hope he will have rheumatism after that. Then I go

back to my hut and I sleep well. The stout makes me sleep well. Good stuff, that stout."

The sergeant, who had taken down the whole of this statement in short-hand, glanced at the inspector.

"Thank you, Mr. Kost," said the latter smoothly. "You are sure of all the times you mentioned? What about the last one?"

"Well, I leave the inn at about twenty minutes to ten. That is to say, at twenty minutes to ten by my time, but at ten minutes to ten by their time. I compared the clock in the bar with my watch, and they say ten minutes apart, so I believe my own."

The usual idiosyncrasy of a public-house clock in being ten minutes fast, if not more, was well known to both inspector and sergeant, and they nodded without speaking, and waited for Kost to go on.

"Well, I have my wristwatch with its luminous dial, and I think the night is fine, and so I will go for a brisk walk, perhaps. I walk the other way of the road, out towards Warlock Hill for a quarter of an hour, then I look at my watch and it says five minutes to ten. Then I return and I walk fast and I compute—a quarter of an hour back to the inn, and from the inn to the gate about six minutes at that pace, then from the gate to the sunk garden to see why the noise—and I arrive at the conclusion that it was between a quarter and twenty past ten when I find the man Hobson. That is Q.E.D., perhaps?" He grinned triumphantly.

"Perhaps it is," said the inspector, turning to go. "And perhaps it isn't," he added to the sergeant as they returned to the house. "Anything strike you about that yarn of his?"

"Well," replied the sergeant, treading cautiously. "Hobson *might* 'ave been murdered by somebody in the road and brought 'ere afterwards."

"Then what about the blood in the unfinished fishpond in the sunk garden? Why no blood on the gravel path? And why, in the name of goodness, all the rest of the fandango? Why not kill him and be done with it? Why tie him to the statue and chuck him in the lake? Oh, and that's another thing, sergeant. How *did* the murderer get the body out that far? I've thought myself sick, tired, and silly over that. Of course, the way I look at it, we can cut out the village people to a man. Even if there was a possible suspect among 'em—which there isn't at present—I should only follow him up as a matter of routine, and not from real conviction that he might have done it."

"You mean this 'ere is a toff's job, sir?"

"I do. What's more, it's somebody in this house."

"What *about* Kost, sir? He's a foreigner, you know."

"Yes," said the inspector, allowing to pass unchallenged the usual English implication that foreigners are always either lunatics or criminals or both, "but the motive?"

"Well, what might any of their motives be, come to that, Mr. Bloxham?" said the sergeant, with great earnestness. "You see, sir, it all comes back to this: we ain't found no one with a motive except that sixpenn'orth of misery down in the village, poor little cat. And, as you said yourself, *she* hadn't either the brains or the guts—although"—he paused as a new thought struck him—"she might 'ave helped *someone else* do it! The whole job, as I see it, would be a sight easier for two than for one, sir."

Inspector Bloxham nodded.

"That's an idea I've had for a few hours myself," he said. "We'll get on to Mrs. Hobson again when I've worked through the household here. Personally, that young Anthony doesn't impress me very favorably. And the fact also remains, sergeant, that this is his home, and so he'd be bound to know Hobson a good deal better than the other people here in the house."

"Dirty work between him and Mrs. Hobson," said the sergeant, nodding wisely. "Well, she's not been a bad-looker in her time, I should judge. Stranger things 'ave happened, and will happen again with human nature what it is today, sir."

With this sententious remark he followed the inspector through the doorway of the sunk garden, and they mounted the steps to the house.

"Well, inspector," said Miss Caddick, fluttering to meet them, "have you made your arrest? I do *hope* we shall soon be out of this terrible suspense and trouble. I declare I shall soon *give up* going to bed at night. I seem to become more and more nervous as time goes on."

"Well, Miss Caddick," replied the inspector, "I hope you will soon be at peace again. The only suspect so far is Mrs. Hobson, but we hope to complete our case shortly now. Could I get hold of Miss Amaris Cowes, do you think?"

"Oh, but inspector!" Miss Caddick clasped her hands in affected consternation and horror. "*She* knows nothing of this dreadful affair! She did not arrive here until four o'clock the next morning. By a *milk train*! Are not the modern young women extraordinary!"

"Precisely," replied the inspector, following her into the dining room and selecting a chair.

Amaris Cowes seemed to have been gardening. She was wearing breeches and gaiters, enormous shapeless gloves consisting of a compartment of honor for the thumb and one large roomy bag for all the fingers, very muddy boots—the property of Clive Brown-Jenkins, as her brother took a size smaller than she did—and a trenchcoat which smelt strongly of dogs, and was the kennel jacket of Timon Anthony.

She seated herself gingerly on the edge of a chair and gazed serenely at the inspector.

"Yes, I did really come on the milk train. It gets into Market Longer just

about three," she said. "The stationmaster will remember me, I expect. He said I was a stowaway and must pay my fare."

"Oh," said the inspector, nonplussed. "And—er—what did you say?"

"I said nothing. I never waste words. I pushed him out of my way and came here."

"Oh?" said the inspector, for the second time.

"I shall report you, my man, for insubordination," added Amaris, staring at the sergeant with disconcerting gravity. "You are grinning at your superior officer."

"And you don't know—you had no knowledge of the man Hobson before you came down here?" asked the inspector hopelessly.

Amaris Cowes laughed.

"I suppose you are expected to ask people that sort of thing," she said. "It must be awfully trying. No, I knew nothing of the man until I heard that he was dead. Oh, and my hobbies are painting and gardening, my birthday is in September, and my favorite color is tomato-red. I was born in the year that Thingummy won the Derby. They wore them mottled that season, you remember; and my published works include the *Encyclopedia Britannica* and *Barnaby Rudge*. Oh, and I spent the night in the gymnasium," she added.

Joseph Herring scratched his jaw. Then he counted the rabbits again.

"There's the two white Angoras and two lots of Flemish Giants, three in each 'utch," he said to himself, screwing up his apelike visage and squinting through the wire mesh. "But there's only two Belgian 'ares. Now, what can you make o' that?"

He opened the hutch and lifted them out. There could be no doubt about it. There were only two. Joe apostrophized them softly, as they tentatively explored the grass at his feet.

"Now, why the 'ell can't you let me know what's 'appened to your brother, drat you! 'E could 'ave nibbled 'is way out of the b— 'utch. Yes. I knows that. But 'e couldn't 'ardly turn round and block up the 'ole be'ind 'im, could 'e! What's the game? And what 'ad I better—oh, cripes! 'Ere comes the old gal!"

The bathchair, propelled this time by Miss Caddick, and attended by Celia Brown-Jenkins in a canary-colored frock, and by Priscilla Yeomond in a green one, came slowly up the paved path of the kitchen garden. A cluster of gooseberry bushes hid Joe's nefarious activities from view, so that by the time that Great-aunt Puddequet came within sight of the rabbit hutches there was only one Belgian hare on the ground.

The other, in a large spare hutch covered with a piece of clean sacking, was probably wondering what had happened to him.

Great-aunt Puddequet's rabbits were one of her chief diversions, and Joe,

as rabbit-fancier-in-chief, was a marked man. His employer regarded him with a mixture of dark suspicion and grudging respect. She sensed that his passion for rabbits was inferior to her own. In knowledge of their needs and habits, however, she realized that he was distinctly her superior. She leaned forward and addressed him.

"Keeper!"

"Yes, mam?"

"Exhibit the animals."

"Very good, mam."

"This Flemish Giant, keeper, is getting a little too thin."

Joe, immediately recognizing stolen property, smiled in tolerant good-humor.

" 'E 'as missed you, mam. 'E's bin pinin' away."

"Explain yourself." Great-aunt Puddequet looked pleased.

"It's this way, mam. Ever since you took such a fancy to that there bit of sunk garding t'other side the 'ouse, seems as if that rabbit knowed it. Don't seem to take to 'is food nor nothink. I dessay 'e'll be as right as rain *now*."

Great-aunt Puddequet stroked the blue-gray creature's long ears, and gave it back into Joe's large, gnarled hands.

"Now the Angoras, keeper," she suggested. Joe, on safe ground here, handed them out. They were nervous and scrabbly, however, so that she very quickly had them put back into their hutch.

"And now," said Great-aunt Puddequet in pleased anticipation, "for my dear little Belgians, keeper."

Joe coughed discreetly, and handed out a solitary little bunny.

"Beg pardon, mam," said Joe, "but I took the opportunity with the other two, seeing that they was that way inclined—" He jerked his head suggestively towards the covered hutch and winked solemnly.

"Enough, keeper. Refrain from indelicacy. Nothing is gained by loose conversation. You have done very creditably, keeper."

The bathchair moved on, and disappeared. Joe took out his handkerchief and wiped his face. Then he removed the sacking from the large spare hutch and tenderly returned the solitary little Belgian hare to his companion.

"And where the 'ell your b— brother 'as gorn, 'as me licked," he confided to the pair of them. "Seems like I'll 'ave to find you another. But it'll 'ave to be a sister if I'm to keep me end up with the old gal."

He turned again to the hutches and went on with the work of hygienic importance. From the kitchen, and pursued by the maledictions of the cook, came Timon Anthony. He was eating a large and rather unmanageable slice of game-pie. With him was Richard Cowes.

"Hullo, Joe," said Anthony, as he came up with Herring. "The old lady been round here this morning?"

"It's a funny thing, sir, but she 'as."

"Why funny? Thought she often came along to have a look at the bunnies and make sure you didn't sneak one for the Sunday dinner!"

"Mister Anthony," said Joe sorrowfully, "she do come round to see 'em pretty often. But what I notice, sir, is this: she always chooses 'er time."

"Meaning?"

"Meaning, sir, as I've suffered another misfortune with these 'ere rabbits. Takes me all me time to think out quick enough what to say to 'er, because, once she got wind there was anything wrong, I'd get the sack without any manner of doubt at all. It's cruel, the lies an honest working man 'as to tell to keep 'is head above water and the wolf from the door."

"Why, what's happened now?"

Anthony put the last piece of pie-crust into his mouth, leaned against the bole of an apple tree, and prepared to listen to a long tale of woe. The tale was not long.

"Why, somebody's pinched one of them Belgian 'ares."

"What, again?"

"What d'you mean—again?"

"Thought you lost one before—a few days ago. Why, it was the day of the murder, wasn't it?"

"Ah, that wasn't a Belgian 'are. That was a Flemish Giant. They're nothink alike, nothink. Look for yourself."

Timon solemnly investigated. So did Richard.

"And now you've lost one of the hares," he said. "When did it go?"

"Well," said Joe, rubbing his hands on a wisp of straw, "if I knowed that, I might make a guess at who took it. But one thing I do know. And that is— none of this 'ere thieving used to go on before the old lady 'ad this last dotty turn of 'ers."

"How do you mean?" asked Anthony.

"Well, sir, you oughter know bettern anyone, I should say. What can you call it but dotty, this athletics business?"

"Oh, that!"

"Yes, sir—that. And d'you know what I think? I think? I believe that there Kost knows all about my rabbit. I reckon 'e eats 'em."

"Oh, come," said Timon Anthony, laughing, "you couldn't prove that, you know, Joe. Besides, the chap's a vegetarian. And, if you couldn't prove it, you shouldn't say it. By the way, didn't my grandmother spot that one was missing?"

"No, sir. I was give an idea, and I won through on it. If I'm lucky she won't bother me again today. But if she asks a lot of questions tomorrow I'm liable to slip up, so before then I got to replace him with a her."

"With a her?"

"A doe, sir."

"Oh."

"Yes. This very night that job 'as got to be done."

"Where will you go? Market Longer?"

"I might. And I might slip up to London on the quiet."

"I should make it London for safety's sake. How about cash?"

"I got what me ferrets makes. More than enough."

"Oh well, look here," interpolated Richard Cowes. "Ten bob. All I've got on me. You take that."

"If my grandmother didn't keep me so beastly short, I'm hanged if I wouldn't go up to Town myself tonight and have a look round. I'm fit to die of doing nothing down here," said Anthony, peevishly. "Even raking round to get evidence against Hobson's murderer bores me stiff."

He strolled off, following the trail of old Mrs. Puddequet's bathchair. Joe looked after him thoughtfully, and then rubbed the top of his nose with the back of his hand. Richard went back to the house.

In his perambulations Timon encountered Amaris Cowes. She had set up her easel near the bathing hut and was painting a group of pollard willows on the opposite bank of the mere.

For some time Anthony stood and watched her. Then he said abruptly:

"Joe's lost another rabbit."

Amaris, one brush between her teeth and the other daubing away busily, nodded.

Undaunted by her preoccupied air, Anthony pursued the subject.

"Funny thing, what?"

Amaris nodded again, laid down the one brush and removed the other from between her teeth.

"Expound," she said.

Timon expounded. When he had finished she nodded again.

"Wonder whether he's right," said Anthony.

"Right about Kost?"

"Yes."

"No."

"Eh?"

"Kost is a vegetarian," said Amaris.

"How do you know?"

"Great-aunt told me so. It was the only thing, so far as they could discover, which singled him out from all the other trainers who applied, so Miss Caddick chose him on the strength of it."

"By Jove!" said Timon admiringly. "Quite the knack of it, haven't you?"

"Of what?"

"Winning people's hearts."

"Great-aunt confides in me about unimportant matters, if that is what you mean."

"Only in unimportant ones?"

"I think so. She hasn't told me yet who murdered that wretched man."

"Hobson?"

"Who else has been murdered here?"

"But do you think she knows who did it?"

"Oh, yes. Of course she knows. At any rate, she is very anxious that no one else shall find out anything."

"Well, I mean, she probably disliked the fellow."

"Yes. Pity anyone should be taken up for stamping on a crawling thing of that type. They'll arrest the wife in the end, I expect."

"The wife? Whatever for?"

"Motive."

"Oh. Important thing, of course, the motive. She must have had a pretty good one. He led her the deuce of a life, they say."

"Poor creature."

"Yes."

From the distant house a shrill whistle, blown three times in succession, announced that it was lunchtime. Amaris packed up her belongings, and, Timon helping her, carried them up to the house. On the way, Timon paused.

"Faint with hunger?" asked Amaris.

"No."

"What, then?"

"I wish you'd marry me."

"Why?"

"Oh, I don't know. I feel you'd buck me up."

Amaris walked on again. After a fraction of a second, Timon followed her example. As they reached the sports ground and began to walk across it, she said.

"I shouldn't have time."

"Time?"

"To buck you up. My career, you know. I paint."

"Yes."

"No."

"Eh?"

"No, I shouldn't have time, I meant."

"No, I'd be your life-work, wouldn't I?" He grinned self-consciously.

Amaris considered him with unflattering detachment, and then slowly shook her head.

"I should hate to think so," she said gently.

She stumbled as she spoke, and swiftly bent to pick up the object which

her foot had touched. It was one of the sports javelins. Amaris held it at full length and shook it in a playfully warlike manner.

"I say," exclaimed Anthony in admiration, "you remind me of that goddess—what's-her-name?—you know who I mean!"

"Artemis," said Richard Cowes's Amazonian sister. "You are mistaken, though. My hips are too big. And I don't look a scrap 'chaste and fair.' Don't trouble to deny it! I'm more like a picture by Augustus John than anything you ever saw in the Artemis line."

She balanced the javelin carefully, the corded grip resting in the center of her slim, well-shaped, grubby, paint-stained palm. Her fingers closed round the shaft. The metal point of the mock spear glittered in the April sunshine.

"Oh!" cried Amaris. She drew back her arm and sent the long, straight, slender, finely balanced missile hurtling high and sure. At the termination of its swift and graceful flight, it came to earth true as a bird, its metal point embedded in the ground.

"I say, I wonder whether there is blood on it?" said Anthony, running forward. He seized the long white shaft and jerked the point out of the ground. Feverishly he scraped the damp earth from the metal.

"Hum! Difficult to say," he said. "I'd better take it back to the gym., I suppose. There's been enough strafe over the beastly things already."

"Yes, so I heard." Amaris regarded him queerly. "I won't wait for you. See you at lunch. I'll take my things now, if you're going to take the javelin."

She stalked away towards the sunk garden, her painting materials hung about her until they looked like the paraphernalia of the White Knight.

"And see whether you can find the gymnasium rope that the murderers took!" she shouted over her shoulder.

Timon Anthony, a singularly perturbed Alice, walked on without finding sufficient spirit to make any reply. When he did pluck up courage and glance back, Amaris had disappeared.

CHAPTER VIII

Irritating Attitude of a Lady Old Enough to Know Better

"WELL," said Inspector Bloxham, seating himself on the large roller at the western side of the sports field, "I don't say we progress, exactly. But at least we don't go backwards. And one thing I'm certain about, and that is, my lad, somebody in this place killed Jacob Hobson. I reckon that we are now exactly half-way through the investigation. I've heard seven yarns about what people were doing and why on the night of the murder, and, as I see it, I've got to hear seven more. I've now interrogated young Brown-Jenkins, Miss Yeomond, Mrs. Hobson, all the Mr. Yeomonds, Mr. Anthony—a very suspicious bird, that one, I might say—Kost the trainer, and Miss Cowes. I must have another go at her later, I think. Clever as a cartload of monkeys that one, I reckon." He stuck his hands in his trouser pockets. Neither man was in uniform.

"Oh, I don't know, Mr. Bloxham," objected the sergeant. "Them sort of large, blowsy females are seldom strong in the brain-line, sir. Sort of passionate and excitable underneath an otherwise placid exterior, if you get me, inspector, but real bright, no."

"Boy," said the inspector, eyeing his henchman and supporter with grave concern, "those talkies are doing you no good. Take my tip, and spend your evenings at home. Help the missus wind the wool. It'll do your nerves good."

A dark flush suffused the sergeant's bovine and ingenuous countenance; he changed the subject.

" 'Ave you ever thought any more of the bathchair business that Friday night or Saturday morning, Mr. Bloxham?" he asked.

"Bathchair business?"

"Ah! As swore to by two independent witnesses, Miss Yeomond and Mr. Jenkins, sir?"

"The point is, were they independent witnesses? I've my suspicions of Mr. Brown-Jenkins. I can't make up my mind how much of a liar that young man is."

"Liar, sir?"

"Champion cyclist, sergeant. There are several advanced classes in the university of liars. Golfers and fishermen rank very high in the sporting grades, and champion cyclists run them close. Then come those Irish country lads

who tell you the size of the fox that's just gone to ground, and the fellow who was Not Out l.b.w. After these comes the man from Maida Vale whose dog always outruns the electric hare; and, of course, right at the end of the list come the simple-minded souls such as water polo players who indulge in foul deeds with artless joy and complete lack of finesse, and then immediately and clamorously claim a free pass against the man they've just fouled. Luckily a competent referee can usually deal with humorists of that sort."

"You seem to have studied your subjick, sir," said the sergeant with heavy irony. The inspector nodded.

"I was not always a policeman, sergeant," he replied sadly. "Time was when they destined me for Sandhurst and a career of death or glory. The war stepped in, however, and made another kind of soldier out of me. Then the family heirlooms went the way such trifles will, and I came out of the Army quite whole and extraordinarily tired, and with no money and no training to speak of, and joined the noble force of which we two are shining ornaments. And now, do you think you can defend me from an umbrella attack if I interview old Mrs. Puddequet?"

"Seems to me, sir," said the sergeant as they walked along the cinder track towards old Mrs. Puddequet's bathchair, which had just emerged from the opposite gateway and was being propelled at a dignified pace towards them, "as you ain't so serious over this 'ere murder as you was over the Merridale case fifteen months back."

"Sergeant," said the inspector, "you're a good chap, and so I'll tell you something I wouldn't repeat, nor care for you to repeat, to anyone else. I'm doing my duty, in a sense, over this case, but my heart isn't in it. I know the police aren't paid to be sentimental, but it upsets me badly to know that through me some perfectly decent and humane person is going to be convicted for bouncing a brick on that filthy animal Hobson. If I had any guts in me, I'd throw up the case—at least, if it weren't for my insatiable curiosity I would. But I want to know who did it—and yet I don't! As soon as I know, duty compels me to pass on the information and make an arrest, you see, and that—"

The bathchair, accelerating its speed, now drew near enough for its occupant to overhear any further conversation, and so the inspector stopped short.

Great-aunt Puddequet, craning her head forward from the bathchair like a peculiarly malignant-looking tortoise, greeted the police with mild derision.

"Well! well! Here we come, with our notebooks and pencils! And what have we found out today?" she enquired, blinking her yellowish eyes at them. The inspector smiled politely.

"We are depending upon you to assist us in our enquiries today, Mrs. Puddequet," said he. "To begin with—"

"To begin with, attendant," shrieked old Mrs. Puddequet, glaring round at

Joe the rabbit-fancier, who was her escort and propeller that afternoon, "leave the equipage and retire to a distance not exceeding ten yards. Deploy."

Joe shrugged his shoulders and removed himself to the motor lawnmower, on the box of which he sat to smoke a cigarette.

"To begin with," said the inspector, "I wonder whether you have come to any conclusion about the use of the bathchair on the night of the murder?"

"I do not understand you, inspector. Are you sure you mean on the night of the murder?"

"Well, to be exact—" began Bloxham.

Old Mrs. Puddequet laughed shortly, sharply, and offensively.

"To be exact," the inspector repeated loudly, for he was annoyed, "I mean the very—the extremely early hours of the following morning. At one o'clock, in fact—or thereabouts."

"What about the bathchair?" enquired the old lady testily. "Come to the point, man!"

"Were you in your bathchair at one o'clock in the morning on Saturday, April the nineteenth?" snapped the inspector.

Great-aunt Puddequet produced from the recesses of the bathchair a tortoiseshell lorgnette, and, with its aid, studied first the inspector and then the sergeant, and then the inspector again. Apparently satisfied that, although curious variants of an existing type, they could still be classed among the known mammals, she lowered the absurd lens and spoke with dignity.

"May I ask whether the police have any objection to make concerning the conduct of a householder, voter, citizen, and ratepayer who chooses to take early morning exercise in her own grounds, in her own bathchair, in her own sufficient clothing, and in her own time?" she enquired. "If so, say so, officers, and we will go into the matter at greater length and at a more convenient hour."

She looked round the side of the bathchair and squealed shrilly for Joseph Herring. The Scrounger put a reluctant boot on the stump of his cigarette and stood up.

"Attendant," said Great-aunt Puddequet, "take me in."

The inspector gazed after the bathchair with mixed feelings. The sergeant broke the silence.

"Well, I'm damned!" he said. "She was in it all the time."

"Was she?" said the inspector, his blue eyes narrowing. "That's what we've got to find out, my lad. Hullo! She's hove to! Coming back to us, by gum! Now what?"

The bathchair drew up smartly, and Joseph Herring skilfully inserted a cigarette between his lips and lit it before his employer bade him once more retire to the box of the mowing-machine.

"I ought to say, officers," said old Mrs. Puddequet, investigating the turn-

ups of the sergeant's trousers with the ferrule of her umbrella and muttering "Permanent!" to herself in a disgruntled tone as she did so, "that a special service of motor-coaches is being run from Market Longer to the gate of these grounds to bring here persons who have a desire to see the spot whence the body was recovered. Pieces of stone and handfuls of gravel are being stolen from the sunk garden as souvenirs from the actual scene of the crime, and one enthusiastic collector has gone so far as to poison the small coarse fish which inhabit the mere in a determined effort to secure one of them as a unique reminder of an exciting occasion. I say no more."

She peered round for Herring. Joseph removed his cigarette, extinguished it carefully, and placed the half of it which remained behind his right ear.

"Attendant," said Great-aunt Puddequet, who had witnessed this proceeding, "are you there?"

"Yes, mam!" replied Joe, establishing himself in her line of vision.

"Remove that disgusting appendage."

"You don't mean me fag, mam?"

Great-aunt Puddequet closed her lips and stared unwinkingly at him out of her baleful eyes.

"Oh, 'ave it your own way," muttered Joe. He took the cigarette from behind his ear, and, by a dexterous sleight of hand, shot it up the sleeve of his jacket, whence it slid confidingly back into the palm of his hand when the old lady turned her head.

"Of course," said Mrs. Puddequet to the police officers, "it is not for a mere defenseless member of the general public to complain that there are two police officers spending all their time, both morning *and* afternoon, about the house and grounds, and that *still* her property is stolen under their very noses! Stone from the sunk garden, gravel from the paths, chub from the mere—disgraceful!"

At the end of this remarkable outburst she suddenly switched round in the bathchair and screamed to Joseph Herring to take her indoors.

"Well," said the inspector, gazing after her with a mixture of amusement and exasperation in his eyes, "so that's that."

"And she was out in that bathchair—" began the sergeant.

"Haring along at twenty m.p.h.," grinned the inspector.

"At one o'clock in the morning," chuckled the sergeant.

"Yes. It only remains to find out whether it was the devil himself or merely one of his angels pushing behind, and then we can forget all about it," concluded the inspector. Then his tone changed.

"I don't like her attitude a bit," he said, frowning. "And the worst of it is that I really don't feel equal to browbeating an old woman of ninety. What's her idea, I wonder, in telling us a lie like that? Oh, well. Never mind that now. Let's follow her up to the house, and then I'll get on to Miss Brown-

Jenkins again. She's the one who spotted her brother bending over the empty bed in Miss Yeomond's room."

"You don't suspect young Jenkins, sir?"

"As I said before, I'm not certain how much of his yarn I can believe. After I've tackled his sister again I may be a little more certain on the point."

Celia Brown-Jenkins could add little to the inspector's knowledge. She had talked with Priscilla until nearly one o'clock, and a few moments later Priscilla had appeared at the bedroom door and demanded to be allowed to share her room for the night as she had been frightened out of her own. Celia then went on to repeat her story of finding her brother in Priscilla's room at about half-past one, and of his subsequent tumble downstairs.

The inspector tapped his front teeth with his pencil and asked to see Miss Caddick. She, fluttering and alarmed, could say nothing beyond the fact that she had sat as usual, in the morning room, doing her crochet work, and had retired to bed at ten-thirty, her usual time. She had heard no more until she was awakened by the noise occasioned by the fall of Clive Brown-Jenkins.

"Well," said the inspector to the sergeant when Miss Caddick, chafing her wrists to make certain that the handcuffs were not even then upon them, had been sent in search of Richard Cowes, "we don't get much forrader, do we? You see, if the old lady sticks to that yarn of hers about being out in the bathchair at that time of night, my pet theory about the case falls to the ground."

"And what might your theory be, sir?" enquired the sergeant respectfully.

"Well, in the murderer's place, I should certainly have obtained possession of that bathchair as a convenient means of transporting the body to the lake. But, of course, if old Mrs. Puddequet's story *did* happen to be true, that would knock that idea on the head immediately."

"But her story isn't the truth!" said the sergeant indignantly.

"Well, we believe it isn't. Still, there's just the bare chance that it might be. These old ladies get some cranky ideas into their heads at times."

"Yes. But, if it isn't true," persisted the sergeant, "it means she knows who the murderer is, and is trying to shield him, as we said before."

"Oh," said Richard Cowes at the door, "you know, sergeant, I hardly think that. She doesn't know who the murderer is, but she doesn't want you official people to know either. She thinks that, as long as the murderer goes undetected, so long will she enjoy the company of reporters, policemen, and morbid sightseers. She's basking in the limelight of twentieth-century publicity, and she just revels in it. So do go slow with the brain-waves, I beg of you! Don't curtail the pleasures of the aged!"

He advanced into the room, holding a large pheasant-eye narcissus in one hand and a stick of rhubarb in the other. Alternately and very delicately he sniffed at the one and bit a portion off the end of the other.

"Mr. Cowes," said the inspector abruptly, when Richard had seated himself, "I want you to tell me, as exactly as you can, your movements on Friday, April the eighteenth, from half-past nine in the evening onwards."

Richard meditated.

"At half-past nine," he said, "I was in the library. I remained there until nearly half-past ten. Then I returned to my hut with the book I had begun to read, and sat there until nearly half-past eleven, when my companion in distress, Mr. Malpas Yeomond, came in and retired to bed. At just after twelve I also retired to bed. I awoke at just after six o'clock on the Saturday morning, except for a short interval of wakefulness between one and two a.m., and another between four and five."

"Did you see or hear anything of the man Hobson while you were in the library? The windows overlook the sunk garden."

"I heard an uneducated man's voice below, but I was absorbed in my reading and scarcely gave the matter any consideration."

"You did not go out on to the terrace to find out the cause of the disturbance?"

"There was no disturbance, so far as I know. After about two minutes the voice obtruded itself no more. Whether the man went away then, or whether my conscious mind was so fully occupied with my reading that I did not notice exactly when the voice ceased, I cannot say. There was gramophone music going on in the next room, I remember, but whether that eventually drowned the sound of the man's voice I cannot say."

"What were you reading, Mr. Cowes?"

"I was rereading Mommsen's work on the Romans. A fascinating set of volumes, inspector."

The inspector cordially agreed, and, politely dismissing him, sent again for Malpas Yeomond, and asked him to name the hour at which Richard Cowes had returned to the hut on the night of the murder."

"I don't know," replied Malpas shortly. "He was already in the hut when I myself returned at just after eleven-twenty."

"Did he leave the hut again that night?"

"I shouldn't say so. Why should he?"

"I'll tell you," replied the inspector, leading him to the door.

They walked out at the front door of the house and on to the terrace. Side by side they descended the steps and walked back to the unfinished goldfish pond, which had been left untouched since the murder. The inspector and sergeant drew aside the tarpaulin and disclosed the bloodstains on the concrete bottom of the empty pond.

"Here's where the body lay for a time," said Bloxham, "and from here it had to be transported to the lake. Now, my idea is that the transporting was done with the help of old Mrs. Puddequet's bathchair, and that bathchair was

actually seen in action at about one o'clock on the Saturday morning."

"Oh, if you're asking me whether Cowes was in the hut at one o'clock in the morning, I can tell you at once that he was! It was just before one that he woke me and said that he thought he heard someone knocking at the door, so he opened it and looked out, but there was no one about, so he shut it again and went back to his bunk. Then I must have fallen asleep in the middle of something he was saying, for I remember no more until daylight, when I woke up and found him just in the act of getting up."

The inspector nodded, thanked him, and Malpas returned to the house, while the police officers went back to Market Longer.

"There's something that I haven't got hold of," said Bloxham sorrowfully to the superintendent at Market Longer police station. "Look here, I've charted it according to the statements they've given me, and this is how it works out."

He handed his chart to the superintendent, who glanced at it, and then, frowning, bent over it more closely and checked up the number of names written at the left-hand side.

"You haven't yet got on to the man Herring, I see," he said. "I've had a complaint about him, by the way. He's been stealing rabbits."

He found a letter and handed it across to the inspector. Bloxham perused it, frowning. Then, handing it back, he said:

"Well, if that's true, it either clears him of being suspected of the murder or implicates him pretty thoroughly. I hadn't got on to him simply because I haven't tackled any of the servants yet. And I haven't tackled the servants because I don't believe it was a servant's job. I'm convinced in my own mind that the murder was committed by someone who stood on the terrace and dropped something heavy and hard on to Hobson's head as he stood cursing below in the sunk garden. If you'll have a look at this plan—it's fearfully rough, but I daresay it will serve to show what I mean—you'll be able to take in the position better."

The superintendent studied the chart and plan side by side as Bloxham expressed his theory.

"Hobson stood here, where I've marked in a letter H," said he, "and the murderer would have been up here at M. Hobson had come to the house full of a grievance. He was disgustingly drunk, and that's why he missed the steps in the dark. There was sufficient light in all the rooms—three in number—which open on to the terrace to give him the impression that his loud and repeated imprecations would certainly be heard. They were heard. Somebody came out on to the terrace from one of those three rooms and—well, bumped him off with a brick or something. Now, the three rooms are the drawing room, breakfast room, and library. In the drawing room were Malpas, Francis, and Priscilla Yeomond, with Celia Brown-Jenkins; in the break-

fast room was Miss Caddick—she seems to make that her special little do-main after dinner until she goes to bed—and in the dining room was Richard Cowes, and in the library was Clive Brown-Jenkins. Now, the first four can all account for each other—"

"Supply each other with an alibi, in short," said the superintendent.

"Yes, if you like. The other three were alone, at any rate for part of the time, so whether one of them is guilty is a matter open to investigation. That leaves Mr. Anthony—oh, well! You can see from the chart what everybody was doing and at what time. Of course, these are their own yarns, investi-gated and corrected by me. I'll just stick in Herring from the report in this letter, though. You see, he could have done it. It would have been possible. And then he would have used the rabbit stealing at Colonel Digot's place as a blind."

The superintendent placed the chart on top of the plan and read the former in an undertone. It ran:

Mrs. Hobson.—Plenty of motive. No alibi. Movements on night of murder unchecked until twelve midnight, when she went and knocked up Constable Copple of Little Longer. *Inferred*: That she could have committed the crime, but that she could not have trans-ported body to lake without assistance. No accomplice, so far as can be traced. Is a nonswimmer.

Mr. Brown-Jenkins.—No motive come to light, but behavior on night of crime very suspicious. Admitted, under cross-examination, took Anthony on back of bicycle to Market Longer station. No alibi until one-thirty a.m. Explains that he was reading in the library until twelve-thirty a.m. or so, but movements unchecked until one a.m., when seen by sister in bedroom (empty) of Miss Yeomond. No alibi after one forty-five a.m. until sunrise. Explanations of own move-ments very unconvincing, but probably could not have heard Hobson's voice from library, if he really was there. Swimmer.

Messrs. Malpas, Francis, and Hilary Yeomond.—No motive. Hole-proof alibi until eleven-twenty p.m. Then Mr. Francis and Mr. Hi-lary no alibi until sunrise, but Mr. Malpas shared hut with Mr. Cowes.

Mr. Anthony.—No actual motive, although probably knew Hobson and wife better than anyone did except for Mrs. Puddequet and the servants at Longer. Suspicious behavior, culminating in refusal to account for himself after nine-four p.m. on night of murder.

Mr. Kost.—No motive, so far as is known, but went every evening to village public house where murdered man was frequent visitor. May have quarreled there, but no evidence to support this hypoth-esis at present. Admits he was drinking in public house at nine-

thirty p.m. Gives time of return to house as being ten-twenty p.m. (Could have committed murder between these times, and this would fit in with medical evidence at inquest relative to time of death.) Tells story of hearing Hobson at gate of sunk garden, and says ran him out into road and heard no more of him. Story of all movements after nine-forty p.m. (nine-fifty p.m. by public-house clock) entirely uncorroborated. No alibi to cover time of murder, or any subsequent hour until sunrise. Swimmer.

Miss Cowes.—No possible motive. Entire stranger to locality. Arrived at Market Longer Station just after three a.m. and walked to Longer. Arrived not earlier than four a.m. Swimmer.

Mrs. Puddequet.—No motive. Physically impossible for her to have

(*a*) committed crime.

(*b*) transported body to lake.

Indicated she was in bathchair being pushed very swiftly round cinder running track at one a.m. on night of murder. Noise of wheels and time sworn (independently) by Miss Yeomond and Mr. Jenkins.

Miss Brown-Jenkins.—No motive. Alibi until one forty-five a.m., and then presumed in room with Miss Yeomond until sunrise. Saw brother bending over bed at one-thirty a.m. Swimmer.

Miss Yeomond.—No motive. Alibi until sunrise (as Miss Jenkins's roommate). Heard suspicious noises at one a.m. Investigated. Saw bathchair, but too dark to recognize occupant. Swimmer.

Miss Caddick.—No known motive. No alibi from end of dinner until sunrise. Opportunity for murder (was in room overlooking sunk garden until ten-thirty according to own undisputed statement), but incapable of transporting body to lake without assistance.

Mr. Cowes.—No motive. No alibi until nearly eleven-thirty. Confesses to hearing noise of Hobson in garden below. Opportunity for murder, but presumably no chance of transporting body to lake, unless did this immediately murder was committed. Is of meager stature, however, and the body that of very heavy man. Also, risky proceeding, because blood might have stained clothing. *N.B.*—Have carried out investigation of clothing of all above gentlemen, assisted by Sergeant Rollins. Nothing suspicious discovered.

Joseph Herring.—From information in possession of headquarters, appears Herring at large on night of murder, engaged in stealing rabbit or rabbits. Suspected to be a blind, but might prove an alibi.

No motive for crime so far as is known, but was probably acquainted with deceased and deceased's wife. Cannot swim.

The superintendent looked up.

"A lot of blank spaces, my lad," he said seriously. "Any number of these people could have done it easily. You'll have to have another go at 'em, and, if I may say so, in the following order."

He drew a sheet of paper towards him, and, consulting the inspector's chart from time to time, wrote the names in a column. He passed the list to the inspector. Bloxham glanced at it and nodded.

"And then, if that gets you no farther, have a go at the servants," urged the superintendent. "We must get a move on, Bloxham, you know. Have you seen the local paper? It's not as charming to us as it was three days ago. Put your back into it, laddie."

Bloxham marched to the door.

"Oh, and by the way," said the superintendent, just as he turned the handle, "find out exactly what that chap Kost *did* do! I don't like these foreigners! There's always something fishy going on when they're about."

With this truly "roast-beef" sentiment, he turned to his own affairs, and bent his bullet head over his papers. Suddenly he rose and walked quickly out after the inspector.

"Oh, Bloxham!" he called.

The inspector turned and came back.

"That swimming stunt. Mrs. Hobson a nonswimmer, you know. That's a good move. Must have been a jolly good swimmer who fixed the body and the statue together. Oh, and why harp on the sunrise when checking everybody's alibi?"

Bloxham grinned.

"Not exactly a daylight job, that planting the body in the brook," he said. "Besides, it was very early in the morning, you remember, when Mr. Hilary Yeomond dived in on top of it."

"Now, those three Yeomonds, for example, and Kost, too," pursued the superintendent, following out the new idea, "jolly good swimmers, all of them. It was Malpas Yeomond and Kost who hiked the corpse out of the lake, wasn't it? And Hilary can certainly swim. We've proof of that. What about Francis?"

"I don't know. I expect he can swim if the others can, but it doesn't always follow," said the inspector.

"No. You know, Bloxham, there was certainly an accomplice. You mention that the women could not have carried the body without assistance, but neither man nor woman could fix it to that statue and place the lot right in the middle of the lake without an accomplice. My advice would be—find the

accomplice as soon as you can. Concentrate on finding him. He may be a squeaker."

"Didn't know you knew that song," said the inspector innocently.

"Song?"

" 'Hats off to Edgar Wallace,' " said Bloxham, making a smart retreat down the passage. "Besides," he called back, "there was the bathchair to transport the body. *I* believe old Mrs. Puddequet's a liar. In fact, I'm sure she is!"

CHAPTER IX

Kost and Caddick, or the Babes in the Wood

THE inspector, despite the flippancy of his tone, felt serious enough as he left the police station at Market Longer and began walking towards the village. He might have found some means of transport other than his own legs, but the action of walking stimulated thought, and he wanted to think.

By the time he gained the gates of Longer he had made up his mind how to proceed. Disregarding the list made by the superintendent, he demanded to see Miss Caddick, and, almost before she was inside the room, he fired his first question at her.

"Miss Caddick, how many times has Mrs. Puddequet's bathchair been used at nights?"

"When you say 'at nights,' inspector," squeaked Miss Caddick, her restless hands giving away the state of her nerves, "what do you mean?"

"After Mrs. Puddequet's usual bedtime," snapped the inspector.

"Oh, yes. Thank you. Well, apart from the night of the—er—apart from the particular and unfortunate—I might say, might I not?—disastrous night that we all know about, the bathchair has been out, at any rate, once during the night."

"Before or after the murder?"

"Oh, before, inspector. Oh, yes, before."

"When?"

"Now, let me see … The murder was on Friday, and this is Tuesday and I told Mr. Hilary about it, and he gave me his *word* it was not them—they—er—them—that is, they had not played a practical joke with it on the Thursday—or was it the Wednesday? Well, it was either the Wednesday or the Thursday because I remember saying to Joseph Herring how *wet* it was, and how *disturbed* I should be if dear Mrs. Puddequet caught cold through sitting in it—on it—er—in it. No, now I come to think of it, it was on the *Thursday* night, because I remember telling Mr. Hilary about it the next day, and the next day was the morning of the murder. Of course, we did not know then that it was the morning of the murder, but, looking back on it now, of course that is the morning it was. Yes. So wet! We dried it by the kitchen fire. Mrs. Macbrae was *so* obliging. Joseph, too. He said he should be dismissed his post if dear Mrs. Puddequet thought that he had been negligent. And, of course, he *had* been negligent. Very negligent indeed, was it not, to forget to

lock the shed door after the bathchair had been put away? Not that Joseph *owned up* to forgetting to lock the shed door after the bathchair had been put away! In fact, he was almost *discourteous* when I ventured to suggest that such had been the case. But if he had done his duty—done his bit, as our *dear* soldiers said in the Great War—how could the bathchair have been taken out? Not—as I pointed out to Mr. Hilary, who was *very* sympathetic—not, I said, through a locked door that *is* locked. What do you say, inspector?"

"I say that you have told me a very important thing, Miss Caddick," replied Bloxham. "This means, you see, that someone else besides Herring had a means of entering the shed where the bathchair is kept, because, having forgotten to lock it on Thursday, it is hardly likely that he would have forgotten to do so on Friday as well, is it? And we know the bathchair was in the grounds on Friday night."

"Herring may have been *bribed* for the key," said Miss Caddick in hushed, ecstatic tones. (The talkie she had been to in London was founded on fact, then, she felt!)

"Possibly," the inspector agreed.

"Or Herring himself," began Miss Caddick, envisaging another, and even more thrilling and perturbing possibility.

"No!" shouted the inspector suddenly. Miss Caddick nearly leapt into the air with shock. By the time she had recovered herself, he had gone.

He found Herring in the kitchen garden hoeing up some potatoes, and called to him.

"Who gave you permission to lend anyone the key of the shed where the bathchair is kept?" he demanded.

Joseph avoided his eye.

"I never asked no permission," he observed in an aggrieved tone, "and I never lent no key."

"No?" said Bloxham, in a peculiarly unpleasant tone. He waited for a moment, but, as the Scrounger volunteered no further information, he continued, "I suppose some clever Ali Baba simply stood outside the door and said, 'Open, Sesame' and open it did! Now, don't be a fool, Herring. Who had the key of the shed on Thursday, April seventeenth, and on Friday, April eighteenth?"

"Nobody never 'ad it," said the Scrounger doggedly.

"Show me the shed," said the inspector curtly.

"Key's in the kitching. You'll 'ave to arst for it yourself, inspector, because that there cuttlefish in there, she'll 'ave my 'ead orf if I pokes it inside 'er door this time in the day."

"Key!" yelled Bloxham, giving him an authoritative thump in the small of the back. The Scrounger went off at the double.

"Oh, two bathchairs," said the inspector, when at last the shed was opened.

"One gone pretty well home, I see. This the one in use? Bring it outside and let's have a look at it. Pity it can't talk, isn't it?"

He straightened himself and looked at Joseph.

"Well, you going to spill it?" he enquired.

"Spill nothing," said Joseph sullenly. "I locks up the shed Thursday and I locks up the shed Friday, and more I can't say. *I* can't 'elp it if somebody's took a wax impression of the key and got a spare one cut, can I?"

"Look here," said Bloxham, with finality in his tones, either you tell me what you know, or I nab you now, this moment, as an accessory after the fact. Know what that means?"

"Ah," said Joseph, expectorating apprehensively. "Spare part in a murder."

"Exactly. And you get a life sentence for that, Herring, my lad. So cough it up, quick, and don't waste my time any longer."

"Well, I don't *know*, mind," said Joseph, clearing his throat again and addressing Miss Caddick's bird bowl, "but what about Mr. Anthony?"

The inspector was off almost before the last word emerged from Herring's mouth. He found Anthony in the gymnasium. He was practicing on the ladder, and seemed dispirited.

"I wish you'd lend me your key to the back shed," said Bloxham casually. "Herring has mislaid his."

"Key?" said Anthony. "I haven't one, I'm afraid, that will fit the back shed. Sorry."

The inspector scowled at him.

"Think again," he said briefly. Anthony shook his head.

"Sorry," he said again.

"Well, if you haven't a key," said Bloxham, "how did you get the bathchair out of the shed on Thursday night and Friday night of last week?"

Anthony shook his head again, and said sadly:

"I haven't the least idea what you're talking about, you know."

"Oh!" said Bloxham.

There was a short pause.

"No," said Anthony. He gave a slight spring and continued his gymnastic exercises.

The inspector went back to Miss Caddick.

"What would you say, Miss Caddick, if I told you that Mr. Anthony gained admission to the shed and took the bathchair out?" he said.

Miss Caddick blinked nervously.

"Well, since you *put* it to me, inspector," she piped, "I should say I am not surprised. Not in the *least* surprised! A dreadfully unsatisfactory young man in every way. I have no doubt that his intention was for *dear* Mrs. Puddequet to catch her death of cold, so that he could inherit her property, which, of

course, according to her new will, he would certainly do if she died *before* one of the grandnephews becomes an international champion."

The inspector gaped at her.

"Say it again," he begged feebly. Miss Caddick said it again.

"Of course, my own little legacy is *secure*," she continued. "I have dear Mrs. Puddequet's word for that. So I do hope, inspector, that you will make it quite *clear* to everyone that *I* have no motive for committing any crime."

The inspector looked at her with new interest.

"And now," he said, "what *were* you doing between nine and eleven-thirty on the night of the murder?"

Miss Caddick gasped and turned pale.

"Oh, but I was *reading,* inspector," she cried. "I assure you that I was reading. And I went to bed at half-past ten—"

"After the murder was committed," said Bloxham brutally. Miss Caddick gave a little scream of terror, and covered her face.

"Oh, please, *please,* inspector!" she said. "*So* unchivalrous to say a thing like that!"

At this interesting moment a knocking on the door as with a stick, or, in this case, Great-aunt Puddequet's beloved umbrella, heralded the approach of the bathchair. Richard Cowes was pushing it.

"Now, now, now!" squealed Great-aunt Puddequet with her usual vigor. She rapped Miss Caddick playfully on the shoulder with the ferrule of the umbrella. "On Friday we entertain the trainer in the morning room at ten o'clock at night, and on Tuesday—"

She stopped. Miss Caddick had fallen fainting to the floor. The inspector and Richard Cowes rendered ineffectual, manlike assistance, and Great-aunt Puddequet improved the shining hour by ejaculating at five-second intervals, "Don't be a fool, Companion Caddick!" until the poor woman recovered. The inspector then left the scene of action, and, sending a maid in search of one of the girls, went to find Kost.

The trainer was reading a newspaper. He looked up when the inspector's shadow dropped across the page.

"About that tale you told me," said Bloxham. He spoke pleasantly, but there was an ill-tempered glint in his eye. "Why didn't you say you paid a visit to Miss Caddick in the morning room, after you left the public house? I know that part of your yarn's true, because I checked it up."

Kost lowered the paper and shrugged his wide shoulders.

"I will tell you, perhaps," he said. "I am sorry you find me a liar, but, sure, I am. It was this way. I am going to tell you about this visit, but later I say to myself: 'Ludwig, you are a fool, perhaps. It was too near the time of the murder, this visit of yours. You go innocently, and you stay the very short time—not fifteen minutes, no; but more than ten, perhaps. And while you

are there, this Hobson, the police make out he is murdered, you see. There is no noise, except the gramophone next door, and they sing the tunes as well, perhaps. Pretty big noise there, but no Hobson. Will the police believe what you say, Ludwig? They will not, perhaps.' "

"Didn't you see the corpse in the sunk garden, then," asked the inspector, "when you left the house?"

"Not me. I don't return through the sunk garden, perhaps. I return through the house, and back through the kitchen garden. That way out. I am afraid I shall be seen and someone will report me to the boss. Cannot risk that."

"And when did you push Hobson into the road?"

"Then. Immediately. He is just arriving at the house, I think. He is in an objectionable condition. I am afraid he will with his shoutings frighten the ladies, perhaps, so I run him out of the gate and I think he falls into the ditch. Then I return to my hut."

"Oh?" said Bloxham stonily. "Let me take you through your tale once more, and see if I can find any flaws in it."

Kost grinned.

"I am a liar, perhaps," he said cheerfully. "Who is not? And I am afraid of your English law, that is why I tell the lies. Now, I am still afraid of your English law, so I tell you the truth, this time."

"Quite," said Bloxham drily. "Now, this is your yarn. You went first to the public house. You then returned to the house and went to call on Miss Caddick. Time—about a quarter to ten. At ten o'clock, or thereabouts, you left her, and came out by way of the kitchen regions into the grounds. You then encountered Hobson and ran him into the road. Later—which must have been almost immediately—he went into the sunk garden and got himself murdered, but by that time you had returned to your hut."

"So," said Kost, with emphasis.

"Ah!" said Bloxham, with more emphasis. "And when did you open the back shed with your key and take out the bathchair?"

Kost looked surprised.

"What for should I require the bathchair, perhaps?" said he.

"To carry Hobson's corpse to the lake," said the inspector.

Kost chuckled gently.

"You should tell that to the mare's nest, perhaps," said he.

"I will, when I've found the horse marines," retorted Bloxham. He turned and walked off in the direction of the house.

Kost gazed after him. Then he gave a peculiar little giggle and picked up the newspaper again.

The inspector went back to the room in which he had left the overcome Miss Caddick. To his relief, her employer had gone, and no one was with her but Amaris Cowes.

"Now, Miss Caddick," said the police officer kindly, "I don't want you to become alarmed and nervous, but I simply must ask you a few more questions."

Miss Caddick gasped, shut her eyes, and waved him feebly away.

"Now, don't be irritating," said Amaris Cowes firmly. "The inspector is quite a nice young man and very kindhearted. Besides, you know you have nothing to fear. You didn't kill the Hobson person, did you?"

Miss Caddick gave a little moan, but whether of fear or denial it was impossible to determine. Amaris patted her encouragingly on the shoulder.

"Now, speak up," she urged. "Tell the truth and hang the consequences!"

"But—but I *can't!*" wailed old Mrs. Puddequet's unfortunate prop-and-stay.

The inspector thought it time to assert himself.

"If you wouldn't mind leaving things to me, Miss Cowes," he said. "Stay within call, by all means, if you think Miss Caddick is likely to require any further assistance, but—er— yes, *outside* the door, if you would be so good."

Miss Caddick gazed in anguish at the departing form of Miss Cowes. Then she turned to the inspector.

"I would willingly tell *you* the truth, inspector," she said, "but there is dear Mrs. Puddequet to be considered. I did all for the best, inspector, but our dear Mrs. Puddequet is apt to be a little *censorious.* Yes, just a *little* censorious. You see, she has not had the freedom that we modern people have acquired."

"Mrs. Puddequet need know nothing of what you tell me, Miss Caddick," said the inspector woodenly. "You mean Kost spent the night with you, I suppose?"

"Oh, but inspector!" wailed Miss Caddick, clasping her hands. "Not *with* me! Oh, indeed, do not imagine anything so *dreadful!* I *never* imagined that the police read the Sunday papers to *that* extent! But he *did* spend the night in the house. I—I admit that!"

"Ah!" said Bloxham. He glanced at her face and then down at the blank page of his notebook.

"You see, it was like this." Once launched, Miss Caddick seemed eager to get the tale told.

"He had confided in me several times how very *spartan* were the arrangements made for the athletes by dear Mrs. Puddequet. The beds, he said, were hard. The food was plentiful but plain. The hours were a disgrace. It was very suitable for the young men, he thought, but the trainer was entitled to more consideration. I sympathized with the man, but, of course, it was not for me to pass on his complaints to dear Mrs. Puddequet. It would have brought on one of her attacks, and that—er—those—er—them I have learned to *dread.* So I said nothing but a few words of womanly consolation such as

may be conceived and uttered in sisterly fashion by any true ornament of her sex, until at last, on the morning of Friday—you know the Friday I mean?—the *fatal* Friday—Kost said that he could stand it no longer, and should give notice at once unless a proper bed could be found for him. Poor fellow! He looked so noble, and he seemed so determined to carry out his dreadful threat, that I felt I must do something to help him."

"What dreadful threat was that?" asked Bloxham.

"Why, to give in his notice, inspector. How awkward for me!"

"Why for you?"

"Well, I engaged him for the post, you see. By letter, of course. Mrs. Puddequet left it all to me, and so just think how *angry* she would be if my choice gave in his notice after less than a fortnight's work!"

"I see."

"So I said to him that I would see him in the morning room at about a quarter to ten that evening, and that he was to bring his—all the things he would require for the night. He came exactly to time, but unfortunately he had forgotten his—er—his apparel. I told him my plan, and then he returned, by way of the kitchen (with Mrs. Macbrae's kind permission), and later came back to the morning room with his things."

"And where did he sleep?" asked the inspector.

"Well," began Miss Caddick, glancing nervously round the room, "there *was* only one bed that could be used, and the *job* I had to purloin sufficient *linen* for it without being discovered!"

"And which bed was it?" enquired the inspector patiently.

"Well," said Miss Caddick, trembling with horror at the recollection of her own daring, "it was the bed in the little dressing room that opens out of dear Mrs. Puddequet's big bedroom. After all, it is *never* used, and the bed, although small, is *exceedingly* comfortable, for I slept on it for a week once when dear Mrs. Puddequet contracted the influenza. I warned him that he must be *very* quiet, and that he *must* not snore, and that he must be prepared to vacate the room at half-past five on the Saturday morning, all of which *instructions* I must say he carried out to the very letter."

"He had to pass through Mrs. Puddequet's bedroom, of course, to get to this small dressing room?" said Bloxham.

"Well, just across one *corner* of it," Miss Caddick admitted. "But she is quite a *sound* sleeper."

"I see. Now, Miss Caddick, we come to the important point in all this. I want you to go on being quite frank with me, because it is only in this way that I can arrive at the whole truth, of which your narrative is just a small part. What about the time of the murder? It seems to me that you and Kost (on the *qui vive* and so on, as you must have been that night) would certainly have heard something of Hobson."

"Did Mr. Kost tell you that he pushed a man out of the gate just before ten o'clock?" asked Miss Caddick.

"He mentioned the fact, yes."

"Well, when we heard Hobson shouting below in that terrifying way, Mr. Kost said to me, 'Here is that fellow back again, I suppose. What a worthless young man. I shall go and give him a piece of my mind.' But I prevented him from doing so, because I did not wish him to betray to *anyone*—not even to one of the villagers—his presence in the house that night. You understand my position in the matter, inspector, don't you?"

"Oh, quite," said Bloxham. "In fact, one more question and then you're through. At what time did his shouting stop?"

"Oh, that I could not say, inspector. You see, there was such a *noise* in the next room, what with the gramophone and the singing and the laughing, and I was so anxious to get Mr. Kost safely into bed that I scarcely know whether it stopped while we were still in the morning-room or whether it was still going on when we went upstairs."

"I see. Well, Miss Caddick, I think you have been very courageous to tell me all this, and I don't think you need fear the results of your frankness."

He was about to go when another thought struck him.

"By the way," he said, "did Kost have any supper before going to bed?"

"He had his usual meal, which corresponds roughly to our own dinner," replied Miss Caddick, obviously surprised. "Why?"

"I just wondered," said Bloxham. "And now would you mind showing me your bedroom door, and then, if it isn't troubling you too much, I would like you to accompany me into the grounds and point out to me your bedroom window. I want to see which way it faces."

Mystified, Miss Caddick did as he had requested. Her bedroom door was next to that of old Mrs. Puddequet. Her bedroom window looked on to the east side of the house.

Thoughtful, but cheerful, the inspector again sought out Kost and confronted him with Miss Caddick's story. Unperturbed, the trainer admitted its truth.

"And now," said Bloxham, "you've given me trouble enough. Don't hide anything else. Why didn't you confess that you got out into the sunk garden at about one o'clock in the morning and chucked a brick at what you thought was Miss Caddick's window in order to attract her attention? Also, why didn't you come clean about these sleeping arrangements and own up to shoving young Brown-Jenkins down the stairs? Also, why didn't you say that in your search for Miss Caddick's door you lost your way about the house and barged into Miss Yeomond's room by mistake? And did *you* see or hear anything of the bathchair that night?"

Kost gazed at him in sheer amazement.

"But why should I do these things, perhaps?" he demanded. "What, the first time in a fortnight that I sleep on a bed that *is* a bed, shall I arise myself at one o'clock in the morning and throw large stones at the window of my benefactress, that disinterested, philanthropic lady who is not beautiful— no! but who overflows with the kindness of a great heart, yes! Shall I alarm and disturb her with stones and wanderings, perhaps? Ask yourself! I spit at the ungratefulness of such an action."

He did so with a wholehearted completeness which was in tune with his remarks.

"Now, look here, Kost," said the inspector, "you've told me so many lies that I'm not going to believe this one. I'm not saying anything more than that you were up, dressed, and acting the fool. I'm not accusing you of anything else, so do just come clean for once, and do yourself a bit of good. Clive Brown-Jenkins says he recognized you! So come on, now. Perhaps you were hungry, and wanted Miss Caddick to find you some food? Be advised by me; tell me the truth, or you'll be in a nasty hole."

Kost gave a howl of fury.

"Get away from here, you fool of a policeman, perhaps!" he yelled. "Or sure as sure I will throw you over my hut. As for Clive Brown-Jenkins, the sulky, lubberly boy, I will twist his neck for him, perhaps! Arrest me for the murder if you like, but for the ungrateful insulting of kind ladies, unbeautiful it is true, but good-hearted like which is never to be comprehended by the big, vulgar policeman, perhaps, no! Get away! Get away, I say!"

CHAPTER X

Night Birds

I

THE Scrounger peered forth into the night. The night was a poet's night—"chilly, but not dark"—luminous with stars. The mere, broad and placid under the sky, stretched away into a ghostly darkness of its own, and between the stems of the reeds it made queer little eerie sucking noises, at once attracting the attention and repelling the imagination of the solitary wanderer on its banks. The pollard willows, fantastic by day, almost unseen under the stars, wagged their ungainly branches in a sudden sharp gust of wind which blew from the southwest, and were as suddenly still again. A water vole swam across the broad stream to some secret opening into wonderland, and the Scrounger, knocking the dottle out of his long-finished pipe, spat in the water for luck and emerged from cover.

Apparently the omens were propitious, for, leaving the shelter of the pollard willow, behind whose gnarled, ancient, and goblin trunk he had been ensconced for the past quarter of an hour, he crept along the bank, dodging from tree to tree, until he was behind the high diving-boards at the upper end of the mere. Under his left arm he held a small wooden box. Inside the box something scratched and scrabbled. The Scrounger sat on the lowest step of the diving-board and wiped his brow with his right cuff.

"Gawd!" said he, with immense feeling. He set the wooden box on the ground and apostrophized it in a whisper.

"Now, what's to be bleedin' well done? *You* dunno! *I* dunno! I'll 'ave to plant yer where you'll grow nicest. That there Caddick! But 'ow's it goin' to be did? If only I knowed the time, it 'ud be some 'elp! Well, I gotter leave yer 'ere for the present, any'ow. So long! Be good till Dadda comes 'ome!"

He placed the box gently on the step above that on which he had been seated, then, very cautiously, he made his way, under cover of the fence, round the sports field and towards the kitchen garden. As he passed the hut in which Hilary Yeomond slept, someone coughed. The Scrounger melted almost into the fence in dismay, for the cough came from outside, not inside the hut. A drop of cold sweat ran down his body and made him shudder.

From the back of the hut a dark shape detached itself and took form as a human being. Silent as a shadow it trotted towards the mere. Joseph Herring

waited while he counted his fingers seven times, then he broke from cover and darted in at the gate of the kitchen garden, which he had left open two hours earlier. In less than three minutes he had gained admission to the outer scullery and was painstakingly and methodically cleaning some yellowish clay and some dark-brown mud off his boots. Many times during his labors he stopped to listen, but all was silent save for the slight sound of water running away down the sink.

Joe finished grooming the left boot and placed it on the stone floor. Then an idea occurred to him. In his stockinged feet he stepped over to where the boots and shoes of the household had been placed in a neat row awaiting his early-morning attentions, and selected a pair of ladies' walking shoes. He picked them up, carried them back to the sink, and then, carefully removing with the blade of a clasp-knife as much of the damp and dirty residue as possible from his own right boot, he plastered it generously about the soles and toecaps of the shoes he had selected. Then he walked over to the windowsill with one of the shoes in his hand, pressed the sole of it firmly down on the clean white sill, and again in the middle of the stone floor, cleaned up all other marks on the floor, and replaced the shoes where he had found them.

He then smiled sweetly, and, boots in hand, admitted himself to the inner scullery, went through it into the kitchen, and so proceeded up the back staircase to bed. His alarm clock showed that the time was five minutes past one.

Joseph was soon between the sheets, where he slept the sleep of a little child.

II

Miss Caddick had had a disturbing evening. To begin with, Miss Celia Brown-Jenkins, a distressingly independent lady of immature years but fully fledged hardihood, had not appeared at dinner, and Miss Caddick, having been beguiled into a promise to conceal guilty knowledge of her whereabouts, had been compelled to sit through what seemed an interminable and tasteless meal listening to old Mrs. Puddequet's diatribes on present-day young madams who flew into a pet over nothing and sulked in their bedrooms. Miss Caddick knew perfectly well that the erring Celia was not in the house at all, but had made clandestine escape from Great-aunt Puddequet's somewhat oppressive mansion into the brilliant life of one of London's dance halls, and would return anon. How much anon Miss Caddick could not determine.

Clive did not appear at dinner either, but Great-aunt Puddequet's convenient assumption that he had been out cycling all the afternoon and had lost his way home relieved the strain of what would have been an intolerable

half-hour had the old lady realized the truth, which was that Clive, also tiring of country solitude, had slipped off on his bicycle to Southampton and was playing billiards with a sportsman named 'Arry in a haunt of vice not far removed from the docks. Clive's natural tastes ran neither to billiards nor to haunts of vice, but he felt that a complete change of surroundings and company would be beneficial to his nerves. Therefore, just as Great-aunt Puddequet was imbibing her bedtime barley water, the sportsman named 'Arry was in process of indicating to Clive Brown-Jenkins that seventeen-and-a-tanner was the amount the umpire declared owing, and Clive, in his pugnacious way, was thrusting forward his powerful jaw, and enquiring exactly where the umpire had learned his bookkeeping. The result of the argument was in the best traditions of the house, and Clive found himself, at ten twenty-four at night, sitting on the most squalid bit of pavement he had ever seen in his life, with an ear that felt like a pumpkin, an eye out of which he could see nothing, thirty-three miles of secondary roads between himself and Little Longer, and no idea of the best way out of town.

Luckily he had left his bicycle at a garage near by, and from the men there he received fairly concise directions as to the route he should follow to get out of town. Clive, furiously conscious of the spectacle he presented, thanked them shortly, mounted, and rode off.

Thirty-three miles is not a long distance, even to a moderate cyclist. To Clive it was a mere hour and a half's spin, given good roads and a fair knowledge of the way. This time, how ever, ill luck dogged him. He had barely left the lights of the town behind, when his own lighting set failed. Attempts to resuscitate it proved futile. He remounted, but was obliged to proceed at little more than a jog-trot pace, for, in the darkness, he was afraid of riding into the ditch. Fifteen miles on his way he picked up a puncture. It was impossible to repair it, for he could see nothing, so for five miserable miles he bumped along on a flat rear tube until he could endure the discomfort no longer; he dismounted and walked the rest of the way. At nearly three o'clock in the early morning, a weary, battered, indescribably angry young man, pushing a bicycle, entered the gates of Longer and made his way to his hut.

III

At the "Romany" fancy-dress dance, Celia Brown-Jenkins enjoyed herself. True, she was not in fancy dress—there had been no time to arrange that—but an affectionate maiden and two polite, well-brilliantined young men had met her at Paddington Station and carried her off in triumph to the almost West End. At precisely twelve-twelve a.m. another sleek-haired young man was waving his hat at a departing train in which sat Celia. She was rather tired, and a little frightened because she had just realized that nobody

had been asked to let her into the house on her return, and that it would be a horribly dark walk from Market Longer Station. Seated there in an otherwise empty compartment, she also recollected that, not so many days before, a man had been murdered in the sunk garden; of course, no one was going to murder *her,* she knew, but, all the same, she felt that she would be just as glad when she was safely in bed.

The train reached Market Longer at twenty minutes past two, and a tired girl of eighteen reached the gates of Longer exactly one hour and twenty minutes later.

She walked up the path to the sports field, opened the wooden door, and skirted the cinder track. On the opposite side of the ground, outside the fence, but rising high above it, she saw the flames of an enormous bonfire.

Celia felt sick.

"It's one of the huts!" she thought. In spite of her weary feet she broke into a trot, and shouted as she ran:

"Fire! Fire! Fire!"

IV

To add to Miss Caddick's sense of impending ill, old Mrs. Puddequet was suddenly and obstinately smitten with the determination to sit up and play bezique. There were two reasons why Miss Caddick dreaded these attacks, which recurred at intervals of about twelve weeks; one reason was that they made the old lady overexcited, so that when she did at last decide to go to bed she could not sleep, and her wretched companion was compelled to spend the hours of beauty sleep in reading aloud to her; the other reason was that Great-aunt Puddequet awoke on the morning following one of these debauches with a splitting headache and the temper of a fiend.

The book chosen by old Mrs. Puddequet on this particular evening was *Little Women,* and she herself turned over the well-worn pages to find the part of the story best suited to her mood. Miss Caddick dreaded the choice of *Little Women* as a bed-book, for the old lady, when once the story was launched, declined to be satisfied until, out of sheer exhaustion, she fell asleep. Miss Caddick outlined the adventures of Meg at the Moffats, followed it with the inauguration of young Lawrence as a member of the Pickwick Club, and had reached the very end of the pleasant chapter describing Camp Lawrence, when the listener suddenly started up in bed and cried:

"What's that?"

Miss Caddick started nervously, her mind divided between trying to decide whether the sound was the noise of a second murder, or whether Celia Brown-Jenkins had returned from London and broken her neck trying to climb the gate leading into the sunk garden.

Both women listened intently.

"There it is again!" said Great-aunt Puddequet. "Go and find out who is throwing stones at the window, companion."

Miss Caddick laid *Little Women* face downwards on the coverlet and blinked nervously at her employer.

"I don't think it is a stone against the window," she demurred. "It didn't sound to me like someone throwing stones against the window. The window overlooks the side of the house, Mrs. Puddequet, and that noise came from the front."

"Then go and see what it is," squealed the old lady, "and don't be such a fool!"

Miss Caddick rose from her chair, and very unwillingly proceeded towards the door.

"I know what it is!" cried old Mrs. Puddequet suddenly. "It's someone banging on the door of the sunk garden. My ridiculous grandson, I expect. What is the hour, Companion Caddick?"

Miss Caddick compared a minute wristwatch with the handsome grandfather clock which stood in the far corner of the room.

"I make it seventeen minutes to twelve," she said, "and Mr. Golightly makes it eleven minutes to twelve." The clock in question was always referred to in this way out of respect for its previous owner, an old gentleman whom Mrs. Puddequet had known in her youth.

"Ah," said Great-aunt Puddequet, shaking her head, "he's fast. At any rate, the gate into the sunk garden is locked by this time, so, if Grandson Timon is on the wrong side of it, he can just stay there, that's all. Go to bed, companion! What are you standing there for?"

Miss Caddick, grateful for any sort of permission to retire, bade her employer a hasty good night, glared nervously both ways on gaining the landing, and then fled like a hare into her own room.

The noise below continued. Someone knocked on Miss Caddick's door, and the voice of the cook uplifted itself, proclaiming that there was racket below enough to waken the dead, and that, for her part, she would see herself drowned before she would consent to remain any longer under a roof which sheltered murderers and thieves, or in a house where at no hour of the night could a poor body get sleep sufficient to recompense her for the vicissitudes of the day that had gone and to give her strength and energy enough to cope with the trials of the day that was to come.

Miss Caddick replied, through an opening two inches wide, that the cook should return to bed and then all would be well. It was only Mr. Timon, she explained. He was locked out, and Mrs. Puddequet would not allow him to be admitted to the house.

The cook, with a dark mutter, withdrew, and Miss Caddick had taken off

her outermost garment and was removing the second hairpin from her coiffure when a louder and more peremptory knock came at the door. By this time the "noises off" had ceased.

"Who's there? You can't come in!" squeaked Miss Caddick in one breath, quite oblivious of the fact that the door was fast locked. "What do you want?"

"I say, Caddie! Who's kicking up that infernal din?"

"Why, Miss Cowes, we think it is Mr. Timon," fluttered Miss Caddick, tripping lightly to the door and speaking with her lips to the keyhole, from which she had that instant removed the key.

"I'm going down to see what they want," said Amaris, and Miss Caddick could hear her retreating footsteps.

"It *is* Celia Brown-Jenkins," was Miss Caddick's final brilliant conclusion, "and dear Amaris will let her in."

Feeling her own responsibility removed in the matter of readmitting Celia to the ancestral hall, Miss Caddick hastily completed her preparations for bed, and scrambled between the sheets.

Great-aunt Puddequet lay awake for a short while, during which time she noted that the noise, whatever its cause, had ceased. The handsome old grandfather clock in the corner struck twelve, and the old lady in bed raised herself on one elbow and remarked in a cracked but friendly voice:

"Good night, Mr. Golightly."

Then she slept the untroubled sleep of the aged until the confused noise made by a household which has been awakened suddenly from slumber aroused her. Great-aunt Puddequet raised herself on one elbow and listened. A cry of "Fire! Fire!" came to her ears. She reached for the bellrope which hung behind the head of the bed and pulled it vigorously.

V

"It's queer," said Amaris Cowes slowly. She contemplated Hilary Yeomond in silence for a moment. "But what a mercy you were not inside the hut," she added.

Hilary laughed.

"Oh, Moggridge would have wakened me in time," he said, patting the dog whose muzzle was on his knee. Moggridge wagged his tail at the mention of his own name, and, against all regulations, Richard Cowes rose and gave him a kidney out of the dish on the sideboard.

"And what a mercy you hadn't left *him* in the hut, either," said Priscilla, caressing Moggridge's left ear.

"The thing that puzzles me," said Richard Cowes, "is how the hut could have caught fire, because I know you put the lamp out before you came up to

the house here with me, Yeomond. It was a lucky thing for you that our great-aunt has the sunk garden gate locked so early, or you might have tried getting back to your hut when we had finished our game."

"Game, Grandnephew?" said old Mrs. Puddequet, whose bathchair was at that moment wheeled into the breakfast room by Miss Caddick.

"Yes, Great-aunt. I invited Yeomond into the dining room last night to play chess. As we did not finish until after one, I persuaded him to camp on the chesterfield instead of breaking out of the house. I myself slept in an arm-chair, and very comfortably too."

Before anyone else could make a remark, Malpas Yeomond dropped a bomb by observing casually:

"Inspector Bloxham is coming up the steps to investigate a case of attempted murder."

"What?" exclaimed his sister.

"Rubbish, Grandnephew," squealed old Mrs. Puddequet. "Refrain from wilful exaggeration."

"I sent for Constable Copple at just after six this morning," said Richard Cowes coolly, "and invited him to look at the burnt-out hut. It has one most suggestive feature. Constable Copple is not a man of great imaginative powers, but even he was roused to quite a show of animation by what I had to show him. Malpas has seen it too."

The announcement that the inspector was in the hall and would be glad of a word with the owner of the house cut short Richard's remarks. Great-aunt Puddequet's bathchair, again propelled by Miss Caddick, went out to give audience to a grave-eyed Bloxham.

"I'd like you to come and take a look at this hut, Mrs. Puddequet," he said shortly. "I don't know whether your house is harboring a maniac, or what."

He addressed a question to Miss Caddick in a low tone as the bathchair crunched over the cinder track three minutes later.

"Oh, yes," replied Miss Caddick, so softly that the inspector was obliged to strain his ears to catch the words, "she *can* get about without it, but only with the help of two sticks and, of course, *always* someone with her. But even then it is very slow work for her, poor thing."

The inspector nodded as though he were satisfied and dropped behind to speak to Joseph Herring, who was wheeling a barrow towards the sunk garden. Immediately he was out of earshot, old Mrs. Puddequet turned round venomously and hissed at her escort, "You're a fool, Companion Caddick! How dare you show your contempt for your employer by calling her a poor thing?"

Miss Caddick gasped in anguish, and exclaimed shrilly:

"Oh, but, Mrs. Puddequet! Oh, but, Mrs. Puddequet, I mean—well, I mean, nothing would be farther from my thoughts, dear Mrs. Puddequet. You must

surely know that. I only meant—well, I mean, we all have our little cross to bear, and I'm quite, *quite* sure, dear Mrs. Puddequet—"

The protestations were cut short by the return of the inspector. The three went through the gate of the sports field and were soon at a point of vantage from which they could view the melancholy remains of Hilary Yeomond's hut.

Here the inspector was joined by the sergeant and by the village policeman, Constable Copple, who had evidently been left on guard at the ruins. Apart from the blackened desolation and the grayish ashes, the attention of the onlooker was chiefly attracted by two tall iron rods which were standing upright in the ground at a distance of eight inches from one another. They were all still warm to the touch.

"Inspector!" squealed Great-aunt Puddequet excitedly. Unable to attract his immediate attention, she prodded him vigorously in the small of the back with her umbrella. The sergeant slid an apologetic hand across a grin and requested her to be patient. Great-aunt Puddequet had no intention of being anything of the kind. She rocked the bathchair dangerously by swaying from side to side in it, raised her cracked old voice still higher, and prodded the unfortunate Bloxham with greater determination than before.

"What the—oh, it's you, Mrs. Puddequet," said the inspector, swinging round. "What is it, ma'am?"

"What are those iron poles, inspector?"

"Witnesses to an attempt at murder, ma'am."

"Don't you be facetious at my expense, young man!" screamed old Mrs. Puddequet.

"Well," retorted the inspector, "from the plan of these grounds, which Mr. Cowes was kind enough to find in the library and hand to me, and from what I myself remember, I see that where those bars stand should be the doorway of the hut. The doors of all these huts, ma'am, open outwards. Do I begin to make myself clear?"

"Attendant, take me in!" cried Great-aunt Puddequet to Joseph Herring, who had abandoned the wheelbarrow and was now an interested spectator of the unusual scene.

"Very good, mam."

"And, attendant!"

"Yes, mam?"

"Return and assist the police in the execution of their duty."

"Very good, mam."

"You understand me, attendant?"

"In a manner of speaking, yes, mam."

"And otherwise?"

"No, mam."

"Tell the police," said Great-aunt Puddequet with great distinctness, "that any article of value they may recover from the effects of the fire is my property."

CHAPTER XI

What Happened to Anthony?

THE inspector drew the sergeant out of earshot of the spectators and spoke quietly.

"Can't see that there's anything more to be gained here. I reckon the whole thing's a plant."

"Plant, sir?"

"Yes. In spite of those two iron bars. They've never been in a fire! Somebody sneaked out early and put 'em in position. Silly practical joke, I consider. Done to put the wind up young Yeomond, that's all. Go and have another look at 'em for yourself. Fingerprints on them, I expect, and so we shall soon know who's the Bright Young Thing of the establishment. I know who I've fixed on."

The sergeant grinned.

"Mr. Brown-Jenkins, sir?"

The inspector made no attempt to confirm or to deny this, and the rest of the party, much intrigued by the official conclave, gravitated towards the two policeman, who, after cautioning them to touch nothing and to return immediately to their several occupations so that footprints might not be confused, set off towards the house, where they asked for an interview with Mrs. Puddequet and her adopted grandson. While they were waiting for the old lady to appear, Bloxham leaned out of the drawing-room window and called to the policeman below:

"Go and get Copple, and the two of you peg a rope round that burnt-out hut. That'll remind people not to go poking round there."

He drew in his head and grinned.

"Nothing like looking thorough in your methods," he said. "But, seriously—"

He was interrupted by the entrance of Great-aunt Puddequet in her bathchair. She was propelled this time by Malpas Yeomond. The inspector regarded them gravely, and then said:

"Mrs. Puddequet, you were right. But the person who played such a foolish and expensive practical joke must be discovered and brought to book. I've my hands full already here. I can't waste my time looking for mare's nests. I am not going to ask whether you know the name of the joker. I am merely going to ask permission to go into your kitchen and interview the cook."

Great-aunt Puddequet shrugged her frail shoulders.

"Anybody who interviews my cook does so at his own risk, inspector," she said. "If this is clearly understood, you have my permission to try."

"Wait here, sergeant," said Bloxham.

To the surprise of the other three, he opened the window, stepped out on to the terrace, closed the window softly behind him, and ran lightly down the stone steps. On the cinder track he encountered Priscilla Yeomond.

"Oh, inspector," she said, "I can't imagine that it's important to you, but such a funny thing has happened."

"Yes?" said Bloxham. "What's that, Miss Yeomond?"

She directed his attention to the top of the stone balustrade of the terrace.

"You see the stone balls that decorate the terrace? How many on each side can you count from here?"

The inspector counted.

"Six," he said.

Priscilla lowered her voice.

"Yesterday there were only five on each side," she said. "What do you make of that?"

Bloxham laughed.

"We know there's a practical joker in the house," he said. "Which are the new stone balls?"

"The two at the head of the steps. There used to be two little cupids standing one on either side. They were there yesterday. Surely you remember them?"

The inspector shuddered.

"I do," he said, hurrying off in the direction of the kitchen garden.

Priscilla frowned thoughtfully after him, and turned and looked again at the new stone balls. Suddenly a javelin whizzed by her and stuck, quivering, into the soft turf which bordered the track.

"Sorry," shouted her brother Hilary. "Hope I didn't startle you. Didn't think it would go quite as far as that. I wanted a change from the high jump."

He pulled on his sweater and fell into step beside her.

"Anything the matter?" he asked.

"No," said Priscilla abruptly. "At least only this beastly house and that stupid murder, and—Timon Anthony—"

"Anthony?"

"Yes. He asked me to marry him yesterday morning."

"Whatever for?"

Priscilla raised her eyebrows. It was not the first time that she had been confronted by the phenomenal lack of tact shown by brothers, who cannot imagine why on earth anyone should wish to marry their sisters and do not hesitate to say so.

"I imagine that in some curious way I attract him favorably," she observed, with suitable *hauteur*.

"Oh, yes, of course, rather," agreed Hilary, hastily recovering ground. "No idea of being rude. I only wondered what the idea might be. I suppose—" He hesitated.

"Well?" Priscilla was mollified, but not by any means appeased.

"I suppose—I mean—well, dash it!—er—Great-aunt hasn't decided that the female line inherits or anything, has she? You know—the Salic law not-withstanding, and so forth."

Priscilla regarded him with a rich mixture of doubt, suspicion, and amusement.

"What exactly are you trying to say, sweetest?" she enquired.

"Oh, I just wondered—you see, it's like this, Priscilla. Or, at least, this is how I work it out. By coming down here and kowtowing to the old dame and so forth, we others queer the pitch of the man Anthony to no small extent. See what I mean?"

Priscilla nodded.

"Don't elaborate, dear," she said, gently but firmly. "It's quite clear. In fact, I've thought it out for myself ages ago."

"Yes. Quite. Well, you see, if Hobson had been me, or Frank, or M., or Cowes, or even Brown-Jenkins, I should say at once that Anthony did him in on the principle of clearing the field for himself. Then, if that had been so, the attempt on me last night would have been the next logical step, and that would be followed now by deep-laid plots against the rest of you in turn."

"*The Greene Murder Case*," said Priscilla, nodding her head sagely. "You might lend it to Celia when you've finished it. She hasn't read it."

"Well, I won't say the book didn't give me the idea," admitted Hilary, "but, you see, the murderer has started all wrong. Instead of laying for one of us, he's only hit a bloke on the head who had nothing to do with the case: to wit, Hobson. Now he makes a rather pie attempt on me, and even gets Cowes to lure me out of danger while Rome burns."

"What *is* it that you're trying to say, angel?" asked his sister plaintively.

"Well, I began by saying that if Anthony thought Great-aunt had decided that the men of the family were a bit of a washout—and don't forget that she's now seen:

(*a*) Malpas muff the high jump at five feet eleven;
(*b*) Frank make his record long jump of nineteen feet seven inches, a distance which a schoolboy champion can equal;
(*c*) Cowes put the shot once on his own toe, twice behind him instead of in front, once into the bathchair—luckily when she'd just got out of it to hobble over to Kost and curse him for letting us get slack—and once a distance of

nearly fifteen feet, after which he retired to bed for two days, suffering from strained eyebrow or something;

(*d*) Brown-Jenkins persistently refuse to make any attempt at mastering the pole-vault action ever since Kost handed him backchat on the subject nearly three weeks ago;

(*e*) Me make my record throw with the discus of fifty-eight feet nine inches—"

"That sounds good to me," said Priscilla meekly.

"Well," returned Hilary, "I know that the world's record figures for the event are one hundred and fifty-eight feet, one and three-quarter inches, that's all."

"Yes, but that wasn't an Englishman," retorted Priscilla.

"U.S.A.," said Hilary patiently. "And M.C. Nokes's English native record is one hundred and twenty-six feet one inch," he added, "so poor H. is a bit of an also-ran, isn't he? No, the point I'm trying to make is this. She might have made up her mind that we men are a dud lot, and so the girls will inherit. Well, if Anthony found that out, you see—"

"Thank you," said Priscilla stiffly. "Your remarks are in rather dubious taste, dear, aren't they? Hullo! The inspector has left the door ajar and that ginger cat has just got into the sunk garden. Great-aunt hates the sight of him, so I'd better chase him out."

She entered the sunk garden and called the cat. Having ejected him and closed the door, she returned to her brother.

"The gardeners must have dumped a fresh load of gravel in there," she said. "What else were you trying to lead up to in your Bright Talks to Young People?"

Hilary considered.

"Oh, ah, yes!" he said. "My second point. As Hobson was murdered instead of one of us, and as it was Cowes who invited me to play chess up at the house and so probably saved my life, Anthony must be the murderer. Especially as he's apparently made a bolt for it."

"What do you mean?" asked Priscilla. "Oh, here comes the inspector again. I wonder whether he's found out anything. What's in the parcel, do you suppose?"

"If they could find the weapon it would be something," said Hilary. "You knew M. and I went to the inquest on Hobson, didn't you?"

"Yes. Was the weapon mentioned?"

"Well, the medical evidence was to the effect that, beyond the fact of its being blunt, smooth, and possibly rounded at the end, and that it seemed unlikely that more than one blow had been struck with it, there was no indication as to the nature of the instrument with which the blow had been delivered."

He hailed the approaching police officer.

"I suppose you haven't discovered the weapon yet," he said.

Bloxham looked grave, and glanced at the brown-paper parcel he was carrying.

"Well, I hope not, sir," he replied, and walked past them and entered the sunk garden.

"Now, what do you suppose he means by that?" enquired Priscilla. "Oh, and by the way," she added, "I'm going to dinner with the Digots tonight. Ought I to ask the inspector's permission, do you think? They are having a most thrilling visitor."

"Who is it?"

"Beatrice Lestrange Bradley. I've heard her lecture. She is marvelously clever."

"Oh, yes. The psychology bird. Evil-looking old dame. She had an honorary degree shoved on her while Frank was up, I remember. Weird kind of creature, rather like a vulture to look at, and with much the same sort of nature. Has a brilliant son, hasn't she?"

"Nothing like as brilliant as herself," retorted Priscilla, quick to defend her sex. "And, talking of dinner, there's the whistle for lunch. I do hope Mr. Bloxham didn't annoy cook, because I'm frightfully hungry, but only if there's something nice to eat."

Mr. Bloxham had not annoyed the cook. He had tapped on the door of the outer scullery and had been bidden to step within. Confronting him was a smallish kitchenmaid, and behind her, with a soup ladle grasped menacingly in her right hand and a gigantic pepperpot in her left, was the formidable Mrs. Macbrae.

"Ou, come ben," she observed, replacing her weapons on the kitchen table much as her forbears might have laid aside their arms upon perceiving the form of friend where they had expected foe. "Ye'll be the police."

The inspector acknowledged the compliment of being referred to in the plural by a genial smile which widened as Mrs. Macbrae continued judicially, "I doubt ye'r ower young tae tak' sic responsibeelity on ye tae be speirin' at a wumman auld eneugh tae be your mither. I thocht ye were that sneakin' devil of a Herrin' that I wis takin' the pepper tae ye. But come ben. Ye're a braw bonnie laddie, though no ower gifted, I'm thinking. What will ye be speirin' aboot this time? Ou, ay, and whiles I'm thinkin' aboot it—will a footprint be ony manner o' guid tae ye? Forbye, I hae a grrand ane I'll show ye."

She led him into the outer scullery. On the windowsill a large aluminium dish-cover had been placed. She lifted it and disclosed the muddy print of a shoe.

" 'Twas no there when I went to my bed the night, forbye I always shine my electric torch on the ledge to drive off the old tomcat that gets roosting

there, and the sill was white as the snaw. Look for yoursel'. There's no onything but the footprint. Very exceptional, that, ye'll be thinkin', and ye'll be thinkin' right. I ken verra well wha made yon track, and I doubt 'twas no leddy."

"It's the print of a lady's shoe," said Bloxham, eyeing it through a magnifying glass.

"Ou, ay. Nae doubt aboot it. But no leddy made it. Noo, ask yoursel", as a sensible laddie, dae ye see Miss Caddick climbing windowsills and sic havers? Weel, 'tis her print. I wouldna let her have the shoon till I'd shown ye the marks. But 'tis Herrin' did that same, the smotherin' kelpie. Here's the shoon. Do ye look them weel ower."

"Yes," said Bloxham. "I see your point, Mrs. Macbrae, but—" He replaced the shoes on the floor.

"Dinna ye see? He was oot last nicht! Look at the dirrt! Where will ye find dirrt like yon? I'll no deceive ye, ye puir haverin' body that canna credit the evidence o' your ain senses! 'Tis by the water. Soople your limbs, and rin doon there. 'Twill na tak' ye mair than a meenute. See for yoursel', mon! See for yoursel'! And, if he was oot, he could hae set light to the wee hoose! Ou, ay! And speir at him aboot the wee beasties! I'm thinking he'll be too frightened tae lee. Ask him did he no gang for the wee beasties!"

"The rabbits?"

"Ay, laddie! The rabbits! He was oot the nicht the wee hoose burned. And he was oot the nicht Hobson deid."

"Look here," said Bloxham, abandoning the unprofitable footprint, which he had turned to reexamine, "what are you insinuating?"

"I'm no insinuating onything, in a way o' speaking," replied Mrs. Macbrae, with dignity. "I'm plying your puir brain wi' a few random suggestions. And if ye're going tae turn ungrateful, I'll tell ye nae mair. Na, na—I'll see masel' drooned first!"

The inspector grinned good-naturedly, and was about to leave her and walk out into the kitchen garden when his eye chanced to fall upon a curious instrument hanging by a leather thong from one of the great beams of the ceiling.

"What's that thing?" he asked, as casually as he could for excitement.

Mrs. Macbrae glanced up at it.

"I'm thinking it's twae things in ane, laddie," she said solemnly. "I wouldna hae spoken o't had ye no spoken first. Yon club was brocht hame frae Jerusalem by my sailor son, and is thocht tae be a weapon left behind by ane of the Crusaders wha focht in the Holy Wars. Masel' I'm no all that sure that the same wasna used to knock the man Hobson on the heid. It would hae daen that fine, ye ken. It's fu' weighty, and verra bonnie tae the hand."

She reached up and slipped the weapon from its strap. Bloxham took it in his hands.

"Why, the top must be solid iron," he said, testing it for weight and balance.

"Ay, verra likely," agreed Mrs. Macbrae unemotionally. "Well, there y' are. I've helpit ye all I can. Good day tae ye. Mind and speir at the man Herrin'. Herself climb ower windowsills! The puir haverin' creature must hae been daft tae think he could tak in Janet Macbrae like that!"

"I must keep this for the present," said Bloxham, still holding the iron-headed club.

"Emily, do ye be bringing a wee bit o' brown paper for the gentleman," commanded Mrs. Macbrae. "Ye'll no be breakin' it?" she enquired anxiously of Bloxham, as she wrapped up the weapon for him. "My laddie's a braw laddie, and I wouldna like him tae be thinkin' I was ower fou wi' his gifties."

It was an exceedingly thoughtful inspector of police who passed Hilary Yeomond and his sister, and walked up the steps of the front garden. Having gained the terrace, he paused and glanced back. The heap of sand left by the gardeners seemed to have grown larger. Annoying of Mrs. Puddequet to allow people all over the sunk garden. What had the man on duty been up to, to allow people to throw loads of gravel all over what might prove to be valuable clues? Still fuming, he thundered at the front door of the house, and was readmitted to the drawing-room.

Old Mrs. Puddequet was still there, although Malpas had gone, and the inspector was invited to remain for lunch. He declined the invitation, and said abruptly:

"I must return immediately to Market Longer. I shall be glad if you will arrange for all your household—family, servants, everybody—to be at home this afternoon."

After his departure, Great-aunt Puddequet was wheeled in to lunch, where she made known the inspector's decree to the assembled members of the family.

"Bother him!" said Priscilla. "I do hope he won't be long over it, whatever it is. I'm going to dinner at the Digots'. Will you drive me over, H.?"

Lunch over, Great-aunt Puddequet was proceeding to her room, where she proposed to rest until the arrival of the inspector, when one of the maids came up to the bathchair and said breathlessly:

"If you please, mam, could you give us some idea what to do with Mr. Timon's food until he comes back?"

"Comes back?" squealed Great-aunt Puddequet, who had not enjoyed the lunch. "Comes back where?"

"To his lunch, mam. If you please, mam, his bed haven't been slept in and he was not there to take his breakfast, and he isn't here to have his lunch, either. We only wondered whether cook ought to keep something hot for him, like, or whether perhaps he wouldn't be back until tonight or anything."

"What *is* the girl talking about, Companion Caddick?" squealed Great-

aunt Puddequet. "Here, take me to my room, and get me settled, and then you can come back and find out all about the matter. If that boy has taken my checkbook without my permission he can take himself off for good, but he must be found by the time the inspector arrives. Mind that!"

Miss Caddick pushed the bathchair into the bedroom, and prepared her mistress for a short siesta, then, dutifully, she returned to the girl.

"Now then, Emily," she said, "you must tell me when Mr. Anthony was last seen."

"Well, miss, he was not at dinner, was he? He changed his clothes, and then he went to the lecture with Mr. Kost in the village hall."

"Lecture? Oh, yes, I know. Mr. Kost wanted some of the young gentlemen to accompany him. It was a lantern lecture about sport or something, wasn't it?"

"That's right, miss. That's why Mr. Kost had his supper so early. Quarter to seven instead of quarter-past eight. But Mr. Anthony never come back to sleep. Couldn't 'a' done. His bed's not been touched."

"Never came back to sleep," repeated Miss Caddick, thoughtfully. Suddenly her pale eyes lighted up. "All right, Emily. I will tell Mrs. Puddequet what you say. Keep a lookout in case he returns, because the inspector is coming to question us all again."

The maid disappeared below stairs, and Miss Caddick, filled with the joy of the huntress, hastened on to the terrace.

"Of course," she thought as she traversed the hall, "Mr. Anthony set fire to Mr. Hilary Yeomond's hut, and has fled the consequences. What a bad boy! I must be on the spot to break this momentous news to the inspector as soon as he appears."

She had not long to wait. As soon as she stepped outside the front door of the house she was alarmed to notice Hilary's dog Moggridge scratching busily at a heap of gravel in the sunk garden. Miss Caddick was afraid of dogs, and especially of Moggridge, who was no thoroughbred, and no beauty, and had a strong strain of bloodhound in his makeup. She leaned upon the stone balustrade and called to him to desist. Moggridge raised his great square head for half a second, wagged his tail, and burrowed on at his research work. Miss Caddick was about to call out to him again when the inspector, followed by the sergeant, pushed open the wooden door of the sunk garden and stood watching the dog at his toil. Suddenly Bloxham bent down and peered intently at the heap of gravel which Moggridge was scattering in all directions. The sergeant stood stolidly by.

The next thing Miss Caddick saw was that the sergeant seized Moggridge by the collar and almost flung him through the aperture on to the sports field, closed the wooden door and fastened it. Then he reached for the spade which the gardeners had left on the ground close by.

CHAPTER XII

Mrs. Bradley visits the Scene of Crime

MRS. LESTRANGE BRADLEY grinned evilly upon her luckless chauffeur and settled herself more comfortably in a corner of the car.

"Carry on, George," she observed.

George touched his cap.

"I beg your pardon, madam, but I can't get any farther tonight, I'm afraid. The clutch rod's broken. It's a garage job, and where I shall find a garage about here is more than I can say. I'm very sorry, madam. That's the worst of these hired cars. According to the map we are less than three miles from our destination. I was wondering, madam, supposing I was to escort you, whether you thought you could manage to walk to Colonel Digot's place."

"George," said Mrs. Bradley, widening her mirthless grin, "I really think it is within the bounds of possibility that I could."

George, who had once been to Benares, and whose dreams were sometimes haunted by the crocodiles which lend historic charm to the Ganges River, shuddered slightly, and held open the door while his employer alighted.

"And what do they call this neighborhood, George?" she enquired, as they set off side by side into the darkness of an English country lane.

"We are in the vicinity of Little Longer, madam," he replied, steering her clear of a puddle. "Where the murders have been committed," he added pleasantly.

"Plural, George?" enquired Mrs. Bradley. "Murders?"

"Yes, so the evening paper I purchased in Southampton indicated, madam. Of course, murder has not yet been proved, but it seems that the body of the young man Anthony has been recovered from burial beneath a heap of gravel, and the police are taking decided steps to trace the origin of a pool of blood in the sunk garden. No trace of a weapon had been found at the time of going to press, but it is suspected that a fairly heavy pointed instrument, covered with rust but retaining something of its original keenness, was used for the purpose of killing the unfortunate man, and the impression of the police seems to be that a verdict of murder and not suicide or accident will be brought in at the inquest."

"Really," said Mrs. Bradley thoughtfully. She cackled harshly, and added abruptly:

"Where were you educated, George?"

"At Gallery Street Central School, madam."

"Yes. George, I think you are an advance on Henry Straker."

"I hope so, madam. Straker was mishandled, I consider, by Mr. Shaw. Boys from Sherbrooke Road School do not drop their aitches, madam. We used to play them at football, and I know."

"You read widely, George?" Mrs. Bradley circumnavigated another puddle by instinct, for it was too dark between the high hedges to see anything, and fell into step with him again.

"Fairly widely, madam. History and biography chiefly, although I am fond of books of travel. And, of course, I have read with interest, pleasure, and profit, madam, such of your own work as has found its way into the public libraries."

"You terrify me, George," said Mrs. Bradley sincerely.

For some time they walked on in silence. At length George remarked:

"To the best of my knowledge, madam, we are now passing the grounds of the ill-fated mansion of Longer, owned and occupied by Mrs. Jasper Puddequet."

"I shall stop and peer through the bars of the gate, George," said Mrs. Bradley, in a terrifying stage whisper. She quickened her pace.

"Do you think there is any chance of the murderer spying us and leaping on our necks in a frenzy?" she muttered, skipping adroitly over another large pool in the center of the road.

"I imagine not, madam," replied the chauffeur, glancing over his left shoulder. "I believe that these bloodthirsty persons betray little or no interest in the movements of anyone but their particular protagonists in the drama which their morbid and inordinate vanity causes them to stage. I fancy that you will be quite safe in peering through the bars to your heart's content."

"I'm afraid it will be too dark to see very much," said Mrs. Bradley regretfully. "Never mind!" she added brightly. "I shall be able to tell all my friends that I've been to the place. That's the great thing, isn't it?"

"So the majority of tourists seem to believe, madam," replied George. "But here is the gate, I think, and Colonel Digot's house cannot be more than another mile and a quarter."

Through the gates of Longer nothing could be seen save a light in the window of the nearest hut, and Mrs. Bradley, having feasted her eyes on this for about a minute, turned her back on the ill-fated mansion, and, rejoining George on the road, said no more until they arrived at their destination.

Dinner table talk, in spite of the determined efforts of Mrs. Digot to introduce other topics, ran almost exclusively on the tragedies which had taken place in the neighborhood, and Mrs. Bradley was drawn into a discussion of the relative merits of two interesting and highly original theories put forward by Colonel Digot and his daughter respectively.

At the conclusion of a lively argument in which Miss Digot sought to prove that old Mrs. Puddequet herself was the murderer, and the Colonel that the whole affair was the work of Russian Socialists, Mrs. Bradley asked for further details of the death of Timon Anthony, but just as Margaret Digot was about to paraphrase the news which George the chauffeur had given to his employer, a latecomer to dinner was announced, and Priscilla Yeomond came in.

"I am awfully sorry, Mrs. Digot," she said, "but that beastly inspector has been at Longer until nearly half-past seven. We've all been questioned and cross-questioned until we hardly knew what we were saying and oh, dear, I could sit down and cry!"

"I feel sorry for Bloxham," remarked Colonel Digot later. "A sound young fellow."

"Yes, he's nice," agreed Priscilla. Dinner had cheered her. She lay back in her chair and looked up at the ceiling. "But it was such a shock for him to find someone else had been killed, because he had just made up his mind how the Hobson business was done, and now all his ideas are knocked on the head."

"Why?" asked Mrs. Bradley.

Priscilla sat upright, and her eyes met the keen black ones of the birdlike old lady on the opposite side of the fireplace.

"Well," she replied, "Hobson was hit on the head, but Anthony was stabbed. They wouldn't let us see the body, but we heard about it, of course. It's been a terrible shock to us all."

"Oh, yes," said Mrs. Bradley, nodding her head slowly. "So George told me. Stabbed with a heavy, keen, but rusty implement. And buried in the sunk garden under a heap of gravel. Somebody living in the house, of course."

"Do you really think so!" Priscilla gazed at her in dismay. "That's what the inspector says. And he won't let any of us go home or even up to London until he finds out all about everything. Of course, we all think he's wrong, and that some enemy of Timon's did it. Poor boy. He wasn't very clever or good-humored, and I don't think anybody really liked him very much, but it's dreadful to think—" She broke off.

Mrs. Bradley watched her narrowly. At last she said:

"What did you say your handicap was?"

"Twenty-three," said Priscilla, surprised. "I didn't know I'd mentioned it."

"Perhaps not," said Mrs. Bradley, gazing into the fire of crackling logs. Suddenly she added, "Who else plays golf?"

Priscilla considered.

"My three brothers and Timon Anthony did, of course. Neither of the Brown-Jenkins. I'm not sure about the Cowes. None of us have played since

we've been down here. The boys have been working at their training; and I'm not really very keen, and Margaret doesn't play. Oh, now I come to think of it, I believe Timon Anthony told us that our odd man, Herring, was rather good. He used to be a caddie in his youth, and learned a lot about the game."

"Herring?" said Colonel Digot. "That's the poaching rascal Tom, Bert, and I chased out of the park last night!"

Margaret nodded.

"I believe he came rabbit-stealing again," she said. "Just before that Hobson business I missed Tiny, and your Emily told our Katie that Herring had lost one of the Longer rabbits and would have to replace it before Mrs. Puddequet found out. And when I went down this morning to feed mine, Tink had gone, and I'm certain Herring came to steal it and ran into Tom on his way back."

"Tom, like a fool, loosed off his gun instead of collaring the man," broke in the Colonel, "and that brought up Bert, and the noise of the shot woke me, and I joined in the chase, but, of course, the fellow had had his warning and took a flying start of Tom, who's got a war souvenir in the shape of a gammy leg; and so, although we chased the fellow right into Mrs. Puddequet's grounds and almost up to the mere, we lost him in the end."

"You are sure it was Herring, I suppose?" asked Priscilla.

"Well, Tom swears to him. I'm sending him over with a note to Mrs. Puddequet as soon as this tiresome murder business is over, to find out whether Margaret's rabbits are in Herring's possession. Thieving rogue!"

Young Rex Digot, an unusually silent youth of twenty, now made his contribution to the conversation.

"Might be rather convenient for the fellow to be able to prove an alibi at a certain time last night," he suggested diffidently.

Colonel Digot slapped his knee.

"There's a good deal in that," he said. "Ring the bell, will you?"

The maid who answered it was requested to send for Tom. Tom, a steady-eyed, grizzled fellow of forty, was certain that the man they had chased was Joseph Herring.

"Yes, but it was dark," objected the Colonel.

"I'd take my oath it was Herring, sir," insisted the man. "I know his voice, and I know his run. You see, sir, when I jumped at him with the gun he shouted quite loud, and then made off as smart as he could move. I know it was Herring, sir."

"Interesting," said Mrs. Bradley, when the man had gone. "I wonder how he lost his own two rabbits? Priscilla, I think I must have a short conversation with this man. Do you think it could be managed?"

Priscilla giggled.

"You could come and collect statistics of working men and their depen-

dents," she said. "Herring has heaps of grievances. He'll love to tell you all about them."

At half-past ten Priscilla indicated that it was time for her to return to her great-aunt's house. The Colonel drove her over in the car, and Margaret sat on the back seat with her for the sake of company. Mrs. Digot left the drawing room for a few moments, and Mrs. Bradley and Rex were left alone there.

Mrs. Bradley said quietly and urgently, "Child, I'm almost expiring with curiosity. What *is* this business that's going on at Longer?"

Rex shook his head hopelessly.

"I'm going to find out," said Mrs. Bradley, with a happy but remarkably unmusical cackle. "If I want an assistant I shall depend upon you."

The young man eyed the door helplessly for a moment. Then, almost imperceptibly, he nodded.

"Then, let's start now," said Mrs. Bradley with zest. "The first thing is for me to see all these cousins and things before they find out who I am. I'll collect for charity, I think. A worthy object, suitably—Or, no. Better to be an insurance agent, perhaps. I'll insure them against fire and flood and—what else? Mosquito bites, I should think."

Rex roused himself.

"Not Priscilla," he said slowly. "She had nothing to do with it."

Mrs. Bradley eyed him sharply.

"It must be understood, young man," she observed, in the mellifluous voice which gave the lie to her whole appearance, "that if I enquire into these strange matters I do so with an open mind. It is not my custom to handicap my mental powers with a mass of prejudices and preconceived ideas." She grinned fiendishly, and then added, "Either I start from scratch or not at all," and ended this unexpected sentence with a little screech of laughter.

The next morning was the beginning of a perfect spring day. Immediately after breakfast, Mrs. Bradley assumed her hat, a large, shapeless affair made of coarse, deep-yellow straw and trimmed most unsuitably with a single large blush-pink rose, put on a tweed coat of semi-sporting cut, and a pair of doeskin gloves which hid from view her yellow, clawlike fingers. A walk of about a mile and a quarter along a country road bordered by hawthorn hedges, on which the inflorescences were already in bud, brought her for the second time in her life to the handsome wrought-iron gates of Great-aunt Puddequet's house. Here she halted and surveyed the field of battle.

That wooden fence, she presumed, shut off the sports ground from the rest of the estate. The head of Malpas Yeomond, which suddenly shot into view as he cleared his usual five feet ten over the high jump, confirmed this opinion. She listened, and could hear voices. The death of their so-called cousin appeared to have had a very chastening effect on the spirits of the athletes,

she reflected. They were probably feeling decidedly frightened.

She pushed open the gates, walked in, and closed the gates behind her. Small, thin, unattractive, and intrepid, she made her way to the nearest hut and tapped on the door.

Richard Cowes was reading. He recognized Mrs. Bradley immediately, and greeted her with protestations of delight.

"This is indeed an honor! Amaris will be charmed. We have heard you lecture. Of course, we have read your books. Truly delightful encounter. Truly too delightful!" babbled Richard. "Come and be introduced to my aunt."

This unlooked-for encounter at once assisted and upset Mrs. Bradley's plans. It was impossible now for her to get to know something of the inhabitants of the house before they discovered who she was, but it was truly delightful, as Richard would have expressed it, to be made free of the house and grounds through this immediate recognition by one who was obviously a disciple. Talking amicably, they crossed the corner of the sports field, entered the sunk garden, where two stolid policemen stood on duty, ascended the stone steps, and were admitted to the house.

Great-aunt Puddequet's bathchair was in the hall, but its owner was not with it. Shrill squeals of objurgation which proceeded from the nearest opening indicated that she was in the morning-room.

"But, indeed, dear Mrs. Puddequet," protested poor Miss Caddick's tearful voice, "poor Mr. Kost did go with him to the lecture, but he left him on the way home to go into the public house for his stout. Poor man! He said he couldn't sleep without his stout! How could he know that somebody would—would kill Mr. Anthony?"

Miss Caddick ended on a loud sob.

"You're a fool, Companion Caddick," retorted old Mrs. Puddequet, even more spiritedly than usual. "Go and find Joseph Herring. He must act as attendant this morning. You can't go out looking like that. What was my wretched grandson to you, I'd like to know, or Hobson either, that you must be sobbing and sighing over them like a great baby! We shall all die some time, I suppose!"

Miss Caddick emerged from the room, and almost cannoned into the two who stood in the hall, for the light was dim after the brilliance of the morning-room, which was flooded with sunshine and, besides, she was still weeping.

Without a word Richard tapped on the door, and ushered Mrs. Bradley into the room. Old Mrs. Puddequet was reclining on the settee. She blinked her tigerish yellow eyes at Mrs. Bradley, and held out a much-beringed claw nearly as yellow as Mrs. Bradley's own.

"I don't know who you are," she observed concisely, "and to be a friend of Richard Cowes is not recommendation in this house"—she cast a malevo-

lent glance at her grandnephew—"but you've a sensible face and I like the look of you. Pray be seated."

Richard hastily dragged forward a chair, which Mrs. Bradley took with a graceful inclination of the head.

"I suppose you've heard about my murders," said old Mrs. Puddequet. "Very interesting."

"Very," agreed Mrs. Bradley. Black eyes met yellow eyes for a full thirty seconds. "No, I thought you didn't," said black eyes to the brain behind them.

At this instant Miss Caddick returned and informed her employer that Joseph Herring was just washing his hands, and that the inspector was outside the door and would be glad of a short interview.

"Bother the man," observed Great-aunt Puddequet with vigor. "Show him in."

Mrs. Bradley and Richard Cowes quietly withdrew.

"Is there a public library in Market Longer?" asked Mrs. Bradley, when they gained the hall once more. "And a local newspaper office?"

"Both," replied Richard. "Are you going to incorporate a psychological analysis of my aunt in your next book?"

"As to that," replied Mrs. Bradley solemnly, "I can't say. But I have been visited"—she lowered her voice—"by a Great Thought."

"And what is that?" enquired Richard Cowes deferentially.

"Well," replied Mrs. Bradley, leading him out on to the terrace, "when one visits friends in the country, one is always taken to see the animals on the estate in the following order: the horses, pigs, dogs, pigeons, fowls, ducks—"

"Rabbits," supplied Richard, as she paused for a second.

Mrs. Bradley, who had paused deliberately for him to make the suggestion, opened her black eyes and cackled with joy.

"Rabbits!" she exclaimed. "Childhood! Tom and Maggie Tulliver! Captain Cook! *Alice in Wonderland!* A present on the first day of the month! How delightfully, innocently, superbly rural!"

Richard Cowes beamed with pleasure, and adjusted his pince-nez self-consciously.

"I myself will conduct you," he said. "Horses? I know nothing about them. Pigs? Faugh! Dogs? I have a great respect for dogs. Very intelligent animals, I believe. But, if rabbits delight you, to the rabbits we will go."

They went.

The Scrounger was now seated on an upturned bucket in quiet enjoyment of a cigarette. He scowled at the visitors, but, considerably mollified by the surreptitious present of half a crown, which Richard slid into his ever-ready palm, he took out his charges, and at great length, and with praiseworthy

accuracy, commented upon and displayed their points.

"And which are the two you are taking care of for Colonel Digot?" enquired Mrs. Bradley, with dreadful clearness.

The Scrounger swallowed twice and looked past her. Then he caught her eye.

"Come, come, Joseph," said Mrs. Bradley, with a grin which made him shudder. "You don't want to be arrested for murder, do you?"

The wretched Joseph wilted, and swore softly to steady his nerves.

"You were out for an unlawful purpose on the night Jacob Hobson was murdered," said Mrs. Bradley relentlessly. That this fact was known to all the people in England who took the trouble to peruse the daily papers escaped Joseph for a flabbergasted instant, and he grew red with anguish.

"I—I never said I wasn't, did I?" gulped the ornament of many defaulters' parades.

"Luckily for you, you did not," said Mrs. Bradley crisply. "You admit that on the night of April eighteenth you did feloniously purloin or steal some portable property belonging or appertaining to Colonel Digot, J.P.—viz., to wit, one rabbit—don't you? Which one was it? Show me."

Joseph showed her.

"Very well," said Mrs. Bradley. "Again, on the night of Monday, April twenty-eighth, the night when Mr. Timon Anthony was murdered, you went again to Colonel Digot's kitchen garden and stole a second rabbit. Joseph, I put it to you. You are a hard-working, trustworthy, intelligent man—"

The Scrounger, who was none of these things, and had never been called them before except in company with several hundred other persons, and then only at political meetings, straightened his shoulders and flung out his chest.

"And you are aware," continued Mrs. Bradley, noting these manifestations with secret amusement, "that on the face of it your conduct must look, to say the very least, unpleasantly suspicious. One thing, and one thing only, will divert this suspicion. Joseph, why did you *need* to steal two rabbits? Tell me that. Are you a collector of rabbits? Do you yearn after them? Have you a secret craving for them, or what?"

The Scrounger cleared his throat and his eyes wandered glassily towards the nearest treetop. Mrs. Bradley, who knew a liar when she saw one, added swiftly:

"And don't say that. It isn't true."

Richard Cowes had grown weary of the lecture on rabbits, and had wandered through the gate of the kitchen garden and back to the sports ground, so that the two of them were alone.

" 'Ere—" began Joseph belligerently; but then thought better of it.

"Somebody miked a Belgian 'are and a Flemish Giant off me, and I dursen't let the old lady know, so I 'as to replace 'em, see? And that's the truth, it is."

"I believe you, Joseph," said Mrs. Bradley magnificently. "More. The day you furnish me with information—correct information, please, Joseph!—as to the identity of the person or persons who stole your rabbits from you, I will give you a pound note. Further, if you can discover, not invent, Joseph!—you understand the difference, don't you?—the reason why they were stolen, and the use, if any, to which they were afterwards put, I'll make it thirty shillings. And now go and take Mrs. Puddequet out for a nice walk."

CHAPTER XIII

May Fair

"WHEN in the country, take part in as many country pursuits and diversions as possible," said Margaret Digot on Wednesday, April 30th. She glanced mischievously at Mrs. Bradley. "We always go to the fair at Hilly Longer on May Day," she added, "and that's tomorrow. Would you care to come with us? Of course, it's not what it used to be, but we rather enjoy it."

"Let us go," replied Mrs. Bradley promptly. "I will throw wooden balls at coconuts. Do you like coconuts?"

"I always think I do until I begin eating a bit of one," said Margaret. "Do you mind if Priscilla Yeomond comes with us? They're sick of their murders and policemen and things, and she says she would like a change of scene."

Mrs. Bradley assented with enthusiasm, and also fell in with the further suggestion that she should accompany her hostess's daughter as far as Longer in order to fetch Priscilla.

"Of course," said Margaret when they were upon the road. "I dare say the other girl, the cousin, will come too, and several of the boys. You don't mind going about in gangs, I hope?"

Mrs. Bradley expressed immense pleasure at the idea of going about in gangs, and added that she hoped it would be a fine day. As a matter of fact, she hoped for rain, for, as she explained later to the silent Rex, who accompanied them, there was nothing like a little heavy rain on a little light summer clothing to bring out the worst aspects of human nature.

"And one of them, or two of them, or, possibly, three of them committed murder a short time ago, child," she added, with a chuckle of ghoulish glee, "and I must know who and why."

"I'm afraid," replied Rex somberly, "that a fair on the first of May is not the most promising place for your purpose."

"That's where you show yourself to be in error, child," said Mrs. Bradley, with immense complaisance. "The great thing is to get them all to come with us. Do you think it can be managed?"

"All?" said Margaret, who had been calling her dog from a field, and who now rejoined them on the road.

"Certainly, my dear," said Mrs. Bradley. She dived into the capacious pocket

of her tweed skirt and drew from the depths a small notebook, from which she proceeded to read the names of old Mrs. Puddequet's nephews, nieces, and trainer.

"I should like to have had the enterprising rabbit-tamer with us also," she added, closing the little book and returning it to the limbo whence it had emerged, "but, the social customs of the country being what they are instead of what Clive Brown-Jenkins would like them to be, I suppose we must do the best we can with the material which is supplied to us."

"How do you know Clive Brown-Jenkins is a Socialist?" demanded Margaret.

"Is he one?" enquired Mrs. Bradley, with a hideous grimace at Rex.

The remainder of the walk was occupied by a discussion on Bernard Shaw, carried on exclusively by the brother and sister. One of them walked on one side of the road and the other on the opposite side, for they were of an age when arguments appear to gain in significance by being shouted across an intervening space. Mrs. Bradley occupied the center of the way, and whiled away the time by reciting under her breath short lyrics from the better-known modern poets as she walked along.

"At any rate, you can't get away from *Heartbreak House*," bellowed Margaret as they arrived at the gates of Longer.

" 'In thee, in me,' " concluded Mrs. Bradley, with serious pleasure, as Rex opened the gates for her to pass through.

The first person they encountered upon entering the grounds was Great-aunt Puddequet herself. The bathchair, propelled by Miss Caddick, who looked taller, whiter, and more angular than ever, halted abruptly, and Great-aunt Puddequet stuck the ferrule of her umbrella firmly into the gravel path, and squealed raucously at Margaret.

"Why have you brought people to lunch? You know I have nothing but the lamb! The girl's a fool!"

"We haven't come to lunch, dear Mrs. Puddequet," replied Margaret, in the soothing tones of chivalrous youth confronted by querulous and more-or-less ridiculous age.

"This is Mrs. Lestrange Bradley, the writer and psychoanalyst. I think you have met her, haven't you?"

"Yesterday," said Great-aunt Puddequet. She extended a parchment-colored finger, heavily ringed, and pointed it at Mrs. Bradley.

"I have heard of your work," she said. "More: I have read your books. Utter rubbish. How do you do?"

Mrs. Bradley acknowledged this informal comment on her work with an appreciative leer which gave her never extraordinarily attractive countenance the expression of a satyr.

"I hesitate to commit myself to sentimentality," she observed, in her rich,

deep, beautiful voice, "but my heart goes out to you, Mrs. Puddequet. How you must have enjoyed the murders!"

Great-aunt Puddequet neighed shrilly like an excited horse. Then she placed a jeweled forefinger on her lips and gave a harelike glance backwards to remind her protagonist of the presence of the meek and humble Caddick behind the bathchair.

"Margaret, my dear," she squealed, "push the bathchair, child. Companion, be off. Will you never learn to rouge? Caesar said," she added, as the unfortunate companion relinquished the responsibility of providing motive power for the bathchair, and hurried in the direction of the house—"or one should say Shakespeare, I suppose, except that I don't know whether Shakespeare made Caesar say it or Caesar Shakespeare. You see my point, I hope? So much more profound, to my mind, the argument about authors and their characters. I hate the ancient, vulgar, hopelessly overdone Shakespeare-Bacon controversy."

" 'Let me have men about me that are fat,' " interpolated Mrs. Bradley, nodding her head vigorously. She removed her ridiculous hat, which made vigorous nodding a matter of some difficulty, and laid it at Great-aunt Puddequet's feet. The old lady kicked it tentatively and then ignored it completely.

"How did you know that I was about to quote those words?" she enquired interestedly.

"It was perfectly obvious from the context," said Mrs. Bradley. "Why don't you make one of them practice throwing the javelin?" she enquired, with seeming irrelevance.

"It was Timon's fault," said old Mrs. Puddequet, her yellow eyes flickering angrily. "Annoying of him to annoy me. Still, I prefer that Kost killed him rather than that he should have killed Kost," she added. "Such a good trainer, and, of course, does no harm to the parrots at all."

"No, I suppose not," said Mrs. Bradley, sympathetically interpreting this train of thought. "That's what I think about golf. It's not a game for young children or clergymen, but at least the parrots take no harm from it. It's a comforting reflection, that."

She gave vent to a little scream of hideous laughter, and swung round upon Margaret.

"I'll push the bathchair," she said. "Go and gather the tribes together, child. I want everybody to come to the fair. It will do them a world of good."

By dint of clever strategy, Margaret prevailed upon all but Francis Yeomond, Miss Caddick, and Kost to join the party.

"I can see by your face," began old Mrs. Puddequet in her farewell speech to Mrs. Bradley on the steps of the terrace, "that I am not going to enjoy my murders very much longer. In any case, I shall probably leave my money to

one of the girls. The world will be a woman's world in another twenty years or so. So very annoying of Anthony to allow himself to be killed by Kost," she went on. "Such short-sighted policy, though, to kill the goose who might have laid the golden eggs." She seemed decidedly put out.

Mrs. Bradley leaned over the stone balustrade and gazed benignly down upon the still-unfinished goldfish pond below.

"And bits of brain, I suppose," she murmured to herself. "Very interesting."

"No brains at all," said old Mrs. Puddequet, mistaking her meaning. "A bullet-headed, low-browed, bruising type of person; always in an unpleasantly belligerent state of intoxication or else in a mood of greasy servility which did not, upon any occasion which has passed into history, extend as far as kindliness to his wife. Poor unfortunate woman! I don't wonder she took her chance when she saw it."

Mrs. Bradley eyed the speaker with furtive interest. Then, looking fixedly at one of the ornamental stone balls on the stone baluster near at hand, she said:

"You think so?"

"We used to have two ornamental stone carvings at the head of the steps," said old Mrs. Puddequet, taking absolutely no notice whatever of the question, "but Amaris persuaded me to have them removed."

"I said they gave me a pain in the neck," called out Amaris, who was standing at the gate of the sunk garden with Priscilla, Celia, and Hilary. "They were truly atrocious. If you want to see for yourself, they are in the garage behind the old bathchair."

"Behind what?" said Mrs. Bradley, startled.

"I suppose I may discontinue using a bathchair and order another if I choose?" said old Mrs. Puddequet tartly. "As a matter of fact, the old one has no rubber tires."

Mrs. Bradley nodded, and, for no obvious reason, picked up a small bulb-bowl which was standing on the floor of the terrace between two stone balusters and balanced it carefully on the top of the stone coping. Having placed it to her satisfaction, she was about to step back when her heel touched the wheel of the bathchair. Her fingers slipped on the smooth surface of the bowl, and it fell with a crash of breaking earthenware on to the crazy paving of the sunk garden below.

"There, now," said Mrs. Bradley regretfully. "That comes of meddling with things which don't concern one."

She apologized profusely, and, in an atmosphere rendered somewhat difficult by Great-aunt Puddequet's repeated observations on the clumsiness displayed by people who might be expected to exercise a little reasonable care, the party left the scene of the disaster and set out for the fair.

Hilly Longer, a small historic village with a Norman church designed pos-

sibly by one of the builders of Christchurch Priory, could be reached by a field-path which later struck across an arm of the New Forest, and, the day being fair and the party in excellent spirits at the thought of any change whatsoever in the daily routine of sports practices and police interrogation, it was unanimously decided to walk.

By the time they reached the outskirts of the village Mrs. Bradley had acquired from various members of the party much valuable incidental information about the mysterious happenings of the past weeks. She learned, among other things, the true history of the gathering of the family at Longer; she heard of the two occasions on which a bloodstained javelin had been discovered on the sports field; she heard of the midnight fears of Priscilla Yeomond and of the midnight explorations of Clive Brown-Jenkins. She learned also of the first discovery of Hobson's body at the bottom of the mere; and, more than all this, she was able to form a very shrewd estimate of what everybody thought of everybody else, and the reasons for thinking so. As an item of immediate but passing interest she heard that Timon Anthony, having proposed marriage in turn to Amaris Cowes and Priscilla Yeomond, had even tried his luck with the youthful but intelligent Celia Brown-Jenkins. By each of them he had been repulsed.

"Margaret Digot, too, I suppose," she said, eyeing the unconscious girl with what was intended to be a whimsical smile, but which approached more nearly to the kind of grin with which an alligator on the banks of the Nile might view the coming of a chubby but careless baby.

"Oh, Margaret turned him down ages ago," said Priscilla. "She wrote and told me about it before we came down here. He used to visit there a great deal, but after that he didn't go any more."

"Which of these people have ever been to your house, child?" asked Mrs. Bradley, skilfully losing the rest of the party among the crowds that thronged the fair. She held Margaret's arm and drew her out of the press and into a fortune-teller's booth. The fortune-teller, a young, coarsely good-looking girl of twenty-two or so, welcomed them gladly, but Mrs. Bradley, having presented her with five shillings, waved her away until Margaret had answered the question.

"Take your time," said Mrs. Bradley kindly. "I want you to be very, very sure of what you say. Madame"—she grinned evilly upon the black-browed Medea at the table—"Madame will not mind waiting five minutes, I'm sure."

"At the pretty lady's pleasure," said the sibyl, with an oily smirk.

Mrs. Bradley eyed her with the gaze of a benevolently minded shark, and the woman took a step backward and averted her bold brown eyes.

Margaret sat down on one of the two small chairs with which the booth was furnished and rested her elbow on the table. As she thought of a name she repeated it aloud, and Mrs. Bradley copied it under a cryptic heading,

into her small and ever-ready notebook.

"The man who invented the looseleaf system," she said, recording the name of Timon Anthony in her minute and almost undecipherable handwriting, "probably sprang from parents who were criminals of genius."

"All the Yeomonds," went on Margaret, frowning a little. "Oh, no! Not Francis. I'm sorry."

Mrs. Bradley wrote busily for a few seconds.

"Both the Brown-Jenkins," said Margaret, "and Richard Cowes."

"Not Amaris?" Mrs. Bradley fixed her sloe-black eyes on the fortune-teller, who was inclined to become restless, for she had nothing whatever to do, and not all her native intuition could make head or tail of the conversation.

"No, not Amaris," replied Margaret.

"Then, of course, there is Joseph Herring the rabbit fancier," said Mrs. Bradley thoughtfully, adding his name at the end of her list.

"Is there anything—I suppose there is something at the back of all this?" said Margaret, laughing.

"We will see," said Mrs. Bradley. She extended a yellow, clawlike hand to the woman behind the table.

"Fourteen children, and beware of a tall young fellow with golden hair," she observed, with a ghoulish cackle, before the unfortunate creature could say a single word. She withdrew her hand and seized that of the fortune-teller in a grip of steel.

"Today someone will give you a pound note," she announced, studying the grimy palm closely, "and no change will be required." She let it go, and, opening her purse, drew out the sum she had named, and pressed it into the woman's hand.

"Wherever have you two been?" demanded Priscilla a quarter of an hour later.

"Having our fortunes told," replied Mrs. Bradley, who had spent a profitable five minutes in watching Amaris Cowes and the young man trying their luck at the coconuts. Amaris, who, taking full advantage of the halfway line allowed by the chivalrous proprietor to all ladies participating in the sport, had smashed four nuts to pieces with her first four balls and had then been refused a second threepennyworth of fun by a justly incensed fieldsman in a red-and-black-striped scarf which he wore in lieu, apparently, of either shirt or collar, turned at the sound of Mrs. Bradley's voice and smiled tolerantly.

"What about hoopla?" she enquired richly.

"Not hoopla," said Mrs. Bradley succinctly. "Have you no respect for the laws governing gambling, gaming, and all pastimes having as their avowed object monetary gain or profit in kind? We will fling darts; we will shoot at colored eggshells dancing on jets of water; we will even enter the maze of mir-

rors and make fools of ourselves to amuse the many-headed—but hoopla! No. It is against my principles to attempt to put a square peg into a round hole."

The party laughed and capitulated. Arrived at the booth, Mrs. Bradley demanded darts, and, flinging them one after another as quickly as she could, decorated her chosen target with a capital letter B—a *tour de force* which was applauded wildly by the onlookers, several of whom offered to lay her bets that she could not reproduce the initial letters of their own names with equal celerity. Upon Mrs. Bradley's intimation, however, that she was liable to fits of extreme absentmindedness owing to having been dropped on her head at the age of two months and three days, and was never quite certain where she would begin hurling the darts next, the proprietress kindly but firmly urged the would-be promoters of the affair to desist from their well-meant efforts, and turned her attention to Richard Cowes. Richard, having modestly but effectually scored the minimum number for the purpose, was in process of deciding whether a green or a canary-colored Fluffy Hussy should be his boon companion for the rest of the day. Amaris settled the question for him by seizing the canary-colored doll and thrusting it into his unwilling arms. She then led him away. At this, Mrs. Bradley called for more darts, and, having scored the required number, secured the green doll, and, tucking it under her arm, where its pristine hue shrieked incoherently at her violet and orange woolen jumper suit, she turned to Malpas and Hilary Yeomond, who, with Clive Brown-Jenkins, were debating the important question of lunch, and said:

"I wager that none of you can do as well as Richard Cowes and I. Now, children."

Malpas screwed a monocle into his left eye and regarded the black-eyed old lady with enquiring interest.

"No?" he drawled.

In Mrs. Bradley's small looseleaf notebook that night the following memorandum appeared under the heading: "Darts. In order of throwing."

Richard Cowes. 200. A prize.
Malpas Yeomond. 139.
Clive Brown-Jenkins. 415. A prize. If he had scored another 35, he could have had two prizes.
Priscilla Yeomond. 25.
Celia Brown-Jenkins. 65.
Hilary Yeomond. 110.

 N.B.—What about Francis Yeomond and Joseph Herring?
 Still, nothing could be more deliciously obvious.

The sun rose at five twenty-nine (Summer Time) next morning, and Mrs.

Bradley rose with him. She stole downstairs and into the library. Over the mantelpiece was a heterogeneous collection of weapons belonging to all periods and many different countries. The weapons were arranged to form a large circle whose diameter was determined by half a dozen long spears. Mrs. Bradley carried a stout mahogany chair over to the fireplace, stood on it, and inspected the weapons closely. Inside the large circle was a smaller concentric one formed of shorter spears, javelins, harpoons, throwing sticks and a single, broad-bladed assegai. Mrs. Bradley fingered two or three of them, and finally shook her birdlike black head.

" 'Not there, not there, my child.' Felicia Dorothea Hemans," she observed sorrowfully. "Ah, well."

She got down and restored the mahogany chair to its former position. She thoughtfully gazed out of the window for a moment, and then left the library and ascended the stairs. She knocked at one of the bedroom doors, and, obtaining no answer, turned the handle and walked in. It was Rex's room. The lad lay on his left side so that his face was turned towards her. In spite of the fact that his mouth was wide open he was an attractive spectacle, flushed with sleep, his hair tousled and his slightly curling lashes long and dark. Mrs. Bradley sighed with the instinctive wistfulness of a mother, and stepped softly to the bedside. She stroked his hair with a yellow claw gentle as the touch of roses, and said in her deep, delightful voice, "Wake up, my dear."

Rex grunted, hoglike, and sat up.

"Go over to Longer, Rex, and steal for me a javelin," said Mrs. Bradley crisply, when she judged that he was sufficiently wide awake to take in what she said.

Rex nodded economically.

Satisfied, Mrs. Bradley smiled in her reptilian way and went out into the garden. Rex grinned, leapt out of bed, fell into the bath, and in less than fifteen minutes was cycling at a Clive Brown-Jenkins pace towards Longer.

Breakfast was at nine. Rex sat opposite his sister, and his wolfish enjoyment of the kidneys and bacon did not disguise from her the patent fact that he was very much excited. As soon as the meal was over, Margaret trailed him to the library. Following the direction of his eyes, she noticed that a new shaft had been added to the collection of spears over the mantelpiece.

Rex glanced over his shoulder.

"Shut the door, kid," he said.

"Don't leave me outside," said Mrs. Bradley, entering. She closed the door behind her, and looked enquiringly at Rex, who jerked his head towards the bunch of spears on the wall.

"There's the javelin, then," said Mrs. Bradley, with satisfaction. "Get it down, child."

Rex obediently detached the implement and handed it down to her. Mrs. Bradley laid it on the hearthrug.

"And what else?" she enquired.

Rex glanced at the door and then at the open window. He tiptoed to the latter and closed it. Margaret giggled nervously. Rex glowered at her and tiptoed over to Mrs. Bradley.

"I've found the gym rope," he whispered.

Mrs. Bradley's black eyes snapped with purely esthetic pleasure.

"My dearest child!" she observed, with a hideous leer of delight. "Where?"

"At the bottom of the water-butt that stands by the woodshed door. And it's in two pieces which seem to be about equal in length."

"The water-butt?" enquired Margaret stolidly.

"The gym rope, cuckoo," replied her brother succinctly.

Mrs. Bradley gazed at the young man with reverence.

"The water-butt!" she whispered ecstatically. "Of course! But I should never have thought of it. How did you find out, child?"

Rex grinned.

"A reporter fell in," he replied, with quiet relish, "and the water-butt tipped over. Herring rescued him and resurrected the two lengths of rope. They didn't see me."

"You fill me with amazement and rapture, child," said Mrs. Bradley fondly. "I did not know the rope was in two parts, of course, and I could not imagine where they'd hidden it. And the javelin—" She stooped and picked it up, staring attentively at the metal point.

CHAPTER XIV

The Little Mermaid

I

INSPECTOR BLOXHAM waved the Crusader's club irritably at the superintendent.

"Na-poo!" said he, with the concentrated and sardonic spleen to which that idiom so readily and amply lends itself. "Na-bally-well-poo, dammit!"

"Oh?" said the superintendent, licking an envelope busily, and covertly regarding the clock. "Chief Constable will be here in a minute or two. Hold on to him till I get back. Going out for a bit of grub," continued the superintendent, putting on his coat and sliding a large, hairy hand over his back hair, "would do you a lot of good, too, Bloxham, boy. Still, you keep the old chap busy till I get back, and then I'll take him over. The damned old fool," he added, in an indulgent tone, "is still talking about calling Scotland Yard in, so get to it, boy, because I shan't be able to hold him down much longer."

He went out, and Bloxham could hear him humming as he went towards the outer door. The inspector sat down on the edge of the big desk, tossed the heavy club on to the only easy chair in the room, and tapped his left heel restlessly against the bottom drawer. He stared moodily into the street, and hoped that the Chief Constable's car had broken down. There was nothing to be seen from the window save the figure of a little old lady. The only remarkable thing about her was the almost indecent hue of the mustard-colored sports coat which she was wearing, with terrible effect, on top of a tomato-red dress. The costume was set off in a manner which would have been at once the mingled rapture and despair of Wilkie Bard, Malcolm Scott, and Nellie Wallace, by a small cloche hat which boasted a single, straight, aggressive feather. This feather shot insolently into the air for a matter of twenty inches or so, and, according to the godless Hilary Yeomond, who swore that he had been privileged to witness it in action at the crossroads in Market Longer, was used for directing and controlling traffic, and was worked from the eyebrows and the tips of the ears.

To the inspector's amusement, the apparition crossed the road and began to mount the steps of the police station.

"Lost her parrot," said the inspector aloud, but with no idea that he could be overheard.

Mrs. Bradley, whose hearing was abnormally acute, stopped on the second step and grinned up at him.

"Not now," she said, with the street urchin's gift of ready repartee.

Five seconds later she was shown in.

"The fact is, inspector," said she, removing the curiously startling headgear and dropping it negligently upon the floor, "I've come to tell you something about the Longer cases."

"Thank heaven," murmured the inspector, piously crossing his fingers and surreptitiously touching wood with the other hand. "What about them, madam?"

"My name is Bradley, Lestrange, Beatrice, one, feminine gender, objective case, answering to the name Dodo if accompanied by lumps of sugar," said Mrs. Bradley, grinning at him like a man-eating tiger, and stepping across to the only armchair. She picked up the club, looked it over appraisingly, tested its weight and balance, and then swung it round her head.

"Some wrist," said the inspector to himself. Mrs. Bradley nodded agreeably.

"Yes," she said. "They become exceedingly violent at times, you see."

"Who do?"

"The mentally afflicted."

"Oh, ah, yes! I place you now," said Bloxham. "You're the lady psychoanalyst. I've read your books. Jolly good."

"You overwhelm me, child," murmured Mrs. Bradley, rolling her humorous black eyes. She glanced at the club again before placing it carefully on the bookcase beside her.

"There's a word golfers are supposed to use," she said regretfully. "You know the one I mean?"

"Tut, tut?" suggested Bloxham, helpfully. He sat down in the superintendent's swivel chair and swung round to face her.

"Thank you. Yes. Well, apply it to yourself, my poor lad."

Bloxham grinned.

"Exactly why?" he enquired.

Her eyes directed his towards the weapon on the bookcase, and he blushed.

"Well," he said defensively, "hang it all, it might have been that! Remember, I hadn't the model of Hobson's skull by me when I spotted that thing hanging up in the kitchen at Longer. And, at any rate, the beastly thing is rounded, and I knew it was a rounded implement that did in that wretched bloke."

"Round, not rounded," amended Mrs. Bradley tersely. "Spherical, child, spherical."

"But you didn't see the dead man!" cried the inspector. "So what do you know about it?"

"I read the medical evidence that was given at the inquest," said Mrs. Bradley. "Of course, the medical profession is always a little—reserved, shall we say?—on certain points, but I've since interviewed the two doctors who examined the corpse of Hobson, and I'm fairly well satisfied that I now know how Hobson was killed, and when, and why."

"But you don't know who killed him?" said the inspector, grinning incredulously.

"Yes, I even know who killed him, and I know how the body came to be placed in the middle of a rather wide lake, inspector. Will you come back to Longer with me now?"

A car drew up outside the police station, and Bloxham stood up and glanced out of the window.

"I'd like to, as soon as I've shunted the Chief Constable," he said.

"Not Sir Bertram?" said Mrs. Bradley, grinning with Machiavellian joy.

"Yes; Sir Bertram Pallery," replied the inspector. "You know him?"

"Yes, but I don't want to meet him," said Mrs. Bradley. She seized her headgear and thrust it on, tiptoed across the room, and, before the astonished inspector could say another word, she had thrown up the lower window-sash and crawled out over the sill. The distance to the ground was less than ten feet. Hanging by her claws, Mrs. Bradley grinned once more, in the disquieting manner of the Cheshire Cat, and then dropped out of sight. At the same instant the Chief Constable entered by way of the door.

The interview was fairly short. The Chief Constable drove off without waiting to see the superintendent, and a harassed, irritated, decidedly worried inspector was left to make the best of his way to Longer.

He caught up with Mrs. Bradley at the very gates of the house, and they sauntered in together. Mrs. Bradley led the way to the kitchen garden, and they passed through it and so round to the woodshed door. There stood the water-butt, almost empty, and at the bottom of it, for all and sundry to view, lay the two soaked portions of the gymnasium rope.

The inspector drew them out, and, coiling them, carried them to the sports field. It was deserted. He stretched the two pieces of rope side by side on the grass. Save for a matter of inches they were equal in length. Bloxham grunted, and made an entry in his notebook. Then he slipped it back into his pocket, and looked despairingly at Mrs. Bradley.

"I don't know whether I'm thick-headed or silly with chewing over these cases," he said, "but I confess here and now, that the sight of this damn thing conveys simply nothing to my mind except the somewhat trite observation that it's been hacked into halves by a rather blunt knife."

Mrs. Bradley solemnly patted his broad shoulder.

"That's quite good for a start," she said kindly. "Bring it along to the mere."

Obediently the large young man gathered up the bisected clue, and fol-

lowed the little old woman to the water's edge.

"The second pollard willow will be about right," said Mrs. Bradley, pointing to an ancient, gnarled, and twisted tree whose branches stood out like crazy hair on a wizard's head.

"Just about opposite the spot where the body of Hobson was located," said the inspector.

"How wide do you think it is across the mere at this point?" asked Mrs. Bradley, shading her eyes with her arm.

The inspector drew out his notebook and consulted it.

"Roughly speaking, about twenty-six yards," he answered.

"And the total length of the gymnasium rope?"

The inspector laid the two lengths of rope on the ground and measured them with a folding pocket ruler.

"Eighteen feet, all told," he said.

"Well, go into the village and find out which person or persons bought a coil of rope or a new clothesline or lines, of not less than thirty-two yards in length, all told, since April eighteenth," said Mrs. Bradley briskly.

"You don't think the murder of Hobson was planned beforehand?" cried the inspector.

"I know it was not," replied Mrs. Bradley serenely, "but the disposal of the corpse was very *carefully* planned beforehand—although how much beforehand it is difficult to say. And I don't think it was the murderer who did the planning," she added. "Think that over, child."

"I shall arrest somebody," said Bloxham suddenly, "and see what happens then."

Mrs. Bradley nodded with great approval. "A very sound move," she said. "Do it, and let the world wonder at you!"

The inspector regarded her with deep suspicion, not untinged with downright distrust.

"And when I've found out who's bought a clothesline—" he said disagreeably.

"You'll know—perhaps!—who decanted the body into the lake and who sent the statute of the little mermaid sliding after it."

Mrs. Bradley cackled ironically. Then she added abruptly:

"Do you *like* the statue of the little mermaid, inspector? What is your opinion of it, judged as a work of art?"

"I don't know that I've looked at it from that point of view," confessed Bloxham, knitting his brows in an effort to recall to mind the fashion of the piece of sculpture.

"Lose no time in making good the deficiency," said Mrs. Bradley earnestly. "Oh, child, it was when I set eyes on the statue of the little mermaid that half the truth dawned on me."

"And the other half?" said Bloxham, grinning in boyish derision at her serious face.

"Have you ever read *The Canary Murder Case,* by a man called Van Dine?" demanded Mrs. Bradley.

"Yes, rather."

"You remember the game of poker?"

"I do. Clever idea."

"One thing leads to another," said Mrs. Bradley modestly. "I also had a clever idea. Pinched, as the vulgar would observe, but, still—clever. Darts."

"Darts?" said the inspector, looking round for assistance.

Mrs. Bradley's fiendish grin, the product of perhaps an evil, but undoubtedly a sound, mind, reassured him.

"I mean it," she said solemnly. "Darts. As played for prizes at the Hilly Longer fair. Look at this, child."

She showed him a page in her loose-leaf notebook. The inspector took it, and read the names and scores of those who had played at darts with Mrs. Bradley at the fair. Then he shook his head and handed the book back.

"Very interesting," said he heavily.

Mrs. Bradley cackled, and secreted the book once more.

A quarter of an hour later, Great-aunt Puddequet, craning her ancient head, was permitted to view a great sight. Inspector Bloxham, magnifying-glass in hand, was busily engaged upon a serious critical study of the statue of the little mermaid from every possible angle and at varying distances.

At length he put the glass away and shook his head hopelessly at the idiotically smiling masterpiece.

"Except that you're the last thing on earth that any sane man could look at for more than twenty seconds at a time without being completely overcome by D.T.s," he said aloud, "I can't see that there is anything important to be said about you. Good afternoon, madam."

He saluted it ironically and went away round to the kitchen garden, where he had left Mrs. Bradley in earnest conclave with the lugubrious Joseph Herring.

II

As soon as Bloxham had left them together, the little old lady demanded abruptly,

"Joseph, who killed the two rabbits?"

The Scrounger put down the gardening boot from which he was methodically detaching chunks of earth with the aid of a broken penknife, and regarded her with the stolidity of an old soldier about to tell a thumping good lie.

"Mam, it was 'Obson," said he unanswerably. He picked up the boot again, and spat sidelong into Miss Caddick's bird-bowl.

"Hobson?" said Mrs. Bradley ruminatively. "Where have I heard that name before?"

Joseph regarded her covertly, and with a trace of not unmerited suspicion.

"Bloke as was done in in the bleedin' sunk garding," he observed tersely.

"I thought it was Anthony," said Mrs. Bradley mildly. "What a pretty show the spring onions make, don't they?"

"Well, they *might*," replied their guide, philosopher, and friend morosely, "if people 'ud only let 'em grow, 'stead of always grubbin' 'em up and gettin' 'em down."

"Your idiom," said Mrs. Bradley gently, "is picturesque but obscure. Translate."

"Eh, mam?"

"You mean?"

"Mean? Why, that there Cowes!"

"Richard Cowes?"

"Ah! Pulls 'em up and mastigates of 'em like 'e was a Covent Garding buyer, 'e do! *And* the rhubub! *And* the lettices! *And* the little young carrots what you can peel wiv a rub of your thumb! *And* the reddishes! Eat *me*, 'e would, if I growed in the late spring and was juicy-like and 'ad a bit of a 'ot flavor to me! It's somethink crool!"

Mrs. Bradley expressed her sympathy in a few well-chosen words, but Joseph refused to be comforted, so she harked back to the previous subject of conversation.

"Hobson?" she said. "What, *both* of them?"

A thought struck Herring.

" 'Oo said the two rabbits was killed?" he demanded aggressively.

"You did, by implication," replied Mrs. Bradley, grinning.

"Eh?" Joseph looked nonplussed.

Mrs. Bradley patiently explained.

"I asked who killed the two rabbits, Joseph. You replied, without hesitation, that Hobson killed the two rabbits. I did not know, when I asked the question, that the two rabbits *had* been killed. But now I am certain that they were, and the blood on the two javelins—no, the *one* javelin, Joseph! I remember that the paper corrected itself next day!—was rabbit's blood. But I am also certain, first, that Hobson was not the rabbit-killer, and, secondly, that you know who was! Out with it, man. Who killed those two rabbits?"

"Look 'ere," said Joseph hotly, " 'oo are you callin' a liar, eh?"

"You," replied Mrs. Bradley, with nice effect.

The Scrounger swallowed twice, muttered once, and passed the back of his hand across his lips.

"Not for two hours yet," said Mrs. Bradley, glancing at her watch. "You'll drink my health, though, won't you, when they do?"

And she handed him half a crown.

"Thanking you kindly, mam," said Joseph, with a grateful smirk. He drew a long breath.

"It was Mr. Anthony, mam, *I* think."

"Oh, yes, of course," said Mrs. Bradley, in a matter-of-fact tone. "It would have been."

At this interesting juncture the inspector reappeared at the end of the garden, and Mrs. Bradley went to meet him.

"Well, child?" she said, grinning like a crocodile. "What is the verdict of Burlington House?"

Bloxham shook his head hopelessly.

"Mind, I'm not a critic," he said, "but I confess I wouldn't want it in *my* sunk garden."

"Very ably, discreetly, and tactfully expressed," said Mrs. Bradley with enthusiasm. "Just think of the frightful effect it would have on a *really* sensitive nature, then!"

"I've been thinking over the rope business," said Bloxham. "What was the gymnasium rope used for, do you think?"

"Nothing much. Oh, well—as a possible red herring," replied Mrs. Bradley. "It was cut in the wrong place, for one thing. For another, it was not nearly long enough."

"Long enough?"

"To reach from side to side of the mere by the second pollard willow on this bank," Mrs. Bradley explained.

"Oh! The clotheslines were used for putting the body of Hobson into the water, were they?"

"And the statue of the little mermaid too," said Mrs. Bradley.

"It becomes important to discover who used the lengths of rope, then. I've discovered they were purloined from the woodshed here." And Bloxham knitted his brows. "But I can't see—a bow and arrow, perhaps—?"

"What about a javelin?" said Mrs. Bradley calmly. "One end of the rope tied to the shaft of the javelin, and the implement itself flung from one side of the mere to the other. Come along and let us have another look at the water."

At the second pollard willow on the home bank they halted.

"Climb up to the top diving board and toss in a stone to show me the position of the body," said Mrs. Bradley.

The inspector did this, and soon rejoined her.

"Can you—oh, it doesn't matter about that, though. A stone will do equally well. Prise another one out of the bank. That's right. Now throw it as straight

as you can from where you are standing, across the water. Throw fairly high."

Bloxham obeyed, and the heavy stone struck the trunk of a pollard willow on the opposite bank.

"That's right," said Mrs. Bradley briskly. "Now go and get—oh, never mind. I can show you by a sketch plan, I think. But first: Required: A piece of rope not less than thirty-two yards long, I should say. A javelin. A murderer. An accomplice. A murdered man. A bathchair. The first pale streaks of dawn. A sharp knife or a pair of gardening shears. A good swimmer. An average performer with the javelin."

"Good heavens!" said Bloxham. "Carry on, please."

Mrs. Bradley made a hasty sketch and showed it to him.

"Cut the rope at C," she said, "and there you are. The theory is that the weight, owing to the force of gravity, will descend the slope of the rope until it gets to the middle. As soon as it reaches point X and the rope is cut, down goes the weight—whatever it is—into the middle of the mere."

"Well, I'm damned," said Bloxham.

"The weight was first the statue—to see whether the plan was feasible, I presume," Mrs. Bradley went on, "and then the body followed. Then came like a flash the brilliant notion of binding the two together in order to secure the corpse from drifting. Of course, they had to do the fixing of the rope and the cutting all over again. I'd like to find those bits of rope."

"It sounds very ingenious," said Bloxham doubtfully, studying the sketch again. "I suppose M is the murderer?"

"And A the accomplice," said Mrs. Bradley chattily. "And B is the bathchair, which you must *not* forget, O Best Beloved, because it was not the old bathchair, but the one in present use. Oh, and T, which stands for Timon Anthony, killed the two rabbits and dipped the point of the javelin, J, in their blood on two separate, distinct, awful, unlawful occasions!"

She cackled with eldritch glee until the echoes came back over the water.

"I don't see T marked on the sketch," said Bloxham austerely, conscious that his leg was being pulled.

"Perhaps you would like to rub up your mathematics?" said Mrs. Bradley, happily wiping her eyes.

"Mathematics?" said Bloxham, who was beginning to want his tea.

"Substitution, child," said Mrs. Bradley, tapping him earnestly on the solar plexus. "T stands for M, and all that kind of thing. And, talking of substitution," she added, grinning at his flushed face, "sweet are the uses of psychology! Look up that story, told by Kost, relating to the night of Hobson's death. There is an interesting point in it."

"What about?" asked the inspector, casually slipping Mrs. Bradley's sketch between the pages of his notebook and commencing to walk towards the house.

"Substitution," said Mrs. Bradley again. "Read through the statement made to you by Kost. I kept the cutting from my newspaper, but I haven't it here. Find out, if you can, who it was he really threw out into the road that night!"

III

"You see," said Bloxham to his wife, "these Longer murders are all wrong. It ought to be all to do with the old lady's money, and it isn't."

"What isn't darling?" said wife, who was fairly new to her job.

"It isn't anything to do with her money, and that gets me west. When an old woman has tons of money and umpteen relations," said Bloxham decidedly, "one of them murders her for it and there you are, and the police get a fair field and the chance of a bit of credit. But what the deuce anybody can make out of the murder of a drunk by somebody who couldn't even have known he was coming to the house, and the murder of the young man who ought to have set to and murdered all the other claimants, passes my understanding. If the confounded idiot couldn't rake up the guts to murder the old lady while her will was still in his favor, he might at least have set about the others! Then I could have got a bit of a move on, and the whole thing would be cleared up by this time."

"People are horribly inconsiderate, darling," said his wife. She put his food before him and kissed the top of his head.

CHAPTER XV

Mrs. Bradley Listens In

"I KNEW that old woman was a man-eating shark in disguise," whispered Richard Cowes to Malpas Yeomond.

"Yes. Come out in her true colors with a vengeance, hasn't she?" murmured Priscilla, gazing with ill-concealed amusement at Mrs. Bradley's mauve and orange woolen jumper, which, worn over a skirt of warm brown and embellished by a tartan tie whose principal checks embodied various shades of green and blue, lent a distinctly festive tone to the rather terrifying proceedings of the morning.

"Oh, I didn't mean her getup," said Richard, grinning. He bent his head and bit off the top of some young lettuce leaves which he had managed to smuggle past Great-aunt Puddequet's tigerish gaze by concealing them in the crown of his hat. He raised his head again, and, between Gladstonian mastication of the springtime greenstuff, explained that it was Mrs. Bradley's present position of aide-de-camp to the local police to which he had referred.

"Yes," agreed Malpas. "Of course, if it weren't for the lack of motive, I wouldn't put it past her to have killed Anthony herself."

"Silence, Grandnephew!" squealed old Mrs. Puddequet, from her point of vantage beside the fireplace.

It was an unusual scene. The folding doors between the library and the smaller room next door, which was used by old Mrs. Puddequet as her private sitting room, were partly open, and those seated in the library could see occasionally the figures of the inspector or Mrs. Bradley, who were moving about in the adjoining room. At the opening of the folding doors the sturdy sergeant from Market Longer and the red-faced, almost apologetic Constable Copple from the village were posted with sinister suggestiveness.

The entire family and every servant in the house had been rounded up by the inspector, and sat now, in three expectant, self-conscious rows, waiting to know what was going to happen. The front row consisted of Great-aunt Puddequet, attended by an almost-expiring Miss Caddick, the Cowes, the Yeomonds, and the Brown-Jenkins. The second row was made up of Mrs. Macbrae, grimly, sardonically, majestically patient, and Kost the trainer, who was glad of a chance to sit on a comfortable chair. The third row was occupied by the two housemaids, the parlormaid, and, at a respectful distance, the kitchenmaid and Joseph Herring. The Scrounger had not shaved, and

was uncomfortably aware that his employer had noted the fact. He fingered his stubbly chin with an air of bravado, and glanced surreptitiously to right and left of him. The kitchenmaid, who had made up her mind that she was going to be convicted and hanged for the murder of her young but scarcely beloved master, had given herself up to abandoned weeping until a message sent by Mrs. Puddequet *via* the lips of the parlormaid had turned her dramatic sobbing into an occasional but excessively irritating sniff.

The inspector put his head round the edge of the folding door and handed the sergeant a piece of paper. There was a flutter of interest from the waiting persons, who were affected much as are the audience at a theater when the lights begin to go out. The inspector withdrew his head. The sergeant drew himself up and coughed importantly. Then he read:

"Mrs. Jasper Puddequet."

Old Mrs. Puddequet blinked her great cat's eyes, but said nothing.

"If you will be good enough, mam," said the sergeant, "to proceed into this 'ere room through this 'ere aperture"—he indicated the opening between the folding doors—"the inspector would be glad to have a word with you."

Old Mrs. Puddequet bowed her head, and Miss Caddick pushed the bathchair forward over the carpet.

The others stirred in their seats. The drama had begun.

In a second, Miss Caddick had returned.

"Just like the *Inquisition*, my dear," she confided in a terrified and impressive whisper to Celia Brown-Jenkins. "The inspector seated at a table in the window with sheets upon *sheets* of clean foolscap paper and white blotting-paper—there is something so *nerve-trying* in the sight of white blotting-paper, I always think!—and a tray full of pens and sealing wax and paper knives and red tape and paper clips—oh, a most *fiendish* display! And one police constable standing at his side, and another sitting just that side of the folding doors—"

"Cheer up, Caddie," said Amaris Cowes. "Have a cigarette?"

Miss Caddick declined to have a cigarette, and a very few moments later a police constable wheeled out the bathchair. It still contained old Mrs. Puddequet. Miss Caddick rose in her place, but the constable shook his head at her very slightly, and, opening the door, himself pushed the bathchair into the passage, and did not reappear for some little time.

Miss Caddick's own name was the next on the sergeant's list. When she had been admitted to the inner sanctum, the sergeant observed austerely:

"And the inspector desires me to tell you that he trusts, ladies and gents, as you will not discuss in this room what takes place in this 'ere room through 'ere until he has completed his round of you all. It will"—he referred hastily to his piece of paper—"it will greatly assist his case if you will please be courteous enough to assede to 'is request. And I might say I 'ave my orders,"

he added warningly, "to put outside anyone so offending. Thank you."

The inspector had not supposed that old Mrs. Puddequet would be able to give him a great deal of information about the events of the night on which it appeared that Timon Anthony must have met his death, and so, after obtaining from her the time of the first disturbance of the family peace—she gave it as seventeen minutes to twelve—he had sent the bathchair and its occupant out in charge of a constable and asked for Miss Caddick.

Miss Caddick was not feeling at all well. To begin with, ever since she had confessed to the clandestine occupation of her employer's dressing room by Kost on the night of Hobson's death, she had been exceedingly ill at ease. Suppose the inspector should forget his promise and let out the dreadful information to her irascible and intolerant employer? Suppose—more horrible still!—someone should be arrested for the murder, and the fact that Kost had been smuggled into the house by a maiden lady came out in evidence! She felt inclined to swoon at the thought. What of her spotless reputation? What of the "character"—written in old Mrs. Puddequet's crabbed handwriting—which would accompany her application for another post when old Mrs. Puddequet had dismissed her from Longer with screeched objurgation and calumnious epithet? What of her expectations, potent yet, although not to the extent of twenty-five thousand pounds?

Secondly, there were the two murders. Long and intimate acquaintance with the works of the more sentimental and romantic novelists of the very late nineteenth and the very early twentieth century had caused Miss Caddick habitually to put herself in the place of the heroine of these soul-stirring daydreams. She was the hapless prisoner; she was the blushing bride; she was the deserted sweetheart; and she was the tear-compelling martyr, victim of a cruel, crushing, Philistine environment. Suppose, then—the thought must be faced!—suppose that she herself were already marked down as the next victim of the Killer, as she had begun to style this unknown hand of death! Sick with apprehension, she sat on the chair the inspector indicated, twisted her bony fingers tightly together, opened her pale eyes to their widest extent, and waited, stiff with nervous tension, for the inspector's first question. It was Mrs. Bradley, however, who spoke.

"The prevalence of the bull's-eye-sucking habit among spinsters of a certain age has interested me more than once," said the beaky mouth in the birdlike, darting head. Miss Caddick, considerably affronted by this apparently casual remark, hastily bolted the striped sweetmeat which she had slipped subconsciously into her mouth whilst waiting for the return of Mrs. Puddequet's bathchair from this very room, took a much firmer seat upon the chair, completely forgot her nervousness (which forgetting happened to be the very object of Mrs. Bradley's otherwise tactless remark), and observed frigidly:

"Indeed?"

"Very good for the digestion, ladies," said Bloxham, looking up from his papers, "but time flies."

"My own opinion exactly, inspector," said Miss Caddick, with an unusual degree of tartness. Mrs. Bradley, the first bit of her work accomplished, retired gracefully into the background.

"Now, please, Miss Caddick," said Bloxham easily. "To begin with, I believe it is correct to assume that you did not leave the house from dinnertime onwards on the night of Mr. Anthony's death."

"It is most certainly correct to assume so," replied Miss Caddick, in her best manner. (She would show this extraordinarily unladylike person in the exceedingly *loud* clothes that an undertaker's daughter knew how to conduct herself on public occasions!) "As a matter of complete accuracy, inspector, I was mulcted of my little hour after dinner in the morning room because dear Mrs. Puddequet had one of her *restless* evenings, and I was obliged to sit in her bedroom and read aloud to her. Then, of course, we heard that dreadful noise—"

"What noise?"

"Why, Mr. Anthony. He threw a stone through Miss Cowes's window and nearly kicked all the paint off the outside of the gate leading from the sports ground into the sunk garden."

The inspector glanced at one of the javelins which stood in a far corner of the room.

"It was not a stone he threw," said Mrs. Bradley, interpreting her cue. "It was a javelin."

"Really?" There was no doubt of the genuine excitement in Miss Caddick's voice. "A javelin? Somebody must have a—a—"

"A javelin complex," interpolated Mrs. Bradley, with one of her startling hoots of mirth. "This is the fourth javelin which has appeared in the play."

"I think," said Miss Caddick boldly, "that you speak too flippantly of serious things. Was there—was there *blood* on the javelin, inspector?"

"The inference is that there was not," replied Bloxham gravely. "That doesn't matter for the moment, though. At what time, Miss Caddick, did the first sound of disturbance come to your ears?"

Miss Caddick considered the question. "Well," she said, with judicial impartiality, "I cannot see that there is any harm in telling you that. Mr. Golightly gave it as eleven minutes to twelve, but I happen to know that Mr. Golightly was somewhat fast."

"Er"—Bloxham's mouth twitched ever so slightly—"would you mind explaining who and where that gentleman was?"

"Well, inspector," replied Miss Caddick coquettishly, "to set all your doubts at rest, I must explain that Mr. Golightly is simply the grandfather clock

which stands in Mrs. Puddequet's bedroom."

"I see," said Bloxham. "Thank you. Pray proceed."

"Well, *I* made it *seventeen* minutes to twelve."

"I see. Now, I wonder whether you noticed the time when you were awakened by the cry of fire."

"Oh, but I did," said Miss Caddick eagerly. "As soon as the alarm spread I flew to dear Mrs. Puddequet's room, because, of course, in the very natural *confusion* into which a household is thrown under the circumstances, I could not be certain whether the actual house or only one of the outbuildings was on fire, and dear Mrs. Puddequet is *helpless* when it comes to a question of assuming her garments. Besides, I had to assist her into the bathchair in order that she should make her escape with the rest of us."

"You know," said the inspector, with great sincerity and admiration, "you're a jolly brave woman to think about that cantankerous old body at such a time."

"Oh, but, inspector," said Miss Caddick, opening her pale eyes even more widely than usual, "it's what I'm *paid* to do!"

"At any rate," continued Bloxham, "you can swear to the time?"

"According to Mr. Golightly," said Miss Caddick, "it was exactly eight minutes to four; that is to say, allowing for Mr. Golightly's little idiosyncrasies, it was—eleven from fifty-two equals forty-one—er—twenty-one—no, no!—nineteen minutes to four."

"Thank you very much, Miss Caddick." The inspector finished writing, and then looked up with a smile. "Very helpful indeed. Now I've extracted a promise from Mrs. Puddequet that she wouldn't discuss what was said in here. I wonder whether you'd mind—?"

"Oh, I will be *dumb*, inspector," said Miss Caddick fervently.

Bloxham's eyes twinkled.

"Then so will I," he said, with a meaning wink. With great thankfulness Miss Caddick departed.

The next in order on the sergeant's list were the four maids and the cook. Beyond the fact that they had been considerably alarmed by the sudden disturbances; that the kitchenmaid, who, in her terror, had rushed out into the grounds in her nightdress, had been ordered back to the house to make herself "fit to be seen"—this by the formidable Mrs. Macbrae; and that that redoubtable lady herself, with genuine foresight and courage, had stayed in the house long enough to collect a cold joint, two loaves of bread, and a gigantic jar of pickles from her store in order that, if the house were burnt down, the family might at least be able to have a meal in the morning—none of the five had anything helpful to report.

Malpas and Francis Yeomond next followed one another into the official presence.

"Well, Mr. Yeomond," said Bloxham to each of them in turn, "I might as well tell you that you're down on my list of suspected persons."

Each of the brothers smiled faintly at this piece of information, but with slightly lifted eyebrows, as though he were being told a weak jest which happened also to be in rather questionable taste.

"You see, it's deucedly awkward about you two," went on the inspector, cheerfully. "Can't prove a single thing about you at present. Daren't believe what you tell us! Can't ignore it, either! You *were* in your hut at eleven-forty that night, I suppose?" he asked each of them in turn, and each assented. "Alone?"

"Alone and asleep. I knew Cowes was up at the house, you see, and we never lock the door of the hut, so I didn't worry about his coming in. He could come when he pleased as far as I was concerned." This was the answer given by Malpas.

"Quite alone," was Francis's unhesitating reply. "Didn't know in the least at what time to expect Brown-Jenkins. Knew he was out to paint the town, you see. I suppose I must have been asleep at the time you mention. Of course, the chap woke me with his cursing when he did get back. That was at about three o'clock. He was in a blazing temper about a punctured tire or something, and woke me up to tell me about it. Well, long before he was through, Celia came and nearly kicked in the door of our hut, yelling, 'Fire.' She was in a frightful stew, so out we dashed, and were first on the scene of action. We burst in the door and found H. was not inside, so we didn't sweat much after that. Helped make a chain to the scullery for buckets of water, that's all."

"This is interesting," said Bloxham. "You burst in the door, you say? Did you get burnt?"

"No, not burnt. Got our faces scorched a bit and a blister or so on our hands. The hut was fairly well alight, though. I shouldn't have gone in but for funk about H. Don't know why Brown-Jenkins fagged. Glad he did. Could scarcely have burst the door in by myself."

"There were no iron bars outside the door?" asked Bloxham keenly.

"I really couldn't say for certain, but I don't think so. The first thing I said to Brown-Jenkins when he showed them to us on the following morning was to ask whether he had spotted them the night before, but he couldn't remember one way or the other."

Bloxham nodded, and when Francis had been dismissed he turned to Mrs. Bradley.

"And there aren't even fingerprints on the beastly things," he said mournfully. "Still, we know there *is* a practical joker in the house—"

"*Was*," said Mrs. Bradley, with a hideous leer.

"Not Anthony?"

"Yes, of course."

"Well, but, granted you're right for the javelins and the—er—the bath-chair, and so on—what about Kost's part in the business?"

"Kost," said Mrs. Bradley very decidedly, "had *no* part in the business."

"But Brown-Jenkins *saw* him," persisted Bloxham. "He was on the terrace the night Hobson was murdered."

"Saw his grandmother!" retorted Mrs. Bradley, with spirit. "He saw Anthony, of course, not Kost."

"Yes, but, look here! Those iron bars. A practical joke to try and make me think that the burning of Hilary Yeomond's hut was an attempt on the lad's life. You agree?"

"With certain slight reservations, yes," said Mrs. Bradley.

"Well, you agree that at the time that hut was set on fire we may assume those iron bars were not there? The joker, whoever he or she was—because, of course, we mustn't forget the ladies—"

Mrs. Bradley bowed ironically at this courteous inclusion of her sex. "—came along after the firefighters were gone, and drove those bars into the ground—"

"After the fire was put out," supplied Mrs. Bradley. "If that is so, inspector, how do you account for the fact that, although they had not been damaged by fire, those bars were still warm to the touch early next morning?"

"Yes," agreed Bloxham, after a moment's hesitation, "yes, there is that, of course."

Mrs. Bradley cackled harshly.

"And yet," went on Bloxham, "all the instincts of my turbulent youth rise up and inform me that, whether or not the iron bars were there when the fire actually broke out, the whole thing was either a joke, a plant, or a blind."

"Now," said Mrs. Bradley, nodding her black, birdlike head in approval, "you are talking sense, child. Can't you go one step further?"

"No," said Bloxham. "No, I can't. I've thought until my brains were standing out like cords on the top of my head, but the next bit of that particular crossword defeats me. You see, if only Anthony had not been dead for three hours and more—"

Mrs. Bradley shook her head sadly.

"Ah, well," she said philosophically. "Who is the next victim?"

The sergeant, who had already glanced twice through the opening between the doors to find out whether they were ready to receive their next visitor, now received a nod for his pains, and called in a loud voice for Ludwig Kost.

"Ludovic to you, my friend," said Kost angrily as he passed him. "You have the Anglo-Saxon pronouncement of names, perhaps."

"Sit down, Mr. Kost," said the inspector. "I need not keep you long. It is my duty to warn you that you are on my list of suspected persons, and that

you must be very careful this time not to mislead me. You understand?"

"Indeed, yes," replied Kost good-humoredly. "I must dot the i's."

"No. Just mind the p's and q's, that's all," said the inspector. "Now then. Tell me all that you did from dinnertime onwards on the night of Mr. Anthony's death."

Kost reflected.

"You will not be too hard on me, perhaps, if I go back and put in things I forgot first time?" he asked.

"Go ahead," said the inspector briefly.

"I have my supper very early, perhaps," began Kost, "as I am going to the lecture at the village hall. Mr. Anthony has some food also, because he will not be present at dinner, as he proposes to accompany me."

"Oh, yes. Anthony went with you to the lecture. How long did the lecture last?"

"To the minute I could scarcely say, perhaps. What about nine o'clock?"

The inspector nodded. He had obtained outside and perfectly reliable evidence that the lecture had ended just after nine.

"Good enough," he said. "Go on."

"Mr. Anthony excuses himself when we arrive at the public house. I understand. Gentlemen do not go to the public house with their trainers when it is in their own village where they are lord of the manor, no. I go in. Mr. Anthony walks down the road in the direction of the house. I think he is lucky, perhaps, to be in time for the port and the smokes. Very nice, that. So I drink my stout and laugh with the comrades there in the bar, and pass a little jest with the host, perhaps, and at half-past nine by the public house clock— he is ten minutes fast, you remember"—he grinned in unregenerate manner at the inspector—"I return to my hut. No more comfortable beds in the house!" His grin widened. "Hard bed in the hut now! But I soon fall asleep, perhaps, and I dream I am winning the world's championship at figure skating. Ah, what a notion that! Then I am awakened. Shouting there is. I to the burning hut so quickly run!"

"Ah, yes," said Bloxham pleasantly. "And when did you stick those two iron rods in the ground outside the door of the blazing hut?"

"A great sinfulness, perhaps," said Kost, his face darkening. "Did I for certain know which of them did that, I would wring his neck for him, I think."

"I asked when *you* put them there," said the inspector.

Kost stared at him.

"I did not put them there, as you very well know, perhaps," said he. "Madam believes me!" He turned and made Mrs. Bradley a polite bow.

"I do," said Mrs. Bradley emphatically. "But I believe you have some idea in your head, Mr. Kost, as to the identity of the person who did put them there."

Kost smiled.

"It is only a suspicion, madam. There is no proof, perhaps. It was this way. When Miss Celia Brown-Jenkins cries the cry of 'Fire' I am awakened at once. I sleep well, but lightly, perhaps. I arise. I pull on my trousers and coat. Out to the fire I run. I run very fast. Two hundred meters champion, but sprain my leg just before the Games. I click my tongue at that. Bad luck, Kost. You the laurel wreath have not obtained. Never mind. I run to the fire. But my hut, is it not further off from Mr. Hilary's hut, perhaps, than the hut of Mr. Brown-Jenkins and Mr. Yeomond? So I arrive third. But no! Not third. Lo and behold, perhaps! I, Kost, over two hundred meters the fast runner—am beaten by—whom do you think?—Mr. Cowes! Yes! Now I think to myself how can this be? But I do not think so at the time, because, after all, the hut of Mr. Cowes is very near the hut of Mr. Hilary Yeomond. But later I hear that Mr. Cowes has not slept in his own hut. He has been up here at the house playing chess until too late to get back through the sunk garden. How, then, does he get from the house to Mr. Yeomond's hut before I, Kost, can get from my hut to Mr. Yeomond's hut? There is an answer. He arrives there not only before me, but before Mr. Malpas Yeomond and Mr. Brown-Jenkins, isn't it? He is in hiding. It does not do for him to seem to be first on the scene. Too suspicious, that. So he turns up in the third place, forgetting that I, Kost, can make even seconds always over your English hundred, and so should arrive before anyone from the house can arrive."

"But—Cowes?" said the inspector, frowning. "Would he play a stupid joke like that? And how did he know the hut would be set on fire that night?"

"He set it on fire himself, I suppose," said Mrs. Bradley placidly. "He was the man who decoyed Hilary Yeomond out of danger, you see."

"Yes, but that's exactly my point," said Bloxham. "What was the idea?"

"Ah, now," said Mrs. Bradley seriously. "That is what we must find out. I wonder what opportunity he had for thrusting those iron bars into the ground without being seen?"

"Oh, plenty of opportunity, madam," said Kost. "But, to be just, so had every one of us, perhaps. The shouting, the confusion, the black figures against the flames indistinguishable, the running for water—who is to be certain what anybody did?"

"And there you are, you see," said Bloxham, when Kost had been dismissed. "We can't prove anything."

"Yes, but that was a very good point he made about Cowes being the third person on the scene," said Mrs. Bradley. "You see, the practical joker of the family was certainly Anthony. But at the time the hut caught fire Anthony was certainly dead. There can be no doubt about that, I suppose?"

"Oh, none whatever," replied the inspector. "The medical evidence at the inquest yesterday gave the time of death as before midnight."

"Eleven forty-three," said Mrs. Bradley thoughtfully.

"Yes. And yet it is too much to suppose that the burning of the hut had nothing to do with the more terrible event of the night," said Bloxham. "What about changing the order of interviewing these people and having Richard Cowes in next? I should like to hear what he's got to say for himself before we go any further."

CHAPTER XVI

And the Cowes Jumped Over the Moon

RICHARD COWES came in chewing a piece of rhubarb. At the sight of Mrs. Bradley's revolted countenance, however, he slipped it swordwise into the silk cummerbund he was wearing round his waist, and smiled amiably.

"Good morning, Prophetess," said he.

Mrs. Bradley, who, during a long, checkered, and interestingly varied career, had been addressed in almost all the known ways, in most of the known languages, started visibly and with assumed horror.

" 'Oh, no, oh, no, True Thomas, she said,' " quoted she with a fearful leer, " 'that name does not belong to me. I'm but the queen of fair Elfland—' "

She ended on a hoot of mirth which surprised even the bovine Constable Copple on the other side of the folding doors. He took a step nearer the sergeant and whispered behind a large raw hand:

" 'Ave you 'eard tell o' that there Irish banshee?"

"Ah," replied the sergeant, who disliked Mrs. Bradley intensely, "and I've 'eard tell of that there Orstralian laughing jackass, too, an' all."

Richard Cowes took the chair which the inspector indicated, and hitched it round so that Mrs. Bradley was included in the circle for conversation.

"Now, Mr. Cowes," said the inspector. Richard leaned forward with that air of benign interest best shown by clergymen who are about to listen to dear little Brian's rendering of a piece about the pretty daisies, and beamed encouragingly. "You are on my list of suspected persons," continued Bloxham sternly.

"I beg your pardon," said Richard sweetly. "Suspected of what?"

"Of the murders of Hobson and Anthony, of course," said the inspector shortly.

"Of Hobson *and* Anthony," said Richard thoughtfully. "Oh, well—yes. Very good. I'll plead guilty if it will save you trouble. You see"—he glanced at his wristwatch—"it is now almost eleven-thirty. Lunch is at one, and you have still—excuse me!" He stepped to the opening, and gently but firmly prodded the sergeant in the back to move him out of the way. Then he put his head out between the two doors and swiftly counted the remaining occupants of the library. "You have still six persons to interview besides myself.

139

That is, if you don't recall anyone. But I should almost think you'd be bound to ask one or two of them some more questions, when you've heard what everyone has to say."

The inspector scowled at him.

"Tell me all your movements from dinnertime onwards on the night of Anthony's death, Mr. Cowes," he said coldly. "And leave me to manage my affairs as I think fit. I am not in the habit of receiving gratuitous assistance, except from persons of"—he bowed to Mrs. Bradley—"tact and experience."

"Oh, quite, quite!" said Richard, waving his hands gracefully. "Just as you wish. I thought it might save trouble, that is all."

"You were at dinner with the others, of course?" said Bloxham.

"On the night you mention? Yes ... yes, I must have been. And after dinner was over I accompanied Hilary Yeomond to his hut."

"What did you do there?"

"We remade the bed."

"Remade the bed?"

"Yes, inspector. We removed the bedclothes, turned the camouflaged-po-tato-sack-misrepresented-to-the-general-public-as-a-mattress completely over, and replaced the divots—pillows, I mean—and then the bedclothes."

"But why?"

Richard shrugged his shoulders.

"Are you a married man, inspector?" he asked.

The inspector snorted.

"Well," concluded Richard, "at any rate, that is what we did. Then I asked Yeomond to play chess. Do you play chess, inspector?"

"I do," said Mrs. Bradley, before the inspector could answer. "You must play with me one day."

"Nothing would give me greater pleasure, O Sibyl," replied Richard, gravely inclining his body in a gracious bow. He thrust the stick of rhubarb further round to the left, and faced the inspector again.

"Up to the house we went, and into the dining room we meandered."

"Why the dining room?" asked Bloxham.

" 'Why not?' " quoted Richard under his breath. Aloud, he said:

"Oh, it's comfortable and the table is convenient and the chessmen are kept in the bottom of the sideboard, and the port and the biscuits are easy of access, and the lights are charmingly shaded, and the color of the curtains matches my eyes. That's all, I think."

"Well, go on," snorted Bloxham.

"But I am, inspector. Really and truly I am. Well, we played—do you want a detailed description of the game?"

"No. Get on to the time of the first disturbance."

"The first disturbance," said Cowes obediently, "occurred at the time which

everybody else has stated, but for the accuracy of which statements I myself am quite unable to vouch. You don't mind, do you?"

"Carry on," said Bloxham, who had begun to write in a grim, a steady, and, to a less complacent person than Richard Cowes, a terrifying manner.

"The disturbance took the form of a loud knocking, kicking, and banging at the locked door of the sunk garden, together with a noise of confused, deep-voiced shouting."

"I see. By 'deep-voiced' I suppose you mean that it was a man's voice that you heard?"

"Oh, I couldn't swear to that. It might have been my sister's voice, or even that of the cook. I wouldn't like you to compel me to *swear* that it was a man's voice." And Richard Cowes looked considerably perturbed.

"You're quibbling rather, aren't you?" said Bloxham, looking up from his papers.

Richard smiled nervously and said nothing. Mrs. Bradley said suddenly:

"I wonder whether we could have Miss Caddick here again for a moment?"

"Oh, not yet, not yet!" said Bloxham hastily. "Afterwards, if you like. Make a note of it, will you, and we'll see her again later. I feel we're on to something really important here."

He turned again to Richard Cowes.

"Well, Mr. Cowes," he said, with an unpleasant rasp in his voice, "never mind about the voice. We can go into that, if necessary, later on. Now, then, please be very careful, as everything you say will be most carefully checked. What did you do upon hearing this loud noise at the door of the sunk garden?"

Richard drew the rhubarb from his belt with a flourish, held it vertically in stiff salute to Mrs. Bradley, and then bit off a generous section and chewed it crisply but thoughtfully as he appeared to consider the question.

"Answer the question at once," said Bloxham. "Don't stop and—and—"

Richard finished chewing, and replaced the remainder of the provender in his cummerbund.

"I can't talk with my mouth full," he observed mildly. "The first thing that I did was to listen to a remark made by Yeomond."

"What was that?"

" 'Shall I go and let that idiot in, or will you?' "

"Oh, Yeomond said that, did he?"

"Yes. Then I said that we need not bother. One of the servants could get the key from the kitchen more quickly than we could."

"Oh! That is what you said, is it?"

"Yes. But the noise grew so loud that Yeomond said that, at any rate, we had better go out on to the terrace and yell to the person or persons to be quiet, as our great-aunt, old Mrs. Puddequet, had retired to bed, and might be alarmed by the noise."

"Who went out on to the terrace?"

"Both of us."

"What?"

"Both of us, inspector."

"Sergeant!" yelled Bloxham. "The next, please!"

Richard retired gracefully, taking three steps backwards out of the presence.

"And Mr. Cowes is not to leave the library. I haven't finished with him yet!" the inspector added ferociously.

"The next on the list is Mr. Hilary Yeomond, sir. Is that all right?" asked the sergeant in a hoarse whisper.

"Yes, yes! Of course it's all right. Bring him in!" snarled Bloxham, whose temper seemed to be suffering under the strain.

"Beg pardon, sir!" The sergeant coughed discreetly as he again inserted his head. "Mr. Cowes says may 'e eat 'is rhubub while 'e's waiting?"

"He can eat his hat if he likes," said Bloxham shortly.

Hilary Yeomond came in, looking very youthful and clean in his flannels.

"One question, Mr. Yeomond," snapped the inspector. "Did you and Mr. Cowes go on to the terrace together or separately when you heard that disturbance at the gate of the sunk garden on the night of Anthony's death?"

Hilary frowned thoughtfully. Then his brow cleared.

"Together," he said. "You mean when that fool—when somebody tried to hoof the gate down?"

"Yes. What happened next?"

"Nothing. The row stopped."

"Do you know why?"

"Yes. We both bellowed, 'Shut up your row, Anthony! Someone's coming with the key.' A sort of combined roar."

Mrs. Bradley leaned forward.

"Who made up the form of words you both used?" she asked.

"Oh, I don't mean we settled on the exact words first and then bellowed them out like a college yell. No, we just shouted, and that's about what it amounted to, both yelling together."

"I see." Mrs. Bradley leaned back in her chair and closed her eyes. A pity, she thought, that the inspector was making such a mess of it.

"And now, Mr. Yeomond," she went on, "what happened when you had shouted to the person at the gate?"

"To Anthony?" Hilary frowned at the carpet.

"I did not say that," said Mrs. Bradley very gently.

The inspector sat up with a jerk.

"What's that?" he said.

"We have had no evidence yet to show that the person at the gate *was*

Anthony," said Mrs. Bradley, in a peculiarly expressionless voice.

"But—but look here!" cried Bloxham—"if—er—go back into the library one moment, Mr. Yeomond, if you don't mind—see you again in just a minute—" He turned excitedly to Mrs. Bradley. "But if it were *not* Anthony who made that noise at the gate at eleven forty-three p.m. it would upset all my ideas about the time of the murder!"

"Exactly," said Mrs. Bradley, smoothing out the creases in the sleeve of her violently colored jumper.

"But, I say, you know!" Bloxham was seriously perturbed. "Now you've raised the point it must be cleared up at once. Of course, I think the probabilities are that it *was* Anthony who made the noise. You see, there's the javelin which was flung through Amaris Cowes's bedroom window."

"Ah, yes, that peculiar bedroom window," said Mrs. Bradley drily.

"Exactly." Bloxham took up the new point with vigor. "That's where we get back to the previous crime."

"Crime?" said Mrs. Bradley, with a faint, cynical grin.

"The murder of Jacob Hobson," the inspector austerely explained.

Mrs. Bradley's cynical grin widened slowly.

"Well, you know what I mean!" said Bloxham, somewhat exasperated. "Crime in the technical sense. It takes us back to the night of April eighteenth, anyhow."

"Agreed," said Mrs. Bradley absently. "So curious about Herring," she added, as though to herself. The inspector leapt upon this as a terrier leaps on a rat.

"Ha!" said he in a short, sharp bark. "Yes! Herring. Let's have him in. I'll get the truth out of that man if I have to roast him alive!"

The wretched Joseph was called. He came in as though he were going to his execution, and sagged visibly at the knees as the inspector pointed a finger at him.

"Now, then!" said Bloxham, with a fearful relish which won Mrs. Bradley's admiration for his histrionic talent. "*Sit* down, and let's have it *first* time, if *you* please!"

Joseph sat down and gazed agonizedly at Mrs. Bradley, who grinned like the Fiend himself and clasped her hands in enjoyable anticipation of what was to come.

"Who stole the rabbits?" bellowed Bloxham.

"I—I did," said Joseph, feebly licking his lips.

"*Your* rabbits!" roared Bloxham. "Not Colonel Digot's!"

"I—I worked it out to me own satisfaction it was Mr. Timon, pore young chap," whined the Scrounger miserably. " 'E was the one as wanted to frighten 'em all away. Though it were Miss Cowes planned to set Mr. 'Ilary's 'ut afire."

"Go on." Bloxham scowled fiercely. "I'll hear about the hut later."

"I reckon as 'ow 'e killed 'em and dipped that there javelin in the blood, and frightened Miss Yeomond, I reckon 'e did, and everythink. But I can't prove it, may I drop dead if I can. But Miss Cowes 'erself told me about the 'ut, because it was 'er I see that night."

"Cut that bunk! You'll drop dead all right. From the end of a hemp rope if *I* know anything about it. And shut *up* about that hut!"

A moan of anguish from Joseph preceded his passionate denial of all knowledge of the crimes.

"Oh, get out!" snarled Bloxham. "And stay in the library. I may want you again."

"Anthony, you see, began practicing with the javelin before old Mrs. Puddequet finally cut him off," he went on to Mrs. Bradley when Herring had disappeared.

He called to the sergeant.

"Send Kost back here a minute. Oh, Mr. Kost," he added, as the trainer entered through the narrow opening, "how good was Anthony with the javelin?"

"Not so bad," said Kost. "Surprised, though, he should throw so true right through that bedroom window. Very erratic, perhaps, Mr. Anthony, with the javelin."

"Who else could throw the javelin besides Mr. Anthony?" asked Mrs. Bradley.

"Miss Cowes. Very good, that lady, perhaps. I think could train on for a championship. Then Mr. Malpas Yeomond, and, of course, there is myself. It is not my event, of course, but I throw not so bad."

"You're still hanging on to the idea that it may not have been Anthony at the sunk garden gate?" said Bloxham. "It's an interesting notion, you know. Mr. Kost, haven't you any idea what Anthony did when he left you at the public house the night of his death?"

But Kost was unable to help him.

"I'll have old Mrs. Puddequet back," said the inspector. "No, I won't. Get Miss Caddick again," he yelled to the sergeant.

Miss Caddick, horribly nervous at being recalled, received Mrs. Bradley's encouraging grin with gratitude, and forgot her former animosity towards the shriveled, yellow-clawed old lady.

"Miss Caddick," said Bloxham, "how did you know it was Mr. Anthony who was making all that noise at the gate?"

"Well, Mrs. Puddequet *said* it was," squeaked Miss Caddick.

"Yes. But apart from that? Everybody appears to be so certain that it *was* Anthony who kicked up that fearful shindy, and yet I haven't received what I can call definite proof of the matter."

"Well, but we can *account* for everyone else at that time, inspector, can't we?" said Miss Caddick, advancing the theory timidly.

"Well, *can* we?" said Bloxham mildly. "If we can, then it must have been Anthony or some outsider, but if we can't—" He paused significantly. "So come along, Miss Caddick. This is going to be very helpful. Look here, I'll call out the name and you tell me how you account for that person. Ready?"

Thus encouraged, and much fortified by the inspector's undoubtedly kindly demeanor, Miss Caddick sat on the chair with much the same expression on her face as people assume who are resolved to play the game called "Truth" in strict accordance with the rules, and gazed at the window curtains.

"Malpas Yeomond," said Bloxham, watching her keenly.

"Oh, inspector!" Miss Caddick came to earth. "What an unfortunate first choice!"

"Why?" Bloxham grinned wickedly.

"How *can* I account for his movements? He was not even in the house!"

"Well, there you are, you see," said the inspector. "I can't account for his movements, either; neither can Mr. Cowes, for he was up at the house instead of where he should have been—in his hut with Mr. Malpas; neither can I account for the movements of Mr. Francis Yeomond or of Mr. Brown-Jenkins, or of Miss Brown-Jenkins. What about Miss Cowes?"

"Well, it was through her bedroom window that the dreadful javelin crashed, so I was not at all surprised when she came and spoke to me through the crack of my bedroom door. Her voice was shaking with the shock, inspector."

"No wonder," said Mrs. Bradley, "when a javelin had just sailed in through her bedroom window. Did you hear the breaking glass?"

"I should think we did," exclaimed Miss Caddick. "Such a crash! Just the kind of silly, dangerous, *alarming* trick that poor foolish young man *would* have played!"

The inspector turned to Mrs. Bradley.

"Certainly underlines the theory that it *was* Anthony out there," he said, grinning. Mrs. Bradley looked dubious.

"Don't lose sight of the fact that it may have been to the murderer's advantage to make you think so," said she. "And the doctor was very cautious about giving a definite opinion as to the time of death."

"They often are nowadays," grunted Bloxham discontentedly. "*Rigor mortis* isn't what it used to be. All right, Miss Caddick. Thank you. Send in Miss Cowes," he said to the sergeant, as Miss Caddick walked out.

"You occupy the bedroom which was first allotted to Miss Yeomond, I believe," he went on, immediately Amaris appeared.

"I do," said Amaris, giving him a long stare. She sat down and smiled equably at Mrs. Bradley.

"Except for the—er—passage of the javelin through the window on the night Anthony was killed, have you had cause to complain of the room in any way?"

"I have no cause to complain of the *room* at all," said Amaris, in her large, calm way. "It was the fact that the javelin broke the window when it could so easily have been directed through the opening at the top which annoyed me. I had the window wide open—the top sash was pulled right down. Of course, it would have damaged the wallpaper a bit over the head of the bed, I dare say"—she paused to think it out—"but I felt awfully vexed about the glass being smashed. So unnecessary, that. … Inartistic. The javelin should have come sailing through. I shouldn't have minded then."

"You heard the shouting and kicking at the gate, I presume?" said Bloxham.

"Who could help it? A great deep voice bellowing like that, and all the kicks on the woodwork, as you say, and then that ass Richard and young Hilary shouting and yelling—it was enough to waken the Seven Sleepers."

"But not quite enough to waken the dead," said Mrs. Bradley, to herself.

"Mrs. Bradley has some idea that it was not Anthony who made the noise and threw the javelin," said Amaris. "She thinks he had conked by that time. It's quite a tenable theory, of course, isn't it?"

The inspector grunted. Suddenly a thought occurred to him.

"I suppose it *was* Miss Caddick's voice which replied to you through the crack of her bedroom door?" he said.

Amaris smiled lazily.

"Poor old Caddie," she said. "You don't think *she* put one over our late lamented relation, do you, inspector?"

"Answer the question!" snapped Bloxham.

Amaris raised her eyebrows and glanced whimsically at Mrs. Bradley.

"Of course it was Miss Caddick's voice," she stated. The inspector grunted again, and made a short entry in his notebook. He then dismissed her and sent for Clive Brown-Jenkins. Having listened to the young man's tale of woe, he turned to Mrs. Bradley.

"Nothing I can do with all this"—he tapped the copious notes he had made—"until I've been to Southampton and checked this yarn. What I've heard about the time of this gentleman's return with his punctured bicycle absolutely tallies with the other evidence, so that's something, of course."

Celia followed her brother. Here the inspector was faced with the same kind of delay. Her story of the dance in London must be checked. He obtained the names of the friends she had met and their addresses, and smiled in avuncular manner upon the youthful gadabout as she took her departure in the same optimistic manner as she had effected her entrance.

"And that leaves Miss Yeomond," said Bloxham thoughtfully. "Bring her in, sergeant. I expect she's sick of hanging about."

Priscilla had a sorry tale to tell.

Yes, she had heard all the noises. Yes, she had been terribly scared. No, she was afraid she had not got up to investigate. Yes, she was horribly nervous at night. Yes, extraordinarily so, she would agree. It was frightfully cowardly, but there you were. No, she had done nothing except put the bed-clothes over her ears and hope for the best. Oh, no! She knew it couldn't be Celia making all *that* noise. Yes, she had thought of the murderer. Yes, she would have shrieked had the javelin been flung into *her* bedroom. Yes, she had heard the cry of "Fire!" No, she had stayed in bed. No, it was not carelessness for her own safety. She was terribly afraid; it was just sheer funk. She seemed paralyzed by fear, and had not felt equal to getting out of bed.

"But you know, Miss Yeomond," said Bloxham very gravely, "this looks rather bad."

He turned to Mrs. Bradley with a slip of paper in his hand.

"I'll let you go for the moment, Miss Yeomond," he said, "but don't go away from the library. I may want you again in a minute."

Priscilla, her face very pale and her heart thumping until she felt sick, groped her way back into the library. Amaris, who was still seated in the front row of chairs, looked up in amazement.

"My *dear* child!" she said. "Whatever is the matter?"

"I don't know!" Priscilla's lips were dry. Her hands trembled. "I—I think they're trying to—to fix the murders on me! I can't think what the inspector is going on! I—I—well, I just mean I didn't do it! I *know* I didn't! I—I couldn't forget a thing like that! I mean you *don't* forget things—horrible things—oh, I *didn't do it*! I *didn't* do it!"

And she sank into an armchair and hid her face.

Amaris pursed up her full red mouth into a soundless whistle.

On the other side of the folding doors the inspector was showing Mrs. Bradley a plan of the sunk garden.

"You see," he said, pointing to the unfinished goldfish pond, "we're certain that the corpse of Hobson lay here until it was removed to the mere and disposed of there in accordance with your very clever suggestion. Now this is the window of the bedroom that seems to be the root of the trouble. From that window a heavy article dropped on Hobson's head would have killed him, wouldn't it?"

"It would," agreed Mrs. Bradley, not very enthusiastically. "So it would, though, if it were dropped from the terrace, provided it were heavy enough."

"Yes, but look here." The inspector's voice was eager. "Even supposing Priscilla Yeomond is perfectly innocent—she may be, of course, although her doings on the two nights in question seem rather mysterious!—a plot was made with the object of getting her out of that particular bedroom—"

"I do not agree," said Mrs. Bradley emphatically. "Besides, she did not go

out from that bedroom until one o'clock in the morning, and I thought you had made up your mind that the medical evidence at the inquest on Hobson warranted the supposition that the murder was committed round about ten o'clock at night. Not to mention all the other evidence in favor of such a contention," she added, with her saurian grin.

Bloxham scowled.

"At any rate, there's *something* suspicious about that room," he said, "and I'm going to find out what it is!"

"Hoots and havers!" observed Mrs. Bradley, in what she fondly believed to be the accents of Mrs. Macbrae's native land. "And don't forget there are two bathchairs," she added in English, "and that both may have been out on the night of Hobson's death."

"Eh?" said Bloxham vacantly. He stared at her like a man who has just been awakened from sleep.

"Both may have been out on the night of Hobson's death," repeated Mrs. Bradley firmly. "One may have been used by Anthony as a scare, and the other may have transported the corpse to the mere."

The inspector continued to gaze at Mrs. Bradley, and at last opened his mouth to speak. Before he could say anything, however, the face of the sergeant appeared at the opening.

"I beg pardon, sir," said he, "but this 'ere Herring 'as something more to say to you. Shall I show 'im in?"

"Do," said Mrs. Bradley, with extreme cordiality. "Come along, Joseph."

The wretched Scrounger, thus adjured, walked in, and stood eyeing the inspector with a mixture of fear and bravado which lent anything but a pleasing expression to his simian countenance.

"Well?" said Bloxham roughly. "Spill it, and slippy's the word."

"If me memory don't deceive me," began Joseph fawningly, "which I dessay it do," he continued hastily, falling back a step in face of the inspector's glare, "when I comes 'ome with that there rabbit as I—as I 'arf-inched from the Colonel I seen a dark figure a one o' the 'uts."

"Ho!" snorted Bloxham. "You did, did you? And what time of night was this?"

"Well, inspector, you see, I thought as 'ow you'd work that out for me. Blowed if I can figure it out for meself. I gets back into me doss—me bedroom, when me alarm-clock says five past one. Well, me clock's about free minutes fast. Well, I'd cleaned meself in the scullery—that took me ten minutes I dessay—p'r'aps more—"

"Yes," interrupted Bloxham, "rather more."

"Eh?" Joseph looked seriously perturbed at this interpolation. "I dunno what you're gettin' at," he whined. "May I drop dead if I do."

"Who made the dirty mark with Miss Caddick's shoe on the clean window

ledge in order to annoy the cook?" said Bloxham coldly. "But go on with your precious yarn. I might as well hear *all* the lies you can make up. I suppose you're going to tell me again that Miss Cowes set fire to Mr. Hilary Yeomond's hut. Well, get on with it!"

" 'I lift up my finger and I say tweet, tweet,' " quoted Mrs. Bradley sardonically, under her breath.

"It's the truth, this is," said the Scrounger, legitimately aggrieved. "Well, I see this 'ere figure by the 'ut what Mr. Francis Yeomond and Mr. Brown-Jenkins occupies. That's where I seen it. No, it weren't neither. I've got meself all 'ocused. It *were* by the 'ut where Mr. 'Ilary sleeps."

The inspector caught Mrs. Bradley's eye. Something in its unwinking gaze made him gulp down the burning words which had risen to his lips, and, instead of letting flow the vituperative address he had planned, he merely observed in a strangled voice:

"Well? Go on, can't you?"

" 'Course," continued Joseph, gratified at having got the stuff over at last to this exceedingly unreceptive audience, "I thinks to meself I'm mistook and it's a shadder, when blimey! if the shadder don't cough! I watches it slope orf to the ole duckpond, and then I breaks for 'ome. Not 'arf 'op it I never! But I sees as 'ow it were Miss Cowes, what allows next morning as 'ow it were 'er."

"Very interesting, Joseph," said Mrs. Bradley, with warm approval. "I suppose you haven't invented it all?"

"Mam?" said Joseph, drawing himself up, and preparing to register an expression of injured innocence.

"Here, cut the cackle," interrupted the inspector rudely. "Listen. This is what you've just said."

He read aloud a concise, police-English version of what Joseph had told him.

"That all right? Very well. I suppose you can sign your name to it? Just here. Thank you. That's all."

Joseph paused at the folding doors. "I gives it as me own 'umble opinion as the inspector knows the murderer be now. Course, I may be wrong."

He made an effective exit.

"Of course, we know there was an accomplice for the murder of Hobson, so why not for the murder of Anthony?" said Mrs. Bradley. "By the way, child, I suppose you tested the Roman *gladius* for fingerprints?"

"And found none," replied the inspector. "Still, it was undoubtedly the weapon. I wish I could find the thing that killed Hobson."

Mrs. Bradley grinned. "Try the two stone balls on the balustrade at the head of the steps leading down to the sunk garden," she said.

The inspector looked at her as though he suspected a hoax. Mrs. Bradley's

face, however, was as passive as that of a Tibetan monk, so he contented himself by making a grunt of protest, and then resumed the subject under discussion.

"They used the key they had in their possession to get into the sunk garden and out again when they covered the corpse of Anthony with the gravel," Mrs. Bradley continued. "That seems feasible, I should say."

"Why didn't they try to take the corpse away, as they did the body of Hobson? I see that you take it for granted both murders were committed by the same person," said Bloxham.

"Of course I do, child. Look at the motives."

"But that's just what I'm unable to do," said the inspector resignedly. "I can't find any motive, so far as any person in this house is concerned—no, not for either crime."

"In both cases an objectionable person is done to death," Mrs. Bradley pointed out.

Bloxham shook his head, and drew a face on the blotting-paper. "It's not good enough, Mrs. Bradley," he objected. "Nobody could call that a motive."

"Child," said Mrs. Bradley sorrowfully, "when you've lived as long as I have, you will realize that motives are very queer things. No murder has what the police would term an adequate motive. Think it out for yourself. It is only in fiction that the motive is worthy of the crime."

"And now we'd better tackle Amaris Cowes about this hut business," said Bloxham.

Amaris Cowes entered, smiling pleasantly.

"Set fire to the hut?" she said. "Well, yes, I did. A silly trick, I own. But I was tired of Anthony's fooling, and thought I would go one better. Nuisance that Herring recognized me. I was preparing the thing, you know, when he saw me. I got out of the house through the kitchen regions and returned the same way. I knew Richard had got Hilary Yeomond up at the house and out of harm's way, because I had arranged with him to do so. Richard was early on the scene of the fire, because, of course, he knew it was going to happen."

"What about the iron bars?" asked Bloxham.

"Oh, Richard stuck those in as soon as he arrived, because we meant to make it look like an attempt at murder. Foolish trick, of course. I see that now."

CHAPTER XVII

Noughts and Crosses

THE inspector found no difficulty in checking the movements of Clive and Celia Brown-Jenkins on the night of the murder of Timon Anthony, for it was proved beyond doubt that Clive had visited Southampton and Celia London. The stationmaster at Market Longer remembered Celia's arrival on the late, or rather the very early, train, and it seemed well within the bounds of probability that she had been unable to procure a conveyance from the station to the house.

To check Clive's movements after he had left the garage where his bicycle had been put up proved to be impossible. By careful checking of times, however, the inspector satisfied himself that either the story of the puncture was true or else it had been so carefully thought out that to detect flaws in it would be a matter of great difficulty. He inclined strongly to the belief that it was entirely true.

His next important task was to attempt to ascertain exactly what had happened to Anthony after he had left Kost. The most careful questioning, however, failed to produce the required information, and the inspector was forced to the conclusion that, the murderer excepted, no one had seen Anthony alive after about five minutes past nine on the fatal evening. One thing, and one only, cheered him. He had found the weapon which had killed Jacob Hobson.

Acting on what he privately considered to be the very flippant suggestion made by Mrs. Bradley, he went to old Mrs. Puddequet and informed her that he proposed to smash both the stone balls which decorated the balustrade at the top of the stone steps. Old Mrs. Puddequet squealed in vigorous protest for some minutes, but later she was understood to give her consent, providing that the stone-breaking was done in her presence.

In the ball from the right-hand side of the steps they found one of the twelve-pound shots used in putting the weight.

Amaris Cowes was highly tickled, and informed the inspector that he must arrest her brother without delay.

"And why, Miss Cowes?" enquired Bloxham, in his stolid way, for he was worried. The discovery of what his intelligence convinced him was the agent

of Hobson's death seemed useless except as a newspaper headline.

"Well," said Amaris, with her wide, slow smile, "Richard puts the weight, doesn't he? It's his event, after all."

The inspector grinned, and informed Mrs. Bradley later that he could not tell how she had known what one of the stone balls was concealing, but that he supposed she was clairvoyant.

Mrs. Bradley, whose exposure of a famous medium had been the talk of London less than a year previously, merely grinned and suggested that the ball was not as solid as it had appeared to be.

"No. Baked clay," replied Bloxham, "and painted white. Amaris Cowes thinks the murderer must have substituted it for the one which her great-aunt had had placed there. I suppose that's the truth."

"Pirandello," said old Mrs. Puddequet's harsh, cracked, parrot voice just behind them.

"Oh, quite," said Mrs. Bradley, who, to Mrs. Puddequet's intense and lasting fury, had interpreted correctly "Pippa Passes" the very first time she heard it used as a *te deum laudamus,* and had cackled with joy for several minutes afterwards.

"So tactless," squealed old Mrs. Puddequet to a sympathetic Amaris Cowes, "when I only said it because she said she couldn't stay to dinner!"

"At any rate," the inspector went on—for he had discovered that the only way to manage old Mrs. Puddequet with any degree of success was to ignore her altogether and get on with the business in hand—"it has all boiled down to a case of subtraction now."

"Oh, why?" said Mrs. Bradley. "We know who they are, don't we?"

"Who who are?" enquired Bloxham cautiously. He was never able to determine whether Mrs. Bradley was pulling his leg or whether she was entirely serious in what she said.

"The murderer and his accomplice, of course," said the shriveled little old woman unconcernedly.

Bloxham snorted unhappily.

"I do wish you wouldn't interrupt my train of thought with these light-hearted and entirely frivolous remarks," he said plaintively. "I was about to say that if I get down to my notebook and draw up a list of all the people who could have killed Hobson and all the people who could have killed Anthony, and then weed out all who could have killed both of them, and have another good go at those, we ought to get somewhere, I should think."

Mrs. Bradley looked at him pityingly.

"But it's all so frightfully obvious," she said. "Do use your intelligence, child."

"I am," said Bloxham obstinately. "And the Chief Constable tells me he's sending for help from Scotland Yard tomorrow."

His face hardened. Mrs. Bradley sighed.

"How long will your notebook business take you?" she asked.

"An hour, perhaps."

"At the end of that time you will know who committed these crimes, child?"

"No. I shall know who didn't commit 'em," said Bloxham, his brow darkening. "That's all."

"I'll tell you the rest," said Mrs. Bradley, "when you feel inclined to hear it."

Bloxham laughed harshly and left her.

Two hours later he was showing the superintendent the finished pages in his notebook. They ran:

(a) Persons who could have killed

Hobson	Anthony
Mrs. Hobson	——
Anthony	——
Kost	Kost
Caddick	Caddick (very doubtful)
Herring	Herring
Brown-Jenkins	——
——	Malpas Yeomond
——	Francis Yeomond
Cowes	——
——	Amaris Cowes (very doubtful)
Priscilla Yeomond	Priscilla Yeomond
(very doubtful indeed)	
Celia Brown-Jenkins	——
(very doubtful indeed)	

(b) Persons who could not have killed either Hobson or Anthony
    Mrs. Puddequet
    Hilary Yeomond

(c) Persons who could have killed Hobson but not Anthony
    Mrs. Hobson
    Anthony
    Brown-Jenkins
    Cowes
    Celia Brown-Jenkins

(d) Persons who could have killed Anthony but not Hobson

Malpas Yeomond
Francis Yeomond
Amaris Cowes

(e) *Persons who could have killed Hobson* AND *Anthony*
Kost
Miss Caddick
Herring
Priscilla Yeomond (?)

"And, of course, sir," remarked Bloxham, as the superintendent looked up from the neatly arranged sheets, "the obvious conclusion, seeing that there must have been two murderers, or, at any rate, a murderer and an accomplice, is Kost and Caddick. Thick as thieves, those two. Sleep together and everything."

"Eh?" said the superintendent, interested.

"Well," said the inspector, "they don't say so exactly, but it's to be inferred. She admits that on the night Hobson was murdered she had Kost in the house. She says they heard Hobson's voice from the sunk garden before they went upstairs. She says she parked Kost in the spare bed in old Mrs. Puddequet's dressing room; still, I can't see her taking a risk like that, seeing that he'd have to pass through the old lady's room, where she was already in bed, to get to the dressing room, and out through it again in the morning. What do you say?"

"I don't say anything," replied the superintendent. "Carry on. What would be the motive for the murder of Hobson? I should fancy, if things are as you say, they would avoid publicity, not court it. I mean, you can't keep a murder quiet, can you?"

"He found out about their going-on and threatened to tell the old lady, I should imagine," said Bloxham. "They couldn't put up with that, you see, because Caddick had considerable expectations of coming in for a nice sum when the old lady died. Used to boast of the fact. I found Caddick's diary the other day when I was snooping about. Plenty down about the money. Twenty-five thousand pounds put down in black and white. Well crossed out, but quite easy to see, for all that. Kost knew he was on a good thing, I imagine, and it got his goat properly to think of a drunken lout like Hobson coming up to the house and giving them away to the old lady. Caddick herself told me that old Mrs. Puddequet would dismiss her without a second thought if she found out that Kost had slept in the house that night."

The superintendent nodded.

"Then take Kost," continued the inspector eagerly. "The murder was committed by a heavy shot being dropped on Hobson's head. What would have

been easier than for Kost, an expert at these games, to lean over the stone balustrade and just let the shot fall from his hand on to the head of the man below? Again, take the way the body was tied to the statue of the little mermaid. A good, powerful swimmer was wanted there. Well, don't you remember how Kost and Malpas Yeomond went in on the Saturday morning and fished up body and statue too? You weren't there, but I told you about it afterwards. Then there was the business of getting in and out of the sunk garden after it had been locked at night. Caddick, familiar as she was with the house, could have obtained possession of the key of the sunk garden very easily, and Kost would then lose no time in getting another one cut from it. Incidentally, I think that job must have been done in Southampton or even London. I've combed out all the shops in Market Longer, and even as far afield as Himbridge and Chaffont Emblem, but none of them seem to know anything about it."

"Hum! Well, it all hangs together very well," said the superintendent. "How about Anthony, though?"

"Well, as far as Kost is concerned in that, I can't say more at present than that he's got no alibi later than five minutes past nine that night. He stayed in the public house less than ten minutes. Anthony was a lazy walker, and it is within the bounds of possibility that Kost followed him up—Kost is terrifically fast over a short distance—he told me so himself—boasted of it, in fact—and killed him in the sunk garden. That would account for the fact that I can find no one who saw Anthony alive after he left the lecture hall that night in Kost's company. In any case, I think I'd be justified in holding on to Kost as the last person known to have seen Anthony alive."

The superintendent nodded.

"And Caddick?" he asked.

"Ah, I don't know," the inspector admitted. "I don't know about her at all in connection with the murder of Anthony, unless it was at her instigation that Kost did the deed."

"Oh, the money business again?"

"Yes, sir. We have to remember, superintendent, that Caddick knows the old lady better than anybody. She is her constant companion. It may be that a hint had been dropped to the effect that, after all, Anthony would inherit the fortune and the property instead of one of the others, and Caddick may have thought—knowing the young fellow pretty well, you see—that he would try to do her out of her share. She couldn't afford to go to law, or was afraid of the law—one or other—and Kost settled the point for her by killing Anthony before the old lady died. How's that, sir?"

The superintendent nodded for the third time.

"Well, at least it's better than anything you've dished up yet, sonny," he observed. "I should get them 'safely gathered in ere the winter storms be-

gin'—or, in other and plainer words, before some damned interfering, efficient, forty-round-the-chest London detective gets busy down here."

"I'll see to it at once, sir."

"You're not worrying about the other two, then?" said the superintendent, looking at Bloxham's notebook again.

"The other two?" Bloxham glanced over his superior's shoulder at the page. "Oh, Herring and Miss Yeomond? Well, it's the accomplice, you see. I can't imagine those two helping each other to commit murder, nor Herring and Caddick, nor Kost and Herring, nor Kost and Miss Yeomond. You see what I mean? They—well, they just wouldn't pair up in any way at all. It would be all wrong if they did."

"Yes. I know what you mean. Certainly the fact of the friendship between Kost and Caddick makes a lot of difference. What about there being no connection between the two murders, though? You say yourself that there was no need of an accomplice for the murder of Anthony."

"Well, there again, Kost and Caddick seem the only two that hang together, sir. Take the suspects for that first murder. Take them one by one:

> "*Mrs. Hobson.*—I'd rule her out altogether if it weren't for the fact that she had the best motive of anybody for wishing Hobson out of the way, and that she doesn't happen to possess an alibi before twelve o'clock that night. But then, which of the others in that list would have been her accomplice?"

"What about someone outside?" suggested the superintendent.

"Might be feasible if she had either relations or a lover in the district, but she has nobody. The nearest person to a friend, even, of the type required to put that body and statue in the lake and tie 'em together, is Constable Copple, and he can't swim. Besides—!"

Here both men laughed, and Bloxham took up the next name on the list.

> "*Anthony.*—Can't see any motive. Besides, the question of an accomplice comes in again. Who would have helped him? And had Anthony the brains and the pluck to carry through a murder that has kept the police guessing all this time? He was a proper waster, that young fellow. And that's the devil of it," concluded Bloxham unhappily. "I bet the murderer—Kost or whoever it is—is a fifty times better specimen than that weak-kneed young reprobate. Still, dooty's dooty, I suppose."

"You've almost convinced me of Kost and Caddick," said the superintendent. "Next, I see, you've put down the man Herring. Also, his name appears

in both your columns. That is to say, he could have killed Anthony, according to the evidence in your possession."

"*Herring*," said the inspector, "is a bit of a puzzle to me. But, as I say, I'm inclined to rule him out because I can't fit him up with an accomplice. There is just one explanation of the coincidence of the rabbit-stealing taking place each time on the night when murder was committed; I don't know whether you will consider it farfetched, sir, I'm sure. Just supposing that the rabbit-killing stunt, which seems to have been carried out without Herring's connivance, happened to be a real coincidence the first time, but that the second time it was used as a decoy for Herring."

The superintendent frowned, and tapped on the table with his pencil.

"I'm not sure that I understand you," he said. "Whom do you think killed the first rabbit?"

"I think Anthony did. It seems fairly clear that Anthony started a silly scheme of practical jokes on his relations, perhaps with the intention of scaring them away."

"Oh, yes. The inheritance business again," the superintendent agreed.

"Well, the murderer found out that Herring dared not let the old lady know one of her rabbits was missing, so when he wanted Herring out of the way he simply lifted another bunny, knowing that Herring would replace it."

"Why should he want Herring out of the way?" asked the superintendent. "Any ideas about that?"

"Man," said Bloxham, excitedly, "I see now! He wanted Herring out of the way for the same reason that Anthony had wanted Herring out of the way! In Herring's absence it was easier to obtain possession of the key of the gate into the sunk garden! That must be it! It was Anthony whom Clive Brown-Jenkins saw playing the fool round the house at just after one in the morning. Oh, damn it all! I wonder at what time it rained that night? Or didn't it rain?"

The superintendent picked up the telephone. A few seconds later he said:

"It didn't rain that night. But it rained the night before." He spoke into the telephone again, "Oh, and the night before that too," he said, as he hung up the receiver.

"Thanks," said Bloxham. "As a matter of fact, it doesn't matter much. I'm only going to see whether I can catch old Mrs. Puddequet out. You see, sir, Brown-Jenkins and Priscilla Yeomond both swear that at one o'clock that morning after Hobson's death the one of them heard and the other actually saw a bathchair careering round the sports field. There are two bathchairs in a shed at the back of the house. One was used for some joking purpose on the night of the murder, and the other was used to carry the corpse of Hobson to

the lake. That much seems certain. Old Mrs. Puddequet sticks to the very absurd statement she made to me at the beginning of the enquiry——"

"Absurd statement? Have I heard that one?" enquired the superintendent, interested.

"I fancy so, sir. She swears *she* was out in her bathchair at one o'clock in the morning."

"Wait a minute. How much of a humanitarian is the old lady, in your opinion, boy?"

"How do you mean?" And Bloxham grinned broadly.

"Would she be a party to saving a man's life?" enquired the superintendent.

"Well, I shouldn't care to answer that question one way or the other," said Bloxham. "Why do you ask?"

"Never mind. I suppose I should be treading on your toes if I went up to Longer myself and questioned the old lady on your behalf? Never mind. Wait here. There's tobacco in the cupboard, and, if you howl loud enough out of the backyard window, the sergeant's good lady will bring you a cup of tea. Ta-ta."

With mixed feeling Bloxham stood at the window and watched the superintendent's broad form bending over the starting handle of his car. He was not in uniform, and looked like a bookie who habitually did himself exceptionally well.

The superintendent found old Mrs. Puddequet in the sunk garden. The bathchair was standing empty near by, but the old lady herself was seated on one of the stone benches and was poking idly at the goldfish in the finished pond. She grasped her umbrella like a club when the superintendent appeared, and squealed at him.

"Good afternoon, madam," said the superintendent, with great affability. "A fine day."

"Young man," squealed Great-aunt Puddequet, lowering the ferrule of the umbrella to the ground and blinking her yellow eyes in the strong sunlight, "it is a very fine day. What do you mean by coming philandering here?"

"But I'm—*my* name isn't Kost," said the superintendent, who was quick-witted enough to take immediate advantage of this promising opening.

Old Mrs. Puddequet laughed, and poked him reprovingly in the ribs with her umbrella.

"Who told you about Kost?" squealed she. "Would you believe it? Do you know Companion Caddick? Have you seen Kost? I never thought to admire that woman. When I engaged her I said to myself, 'At any rate, Matilda Puddequet, this poor creature will never cause you a moment's anxiety.' But really! When she came creeping into my room that night with that handsome, manly creature in tow, and gave him the bed in my dressing-room, I

thought I should have died laughing. I've a weak heart, you know. Old women are exceptionally wicked. I am an old woman. I am exceptionally wicked. That is a syllogism. And when, at my age, I ought to be meditating upon my sins—so I do, of course! All old people meditate upon their sins. I needn't finish that syllogism, because you are an intelligent young man and you see already how it will go—I feel nothing but sadness to think how very much more wicked I might have been, if only I had had the pluck. And oh! the pleasant memories of sins I might have committed and actually *did* commit! Rejoice with me! I have been so much more sinful than most of my contemporaries."

"Yes," agreed the superintendent, somewhat hazily, for her harsh, strident, parrot-voice confused him, "it's really wonderful what one can get away with. I suppose *she* spent the night in your dressing room too?"

"That was the curious part of it," said old Mrs. Puddequet, with glee. "She didn't."

"Didn't?"

"No. She came out almost immediately and locked the door on the outside and took the key away with her. At six o'clock next morning she crept into my room again and went up to the dressing-room door and let him out. What can you make of that?"

The superintendent concealed his true feelings in a most creditable manner, and replied:

"Nothing at all." And then, falling in with the old lady's obviously Rabelaisian frame of mind, he added, "Seems to have been rather a waste of time, doesn't it?"

Old Mrs. Puddequet smote him playfully with the umbrella and squealed with joy.

"But I suppose," the superintendent continued, cleverly following up his investigation along the line of least resistance, "you fell asleep or something, and perhaps lost the—er—the second act of the play?" His voice ended on a mark of interrogation.

"Oh, did I?" snorted old Mrs. Puddequet. "People of my age don't get so much amusement, young man, that they can afford to go to sleep and miss things like that! I never would have believed it of Companion Caddick, never! To have sufficient enterprise to smuggle a young and handsome man into the house past my very bed—!"

The recollection of it overcame her. She lay back in the bathchair and squealed and choked until she was exhausted with laughter.

"You managed to pull the inspector's leg pretty well, then," remarked the superintendent, grinning. "You told him you'd been out in this bathchair at one o'clock in the morning, if you remember."

"I don't remember telling him anything of the kind!" retorted old Mrs.

Puddequet, with spirit. "And what is he going to do about the stone balustrade up there, now that he's smashed up my two stone balls, I wonder?"

"I've brought you these to put in place of them," said Mrs. Bradley's voice from behind the statue of a Roman gladiator. She came forward. Under each arm she carried a stone ornament.

"Please take them from me, superintendent," she said pleasantly.

"Superintendent?" squealed old Mrs. Puddequet furiously. "Have I been talking all this time to an eavesdropping policeman?"

"No, to an eavesdropping psychologist," said Mrs. Bradley under her breath, for, by taking advantage of the cover afforded by the statue, she had managed to hear the whole conversation.

"No *bon*, sonny," said the superintendent upon his return to Market Longer. Bloxham looked at him anxiously.

"What isn't?" he asked.

"Kost."

"No *bon*?"

"No earthly *bon*. Fellow was locked in that dressing-room all night. So, even if he killed Hobson, he couldn't possibly have put the body in the water and tied it to that statue. Get out the book of words and let's have another go, because, if Kost wasn't the murderer, we've nothing on Caddick as the accomplice. You've certainly splashed the gravy up the wallpaper this time, boy."

CHAPTER XVIII

Questionable Behavior of a Champion Cyclist

I

"At any rate, we haven't proved that Kost didn't commit the second murder. He was the last person to see Anthony alive—" began Bloxham despairingly.

"You said that before," remarked the superintendent mildly. "I think I should go back to Longer if I were you and find out from Miss Caddick whether she really locked that door."

Bloxham, who had scarcely liked to suggest this obvious proceeding, was gone before the superintendent could say any more.

Miss Caddick received him in the morning room, where she was having her tea.

"You *will* have a cup of tea, inspector, won't you?" she fluttered.

Bloxham said that he would.

"Did you wish to see me about—anything in particular?" enquired Miss Caddick, after he had confessed to a preference for two lumps of sugar.

"Er—yes." Bloxham helped himself to bread and butter. "Why did you lock the door on the outside when you'd shown Kost into Mrs. Puddequet's dressing room on the night of Hobson's murder?"

"Oh, that? Well you see"—she giggled coyly—"I thought it would hardly *do* for anybody to open that door and *find* him there at night. So embarrassing for dear Mrs. Puddequet, you see. I thought it would be so much *simpler* just to lock the door and take away the key."

Bloxham nodded gloomily.

"I see," he said despondently. "Much simpler, of course."

"But in the middle of the night," Miss Caddick continued, "not long before Mr. Clive woke us all up by falling downstairs, it occurred to me what great *danger* poor Mr. Kost would be in supposing the house were to catch on fire. So I tiptoed into dear Mrs. Puddequet's room and unlocked the dressing-room door. Of course Mr. Kost left the house quite early in the morning."

They talked on other matters for the next quarter of an hour, and then Bloxham took his leave. If Kost had been locked in the dressing room until midnight—

At the gate of the sunk garden he encountered Mrs. Bradley.

"Are you going in or coming out?" said he.

"Well, I was going in to return a book I borrowed," replied Mrs. Bradley, regarding him shrewdly with her humorous black eyes. "How goes the arithmetic?"

"Arithmetic?" Bloxham laughed shortly. "It comes out a lemon every time."

Mrs. Bradley blinked over the idiom, and then grinned sympathetically.

"Come into the library, where I have sufficient reason to go without asking for anybody belonging to the house," she said, "and then, whilst I put back this volume and borrow another, you shall tell me about the criminals and when they are to be arrested."

Bloxham followed her into the library.

"Notebook," said Mrs. Bradley, holding out her skinny claw. Bloxham found the page and showed it to her. Mrs. Bradley perused it with little cluckings of approval.

"But this is wonderful!" she exclaimed, as she perused it. "Where are the handcuffs?"

"But it wasn't Kost," said Bloxham sadly. "And, if it wasn't Kost, you see, it wasn't Caddick either."

"Kost? Caddick?" said Mrs. Bradley, puzzled. She looked at the notebook again. "My dear, neither of these could commit murder."

"Well, look at it in black and white," said Bloxham. "What other conclusion could one come to?"

"Why, plenty of other conclusions," said Mrs. Bradley briskly. "Wait just a moment and I'll come back and tell you what they are."

She was gone from the library for less than ten minutes. When she returned, Bloxham was seated on a corner of the table with his notebook in his hands, scowling thoughtfully at the last few entries. Mrs. Bradley took the notebook away from him and seated herself in a chair with the book laid open before her on the smooth, beautifully polished wood.

"Herring, of course, you ruled out as lacking in the necessary brain power and as having no accomplice as far as can be traced," she announced in businesslike tones. "That leaves Priscilla Yeomond still in your last collection of names. What have you against her?"

"Nothing personal," said Bloxham. "A very pretty and charming girl. Besides, as I've put in my notes, it is exceedingly doubtful whether she could have had anything to do with the death of Hobson. I ascertained that Celia and she left the drawing room together at somewhere round about ten o'clock while the gramophone was playing, to tidy their hair and so forth, but that's all. Of course, there's the second murder to be considered, the same as it has to be considered in regard to Kost—"

"I suppose you have taken into consideration with regard to Priscilla Yeo-

mond and Celia Brown-Jenkins the following facts?" said Mrs. Bradley. "First, as you say, either of them could have leaned over the balcony and dropped the weight on to Hobson's head, for the essential point of the first murder is this: Everybody in the house had sufficient strength, and almost everybody had sufficient time and opportunity for it."

"Yes, but the other business of putting the body in the lake," said Bloxham. "You don't mean to tell me—"

"No, of course I don't," said Mrs. Bradley decidedly. "I am coming to that point next. Supposing that Priscilla accomplished Hobson's death, why then Malpas and Hilary Yeomond could have performed that mad trick which gave the game away."

"But Malpas and Hilary—oh, Malpas and Hilary—"

"Both big, daring, chivalrous lads," commented Mrs. Bradley, grinning wickedly. "Both desperately anxious to cover up sister Priscilla's unfortunate peccadillo. Both—Hilary especially—quite clever enough to think out the details—"

Bloxham kicked the leg of the table temperamentally and then glared at the toes of his boots.

"And as for the second murder," said Mrs. Bradley, thoroughly warming to the work and enjoying herself hugely, "you yourself know best how very suspicious Priscilla's admissions appeared to us when you questioned everybody in the little sitting room. Of course, it is another question whether a young female of unremarkable physique could have used that keen and heavy *gladius* with such fell effect as it seems to have been used on Anthony, but, apart from that—"

"The thing was beastly sharp," said Bloxham slowly.

"And the body had been completely impaled on it," said Mrs. Bradley briefly. "The inference, to my mind, is fairly obvious, in spite of the proved sharpness of the weapon. I fancy a clever defending counsel—Ferdinand Lestrange, for example—would make short work of a case against Priscilla Yeomond or Celia Brown-Jenkins."

"The thing that puzzles me," said Bloxham, "is why you are so certain that both the murders were committed by the same person. There's no earthly connection between them, to my mind."

"Well, it would be *too* exciting to suppose that two murderers, each with a Jupiter-like propensity for picking off ill-disposed persons for no other reason, apparently, than that they *were* ill-disposed, should be dwelling together under the same roof through circumstances which neither of them could possibly have foreseen until just over a year ago," said Mrs. Bradley. "However, there is point in your objection, and I will not dismiss the notion lightly now that you have seen fit to put it forward. Let us take, then, the persons who could have killed Anthony, but who could not have killed Hobson. You no-

tice again that we get Malpas Yeomond. The other two names that you have down under this heading have not been mentioned in this enquiry before, so we will deal with Malpas first."

"But I've nothing against Malpas Yeomond except that he has no alibi," protested Bloxham. "As for Francis Yeomond, I've nothing on him, either. Not for either of these affairs."

"And he didn't even come to the May Fair at Hilly Longer with us," said Mrs. Bradley, "so I've nothing against him, either. Disappointing, isn't it? What about Amaris Cowes?"

"Very doubtful," said Bloxham. "She was even inside the house when the disturbance began and everything."

Mrs. Bradley looked surprised.

"But was she?" she asked.

"Of course she was. Didn't she speak to Miss Caddick?"

"Not when the disturbances commenced," said Mrs. Bradley. "She did not speak to Miss Caddick until the disturbances had ceased and Miss Caddick had left Mrs. Puddequet and was back in her own room."

"Well?" said Bloxham.

"Well," returned Mrs. Bradley, "you go up to Miss Caddick's room, and wait outside the door. When you hear a shot from Mr. Kost's starter's pistol, please begin taking the time by your wristwatch. Has it a seconds dial? Yes. Very well."

"Look here, I've not time to waste—" began Bloxham, but before he could conclude the sentence Mrs. Bradley had gone. He grunted sardonically and took the chair she had vacated. He bent over his notebook, rereading the list of names. It was maddening to think that on those pages somewhere was the name of the murderer—for, despite his remark to Mrs. Bradley, he, too, felt certain that the person who had killed the drunken Hobson had also murdered the spendthrift, worthless Anthony.

At the end of four and a half minutes it occurred to him that he might as well fall in with Mrs. Bradley's suggestion. He rose slowly and walked to the door. As he opened it there came the sound of a blank cartridge fired in the sunk garden. He tore up the stairs three at a time after a hasty glance at the seconds hand of his watch, and for forty seconds he waited outside Miss Caddick's bedroom door, his eyes fixed on the seconds hand as it went racing round the tiny circle. Suddenly, a rich, mellifluous voice said in his ear:

"How many, child?"

"Good heavens!" said Bloxham, startled. "Fifty seconds from the sound of the shot. Where the deuce did you come from?"

"The sunk garden," said Mrs. Bradley. "We can go downstairs again now. I just wished to prove that, if it had been Amaris Cowes who made that dreadful noise outside the gate of the sunk garden, she could have run round

the house and come in at the kitchen entrance; then she could have come up here by the way of the back stairs without making a noise, and could have spoken to Miss Caddick, as we know she did. Miss Caddick would not have seen her approach because the door was shut and Miss Caddick was on the farther side of it. Therefore, you see, the illusion that Amaris had merely come along the landing from her own room, because she had been disturbed by the javelin which broke the window, could have been created very easily and artistically."

They reentered the library, and Mrs. Bradley sat down in the chair once more.

"Yes, but that means that she threw the javelin at her own bedroom window," protested Bloxham.

"Well, why not? The moment we asked Kost for the names of persons who understood how to throw the javelin he mentioned Amaris Cowes first. Don't you remember?"

"But you're not proving that Amaris Cowes murdered Anthony," said Bloxham. "You're only proving that she could have played a silly trick—"

"In order to create the impression—successfully, I think you will agree—that Anthony was alive and outside the sunk garden at eleven forty-three that night, instead of being dead and inside it at that hour," concluded Mrs. Bradley. "Don't you remember that Miss Caddick said that to throw the javelin at the window was just the kind of mad, stupid thing Anthony would think of?"

"But why should she want to create such an impression? You don't suppose *she* did murder Anthony?" cried Bloxham.

"Oh, I am quite *sure* she didn't?" said Mrs. Bradley, suitably horrified at the very idea. "And your next question, of course," she added, in the indulgent tone of a paternally minded tutor, "is, who *did* murder him?"

"But half a minute!" cried Bloxham, considerably impressed by Mrs. Bradley's effective demonstration. "Amaris Cowes is an artist."

Mrs. Bradley eyed him with the delighted astonishment of the teacher whose dullest pupil suddenly seems to see a great light.

"Marvelous, child!" she ejaculated fondly.

"And you once asked me"—Bloxham scowled in the effort to remember the incident—"you once asked me— I say!" he suddenly shouted. "It was Amaris Cowes who chucked the little mermaid into the mere!"

"I should imagine so," replied Mrs. Bradley, shaking her head sadly over the extraordinary workings of the artistic mind.

"Because she didn't like it?"

"Undoubtedly she didn't like it, child. Who could?"

"Ah! Then you were wrong when you thought the murderer and his accomplice were the people who chucked it in? They knew it was in there, and

they made use of it." He grinned triumphantly at her.

"So simple," said Mrs. Bradley, under her breath.

"And of course it was Amaris who persuaded old Mrs. Puddequet to dismount those frightful cupids, or whatever they were, and to substitute those two stone balls——" went on Bloxham.

"One of which was made of clay, and contained the shot which killed Hobson," said Mrs. Bradley. "Strange, but true."

"Oh, but we decided that clay ball must have been substituted later by the murderer," said Bloxham.

"Please don't associate me with that particular finding," said Mrs. Bradley, with finality. "That clay ball was made by Amaris Cowes."

"You don't mean she was the murderer's accomplice?" cried Bloxham.

"Well, everything seems to point to it. And now I must go back to the Digots' and dress for dinner."

"Yes, but you're all wrong, you know," said Bloxham, rising. "You have forgotten, I think, that Amaris Cowes didn't even reach the house until four o'clock on the morning after the murder of Hobson. The man had been dead six hours when she arrived."

"There is that, of course," said Mrs. Bradley, looking considerably less important. She walked to the door, and Bloxham followed her. Both were grinning at secret thoughts; the inspector like a little boy who has cheeked nurse and got away with it successfully; Mrs. Bradley with the gentle grin of the alligator replete with food.

II

"If you are going to stay up all night, darling, I wish you'd say so, and then I could go to bed," said the youthful Mrs. Bloxham plaintively. She came over and sat on the edge of the writing table. "Is it still those silly old murders?"

Bloxham shut his notebook with a snap, tossed the sheets of paper on which he had been working into the basket, sighed heavily, and rose.

"Have we had supper?" he enquired.

"Of course, silly, nearly two hours ago." Mrs. Bloxham stood up and yawned. "I knew you weren't caring whether I'd taken the trouble to cook it or not. Ungrateful old pig, aren't you? Are you hungry again? There's bread and cheese—"

Bloxham pulled her hair.

"Scotland Yard on the ball tomorrow," he said, with affected lightness. "Then we shall learn how to do it."

"If *you* can't work it out, I'm sure those London smart alecs won't be any

good," said Mrs. Bloxham defiantly. "It's your turn to use the bathroom first, so hurry up, old sleepy-head."

III

At three o'clock in the morning Bloxham woke.

"Of course," he said aloud. "Damn fool!" He turned over and went to sleep again. At half-past eight he was knocking at the door of the superintendent's quarters.

"I'm going over to Longer to make an arrest in connection with the murders of Hobson and Anthony," he said. "I'm taking the sergeant and two men, as he's such a very powerful and athletic chap."

"Who?" asked the superintendent, looking over the top of the morning paper.

"Comrade Kost."

"And what about the accomplice?"

"Companion Caddick. It's true she locked him in the dressing room until midnight, but he could have killed Hobson before they ever went upstairs at all, and he could have put the body in the lake after twelve. Shan't be long."

When he arrived at Longer, however, the two he sought had not appeared at breakfast, although it was more than half-past nine. Priscilla Yeomond, pale and anxious-eyed, said hesitatingly,

"You don't think—oh, but no! No! It is impossible!"

"What is?"

"That they've been murdered," said Celia Brown-Jenkins, grinning. "I'll go up to Great-aunt's bedroom and get Miss Caddick to hurry up."

She put down her knife and fork and left the table. In a few moments, flushed and trembling, she returned.

"She's just coming," she said, with a curious catch in her voice. "Won't you have some breakfast, inspector?"

Bloxham refused, and sat waiting in a fever of impatience like a terrier at the mouth of a rat-hole.

The family champed its extraordinarily English breakfast stolidly, save for Celia; she merely drank three cups of coffee in quick succession, and then hid herself behind the morning paper.

"Is Kost in his hut?" demanded Bloxham at last.

"I'll go round and see," said Clive Brown-Jenkins obligingly. "He's often late for breakfast," he added carelessly, as he walked on to the terrace by stepping out through the open window.

"Have breakfast so devilishly early here," said Malpas, kicking first Francis and then Hilary under the table, and treating Priscilla to a warning scowl.

After an absence of almost a quarter of an hour, Clive returned.

"Sorry. Can't find him. Probably out for a long run or walk or something devilish energetic," he said. He reseated himself indifferently at the breakfast-table and reached for a third boiled egg.

"How did the Bedouins do?" he enquired of his sister Celia.

"The Bedouins?" Celia turned over the pages. "Ch—er—they lost by three wickets."

"Good egg!" said Hilary. "Lend me the page, Celia. Oh, never mind. Here's aunt. I'll get her some brekker."

He went to the sideboard and stood idiotically at attention as his great-aunt, in her bathchair, propelled by Amaris Cowes, entered the room.

"Why, inspector?" said Great-aunt Puddequet, in surprise. "This is indeed an honor."

"Scarcely an honor, I'm afraid, Mrs. Puddequet," said Bloxham. "The fact is, I'm here very much on business, and it is absolutely essential that I speak to Miss Caddick and the trainer Kost immediately."

"Breakfast first," said Great-aunt Puddequet implacably, "and all unpleasantness afterwards. Kidneys and bacon, Grandnephew Hilary," she added, turning towards the sideboard. "And sit still, inspector. You'll spoil my digestive powers if you scowl and fidget like that. If you must see Companion Caddick and Trainer Kost, you must wait until they see fit to grace the room with their presence. They will be late this morning. He is teaching her to drive a motorcycle. Very creditable of him."

Another quarter of an hour passed. Bloxham rose, his patience quite exhausted.

"Mrs. Puddequet," he said, "I must ask you to allow one of the ladies to accompany me to Miss Caddick's room at once."

A strong feeling that the catch was going to slip through the meshes of the net was presenting itself with alarming insistence.

"I'll come," said Celia, in return for a nod from her great-aunt.

Outside Miss Caddick's bedroom door she halted and tapped. There was no answer, so she called the occupant by name. At last she turned the handle and went in, only to reappear immediately.

"She is still out with the trainer, apparently," she said lightly. Bloxham strode past her into the room. The bed had been slept in, but otherwise the room was in order. Bloxham walked to the window, which had been mended since the night of Anthony's death, and leaned out.

"Anybody been through into the sports ground?" he called to the sergeant, whom he had left in the sunk garden whilst he himself was in the house.

"No one, sir."

"No. She would have gone down the back stairs and out through the kitchen garden," said Celia, striving to keep her voice steady.

Bloxham pushed past her and tore down the stairs and out through the sunk garden, bellowing to the sergeant to allow no one to leave the house.

The trainer's hut was empty. The sports field was deserted. The gymnasium was untenanted, and the mere a width of placid, shining water.

Bloxham ran back to the house.

"I *must* see them," he said shortly. "You don't know which direction they are most likely to have taken, Mrs. Puddequet?"

"No, young man," said old Mrs. Puddequet tartly. "I do not."

"Towards Hilly Longer," said Clive shortly. "Look here, I'm going out for a spin that way now, this minute. I'll send them back here to you at the double."

The inspector scribbled on a leaf out of his notebook.

"If you wouldn't mind handing that in at the police station at Hilly Longer," he said, "the sergeant and constable will get a conveyance in the village and follow up Mr. Brown-Jenkins, and I shall sheer off in the other direction. Those two must be found. I'll send Constable Copple along here to keep my other man company."

Clive, without waiting to hear any more, mounted his racing bicycle with all possible speed, and tore through the gates of the grounds.

Kost and Miss Caddick had almost reached the outskirts of Little Longer on their way home. Clive stopped them, and said urgently, "Can she drive that scrap-heap?"

"Plenty, perhaps," said Kost.

"Then get away on it, Miss Caddick. The police are after you," said Clive Brown-Jenkins earnestly. "Don't stop to argue. And you get on to the cross-bar, Carver Doone," he added to the trainer when they had given the terrified Miss Caddick a good push off for luck, "and keep your damned hoofs off the front wheel. I'm going to hurry."

"I shall go by train from Market Longer Station," said Kost, as the racing bicycle with its double burden went hurtling through the main street of the quiet country town.

"More fool you," retorted Clive. "Southampton's the place for you. Half a minute. I've got a note to push through the letterbox at this police station. They'll never suspect it's you on the bar, so sit tight and Uncle Cliffy will save your blinking neck. This is doing me more good than anything since I won the Harriers' hundred miles tourist. Not that I like you, Kost. I'm not doing this because I like you. I'm doing it to get old Aunt Puddequet's cash. So mind you don't go and bungle matters when I leave you. I want that money badly."

Kost chuckled tolerantly. He had attained a precarious balance on the cross-bar by this time. He let go very cautiously with one hand, and felt in his left-side trousers pocket. Gingerly he produced a huntsman's horn, and com-

menced to blow it with a kind of solemn gusto.

IV

Miss Caddick felt exhilarated, but unsafe. It was the very first time she had been out alone on the motorcycle. She was also exceedingly hungry, and, now that she had recovered from the state of panic into which Clive Brown-Jenkins's startling words had thrown her, she felt somewhat puzzled.

It occurred to her that she had not the slightest idea whither she was bound, and that she had no luggage, and only about two and tenpence in money. Her clothes were suited to early morning practice in the art, science, metaphysics, and philosophy of driving a motorcycle, but for all other conceivable purposes she judged them singularly inappropriate and decidedly unbecoming.

The motorcycle grunted its way up a long hill. At the top were crossroads. One, slanting back to the southwest across a beautiful common which bordered the New Forest, led to Little Longer village and the kindly house where breakfast was awaiting her.

"A foolish and ill-natured jest on the part of Clive Brown-Jenkins," said Miss Caddick, mildly indignant. "But what a magnificent morning!"

Greatly daring, for she feared corners and detested turning the motorcycle out of the straight, Miss Caddick urged her iron steed round into the homeward way. The road was narrow, but ran straight and open across the white and golden common. The scent of gorse and hawthorn and the pungent odor of her petrol-drinking stallion filled the summer air. A sudden glorious madness filled the soul of Myra Caddick. She burst into glad, full-throated song, and opened the throttle wide.

V

Clive Brown-Jenkins, having satisfied a twenty-years' craving to defeat the forces of law and order, pedaled leisurely homewards. Kost looked after the retreating bicycle and its altruistic rider with mixed feelings until both were out of sight. He then put his hands into his pockets and withdrew the sum of ten and fivepence. This he contemplated for a while. Then, thrusting it back into his pocket, he shrugged his shoulders, walked a short distance along the mean street in which Clive had set him down, and enquired of the first passerby the whereabouts of the nearest police station. To a startled inspector he observed:

"Wanted man. You should telephone to the police at Hilly Longer, perhaps."

Ten minutes later the hungry Kost was being rushed in a police car back to old Mrs. Puddequet's house, where he was hustled into the library. The first person he set eyes on was Miss Caddick.

"Have you had breakfast, perhaps?" he demanded curtly. Miss Caddick smiled and nodded.

"And, believe me or believe me *not*," she giggled coyly, "I really did clock fifty on the Little Longer road."

Kost, who thought she had been drinking, turned to a lynx-eyed Bloxham.

"Breakfast, and I tell you all you ask," he said abruptly. "But breakfast first, perhaps."

CHAPTER XIX

Autobiography of a Murderer

"Oh, well," said Mrs. Bradley, with her dreadful grin, "you must give me credit for one thing, child, if for one thing only."

"And what is that?" enquired Bloxham cheerfully, for he was feeling exceptionally pleased with himself.

"I've extorted a confession—a full confession—from the murderer," replied Mrs. Bradley calmly. "Would you care to hear it?"

"If it can be substantiated it will save a good deal of time at the trial," replied Bloxham, somewhat surprised by the answer to his question. "I take it, then, that they intend to plead guilty?"

"At the trial? Oh, I should imagine that it is most unlikely," Mrs. Bradley replied.

She settled herself comfortably in the armchair which little Mrs. Bloxham had placed for her, and untied the roll of manuscript she had brought.

"I suppose the various members of Mrs. Puddequet's family have returned to their homes?" she said, glancing over the sheets of foolscap and noting with approval the neat, precise writing with which they were covered.

"Well, what with their trainer being in prison and old Mrs. Puddequet being compelled to advertise for another companion-secretary, they hadn't much choice, I imagine," said Bloxham. "Incidentally, I understand that the old lady, with her queer sense of humor, has promised to settle twenty-five thousand pounds on Caddick if she and Kost are declared not guilty at the trial."

"Really?" said Mrs. Bradley drily. "How extremely tantalizing of her. Do they know?"

"Oh, they know all right," replied Bloxham, with a slight shrug. "Where would be the joke for the dear old lady if they didn't? Well, she'll keep her money all right, for our case is foolproof. Besides, if you are really holding in your hand the murderer's confession, that clinches it, doesn't it?"

"Oh, undoubtedly," replied Mrs. Bradley. "You mean you don't want to hear it?"

"Oh, carry on, by all means," said Bloxham cordially. He fingered his pipe.

"Do smoke," said Mrs. Bradley.

"I can't think why he should have given the confession to you, of all people,

if you'll excuse the observation," said Bloxham. "It would have seemed more suitable for his solicitor to have had it, or even myself. How came he to hand it to you? Have you seen him since his arrest?"

"Poor Kost! I've seen him, of course," said Mrs. Bradley, "and tried to cheer him up. He is an exceedingly dejected man. Miss Caddick takes it better. She visualizes herself as the heroine of a talkie who is placed for the moment in extremely unpleasant and dangerous circumstances. The talkies, however, always appear to believe in the happy ending, so she lives in hope of a speedy release!"

"I'm sorry for Caddick," said Bloxham frankly. "She's been the victim of circumstances and of falling in love with a villain."

"Kost?" enquired Mrs. Bradley, grinning like a dragon.

"Well, it's a pretty villainous thing to kill two men, one after the other," said Bloxham. "But I'm keen on hearing the book of words. Is there much of it?"

"Quite a little," said Mrs. Bradley quietly. "One comfort is that I can stop reading as soon as you get bored."

She lay back in the big armchair, held the manuscript between her yellow claws, and began to read aloud.

" 'I was born in the year 1899,' " the manuscript began, " 'and was more or less imperfectly educated. I was subjected, I suppose, to the usual physical, moral, and intellectual risks of youth and early manhood, and in due course I reached, without obvious mishap, the so-called years of discretion.

" 'Nothing noteworthy occurred to me until I decided in the year 1919 to found a new society. Since childhood I had belonged to a church club known to the environs of a certain respectable city as the Sons of Chivalry. Our *raison d'être* was to collect funds for the pauperization of the poor. This object, laudable as it may appear to some, highly immoral as it undoubtedly seems to others—for to give his fellow creatures something for nothing is the most profoundly and devastatingly demoralizing proceeding that man has yet inaugurated—was carried out by us under various charitable pretences. We had a coal and blanket fund, a babies' clothing fund, treats and parties were given to the youth of the neighborhood, and charabanc outings were arranged for the adults.

" 'Upon reviewing the scope of our activities one night after I had acted as assistant chucker-out at a particularly disorderly bun-fight *cum* magic-lantern show, it struck me that as an agent for social service we were both unnecessary and out of date. I yearned to strike a modern note, and, above all, to found a society of real benefit to humanity. I was tired and disgruntled at the moment, and my one immediate desire was to fling myself down upon my bed—clothes, boots, and all—and go to sleep without the troublesome preparations which make the child—wisest of humans (one boy had thrown

lumps of cake at the magic-lantern illustrations for ten minutes whilst I strove to determine in the darkness which was the offender and to eject him)— decide that when it grows up it will never go to bed at all.

" 'I was about to exchange my boots for slippers when the Great Idea sprang to my mind. Why not indulge the impulse? Why not lie down as I was and go to sleep? Why not—greater thought still!—disseminate the doctrine of indulging one's primitive impulses? Why not persuade my fellow-creatures to adapt the notion to their own uses?

" 'I will not claim for the society thus founded that its rules were unique, but they were not, perhaps, common to the majority of societies. We determined never to meet; to have no official premises; to have no subscription except that if letters were sent to me which seemed to call for a reply, a stamped addressed envelope was to be enclosed. I elected myself president and secretary. There were no other officials. I kept a complete list of members in triplicate. One of these lists I kept in my desk; another reposed with other of my private papers at the bank; the third was in the possession of the society's solicitors.

" 'We found it absolutely necessary to keep in close touch with our solicitors, because, from the very nature of the society, it was inevitable that our members should frequently come into violent contact with the law of the land. To begin with, there were the members—chiefly elderly gentlemen with extensive and reputable business connections—who looked to their membership of the society, and to all that that membership implied, to enable them to let off the steam and exuberance for which their daily life of painful decorum and swallowtailed respectability offered them no outlet. These graybeards took to hitting policemen over the helmet with their walking sticks, and to squirting soda-water on to the bald heads of fellow members of their London clubs. One man went so far as to seize a large plaice from its slab of ice at a fishmonger's shop and to smack it round the face of a particularly irritating female acquaintance who was in the act of changing her mind for the fourth time about the poultry she was having sent up for dinner whilst he waited his turn to be served.

" 'The subsequent police-court cases which followed these and similar interpretations of the Freudian gospel of anti-inhibitionism were handled extremely ably by our solicitors, who usually took the line of suggesting that the regrettable lapse was the result of a flippantly conceived wager. The bench, a singularly sporting fraternity, amiably conceded the point as a general rule, and the offenders were let off lightly, and lived to be better and happier men for having pandered to their primitive impulses in this carefree fashion.

" 'Our great difficulty was to deal with members who wanted to indulge an appetite for sadism or morbid cruelty. When such members were detected

they were warned; for a second offense they were expelled from the society; if any further tales of their bestial behaviour came to our knowledge we handed the offenders over to the law, for it was very generally conceded that cruelty is not a primitive impulse, but is the product of a morbid, brooding, and unhealthy mind.

" 'Then we had our cases of theft following the impulse to obtain possession of a desired object. Most of the "kleptomania" cases reported in the daily papers between 1920 and 1930 were those in which our members were involved, and a certain distinguished psychologist, who shall be nameless, was presented with a handsome clock, bought out of thank-offerings voluntarily contributed by grateful persons as a tribute to his genius in inventing a term which covered their misdemeanors and mitigated the punishments dealt out by a paternal government for the same.

" 'Free love, with its attendant embarrassing consequences, also occupied the attention of our members, until the admission, on a sex-equality basis, of women to full membership of the society. This caused considerable readjustments to take place in matrimonial and connubial affairs, and husbands and wives, acting upon the intelligent conception that x sometimes equals o, returned to the paths of domesticity and virtue, until in the year 1928 the percentage of claimants for the Dunmow flitch exceeded all previous records by nearly two hundred percent., a great tribute to the personal influence of our members, both male and female.

" 'Then we had our "occasional" cases—murder and the like. In this category I include the affair at the Grandat Theatre, when a sleeper in the stalls was set upon with vituperative violence by the author and slain by a blow on the head with a brass music stand which the murderer snatched out of the orchestral well. In this connection it is interesting to note that a leading musical-comedy actress performing in Paris was acquitted by a gallant but obviously biased French jury for throttling the author of the piece when he presumed to correct her pronunciation of the word "details." The French, in their logical way, brought it in as a *crime passionelle* and, with their known admiration for the temperamental reactions of the highly strung, refused to proceed further with the matter. An occasion which caused us to feel pride in the activities of the society, and confidence that its doctrines were being disseminated with noteworthy success, was the lynching, by indignant members of a London audience, of two latecomers to the front row of the dress circle.

" 'Captious aunts and stingy uncles came in for a share of attention from our enthusiastic members; so did a brother aged eleven and the pet dog of a rich aunt; and a tram-conductor murdered a passenger who proffered a florin in payment of a penny fare. The ticket-punch—located by X-ray—was found to be completely embedded in the victim's skull. As a counteraction to this,

there was the case of the incensed passenger who received two threepenny bits in his change, and murdered the conductor by suffocating him with his own woolen mittens. This happened in Glasgow, and a canny verdict of "Nonproven" was the result. Our member was publicly cheered.

" 'Of all the cases of murder with which we, as a society, were associated, however, that which won the greatest amount of admiration, approbation, and sympathy from our members—I received upwards of three hundred letters of congratulation on the subject, together with heavy subscriptions towards the cost of the defense—was that of a holiday-maker who saw a large ruddy man (in a bright-blue, double-breasted blazer with brass buttons, new dove-colored flannel trousers, a polo-collared, white woolen sweater, and a loud tweed cap) standing on the top of Beachy Head admiring the Channel view. Our member, succumbing, I suppose, to the most overwhelming primitive impulse there is, crept behind him and pushed him heartily over the edge. The body was recovered by boat.

" 'Talking of murder brings me to the real reason for the writing of these memoirs.' "

Inspector Bloxham grunted.

"Taken him some time to get to the point," he said. "Fellow can write English better than he can speak it, too."

"Well, in a sense, yes," Mrs. Bradley agreed. "But, apart from that, it is interesting to pause here for a moment and notice the impression of the man's character that we get in those few pages I have read to you."

"He certainly has no respect for human life whatsoever," said Bloxham, nodding his head. He knocked out his pipe and proceeded to refill it. "Apart from that, though—"

"You agree, then, that the writer might posses criminal tendencies?" said Mrs. Bradley, grinning in her terrifying, because mirthless, and apparently meaningless, way.

"Tendencies?" cried Bloxham. "The man's an out-and-out bad lot, I should say! The idea of murder appears to *amuse* him!"

"Well, from some points of view, it is amusing, of course," said Mrs. Bradley briskly. She turned again to the manuscript. "The style of writing changes at this point," she added. "The murderer is about to chronicle his own deeds of which he is inordinately proud."

She continued the reading:

" 'My own chance to prove that I was worthy to be the inaugurator, president, and secretary of this great society came on Friday, April eighteenth, of this present year.' "

"Ah!" said Bloxham. "Here it comes!"

Mrs. Bradley nodded, and went on:

" 'I was enjoying the quiet hours of the evening in my own way, doing ill

to none, and improving the pleasantest part of the day and my own mind at one and the same time, when my peace was disturbed by a loud, drunken, raucous, masculine voice below, uncultured, heavy, bullying, thick with beer and anger, bellowing the name of Puddequet. Interested, for it was by order of the ancient lady who bore that name that I worked and sweated daily at an oafish task—' "

"Thought he wasn't too satisfied with his job," said Bloxham sagely. "Wonder he didn't do in the old girl herself while he was about it."

" 'I set myself to listen,' " continued Mrs. Bradley. " 'The voice itself, however, was so irritating, and the sentiments to which it gave expression were so extremely coarse, that an impulse of annoyance moved me to discover my proximity to the debased creature below, and to invite him to remove himself from my vicinity. To this end I opened the long window and stepped out on to the terrace.

" 'With the laudable determination of making myself as perfect as I could in the ridiculous labors to which I had committed myself during my stay at Longer, I had been working out, with the aid of diagrams and mathematical premises, the angle of flight taken by the shot when it is correctly put. The shot itself I was still insensibly grasping in my hand when I stepped out through the window on to the stone terrace.

" 'The voice went on with its indescribably objectionable monologue. It reiterated its unlettered phrases, and continued to perpetrate grammatical error and pot-house idiom until the very night itself was polluted. The blood of a thousand members of our beloved society boiled in me. Without a word—without a sound—I leaned over the broad stone coping and put the shot, with a niceness of accuracy and a deliberation of aim for which no amount of skill or practice can account, on to the head of the disturber of my peace. I heard the body fall. Then I went inside the house again. Godlike Caesar could have done no more.' "

"Queer he doesn't mention Caddick," said the inspector. "Wants to shield her, I suppose. Is the part played by the accomplice mentioned later?"

"Oh, yes. The accomplice is given her due share of praise and blame," said Mrs. Bradley. "He goes on next to describe how apprehensive he began to feel when the first thrills of self-congratulation and artistic pleasure had worn off."

"Oh, well, it seems rather a lengthy effort," said Bloxham. "If that's all it says, perhaps we could leave that piece out and get on to the 'corpse in the mere' bit. I'm keen to know whether you were right there."

Mrs. Bradley turned over a page, and went on:

" 'I realized that before I slept that night'—"

"In old Mrs. Puddequet's dressing room," chuckled Bloxham appreciatively.

"—'I must recover that shot from the sunk garden and hide the body if I could. Torch in hand, I crept down the stone steps to the unfinished goldfish pond. Judge of my joyful surprise when I discovered that a careless workman, having tested whether the newly cemented bottom of the pond had set hard, had left the heavy tarpaulin thrown back, and my victim's body had so fallen that he was stretched along the bottom of the pond! I drew the tarpaulin over him with tenderness, retrieved the shot, and went to my quarters.' "

"His quarters!" said Bloxham, with another chuckle. "That's rather good. Well, what happened next?"

"Next," replied Mrs. Bradley, scanning the closely written sheets, "he appears to have become unduly apprehensive. He describes how the unpleasing spectacle of the murdered man kept rising before him in the darkness, and of how he could not sleep for remembering what he had done. He reiterates, however, that he was glad to know that he had obeyed a strong, primitive impulse—"

"Pah!" said Bloxham, in disgust.

"Quite," Mrs. Bradley mildly agreed. "Well, just before one o'clock in the morning—"

"Hah!" exclaimed Bloxham, with artless satisfaction. "It was just about midnight that Caddick unlocked the dressing-room door."

"—he was unable to resist a craving to visit the scene of his crime and assure himself that the body had not been discovered."

"They're all the same," said Bloxham, with a sigh. "Can't leave well alone! That's how we catch 'em nine times out of ten."

"Just as he reached the sunk garden, however," Mrs. Bradley went on, "he heard the sound of wheels on the cinder track outside. Keeping under cover, he investigated. Shall I go on in his own words now?"

"If you think it necessary," said Bloxham, "but to me this paraphrase is all-sufficing. You're not leaving out anything of importance, I take it?"

"Perhaps I'd better let you have the unexpurgated text," remarked Mrs. Bradley, glancing down the page. "He goes on to say:

" 'Astonished and extremely ill at ease, I hid behind the shadow of the gate—which, to my great surprise, was unlocked—and waited to discover what was going on. The moon came out for a moment and immediately disappeared again behind a cloud, but in that instant I had seen that the person wheeling the bathchair was Anthony. He left it outside when he reached the gate of the sunk garden, and entered, almost treading on my shoe. My heart beat till I thought he must have heard it, but unseeing and unhearing he passed on, and slipped behind the statue of the Roman gladiator. I dropped on to my hands and knees, and quick as thought slipped out of the gate lest I should be discovered for the murderer I was!

" 'Scarcely had I risen to my feet on the safe side of the wall when a great

thought struck me—two great thoughts, indeed, in one! I would steal the bathchair and later return for the corpse and carry it away from the actual scene of the crime; and, when the crime was discovered and I stood in danger of detection, I would testify to having witnessed Anthony visiting the scene of the murder with the suspicious accessory of the bathchair. I could quote time and place; I could supply corroborative detail. ...

" 'I am a good runner. I seized the bathchair by its handle, but before I could get into my stride I distinctly heard a sharp crack as of a stone striking one of the windows of the house. Instinctively I let go of the bathchair and sank crouched against the wall. Suddenly one of the bedroom windows was flung up and Priscilla Yeomond's voice cried out, "Who's there?"

" 'The instantaneous thought that Anthony would fly by way of the open door of the sunk garden, followed immediately by the realization that he might discover me, braced me for flight. I seized the handle of the bathchair again and sprinted strongly round the track. At that unlucky instant out came the moon and discovered me to all the world.' "

"Hum! I suppose Clive Brown-Jenkins was so much interested in watching the antics of Anthony that he missed seeing Kost's performance in and out of the gate of the sunk garden," said Bloxham. "That lad must be pretty slippy, though, because Brown-Jenkins wasn't far inside the gate when he heard that bathchair go by."

"You're so determined to delude yourself," said Mrs. Bradley sweetly. "Do you really think this reads like Kost's confession?"

"Like—*Kost's*—confession?" Bloxham repeated slowly. "Oh!" His facial expression very comically changed. "So—so that's it, is it? ... Or are you pulling my leg? He 'saw' Anthony throw the stone! He 'heard' the bathchair go by!"

Stunned, he drew out his official notebook and reread the notes on his interviews with Clive Brown-Jenkins

CHAPTER XX

The Story of the Second Roman Gladiator

"SHALL I continue?" enquired Mrs. Bradley, as Bloxham closed the notebook and slipped it back into his pocket.

Bloxham hesitated.

"I've got his home address, of course," he said at last. "We can get him any minute. Does he say anything about putting the body in the mere?"

Mrs. Bradley flicked over the pages, glancing down each one with her keen black eyes.

"Yes. He describes it fairly fully," she said. "The method was pretty much as I told you."

"Does he give the name of his accomplice? For, if Kost is not the murderer, I suppose Caddick was not his assistant?"

Mrs. Bradley turned back to the paragraph at which she had discontinued her reading aloud, and said briefly:

"I'd like to read it to you."

The inspector nodded and lay back in his chair.

" 'At last I reached that gate in the sports ground through which one passes in order to gain admission to the gymnasium,' " Mrs. Bradley began. " 'The gates into the ground are always left unlocked because they allow of short cuts from the huts to the house. I made up my mind, as I flew round the track, to leave the bathchair in the shadow of the gymnasium wall so that the moon should not discover it to my pursuers. Pursuers, however, there were none. I cast myself down near the stationary chair and listened. I felt like an animal that knows not which way to break from the hunters. Gone were my feelings of boastful self-congratulation. I would have given years of my life to have had that drunken villager, whose name I did not even know, alive, and offensively verbose, and howling beneath my window. The fact that his corpse should be remaining there beneath the Puddequet tarpaulin to embarrass my waking hours and terrify me in dreams gave me the most terrible nervous qualms imaginable. My immediate necessity, I felt, was to get the body away from the spot where I had—where it was lying. But for hours, or so it seemed to me, I dared not contemplate the thought of going back for it. Besides, the difficulty which confronted me was that I could not think where to *put* the body. ... There were some long lockers for apparatus in the gymnasium, I remembered. ...

" 'Rising cautiously to my hands and knees, I crept round the building until I came to the door. I rose to my feet and tried the handle. The door opened.

" 'It was pitch dark inside. I drew out my torch—we all carried them to assist us in finding our way back from the house to our huts after dinner—' "

"So it couldn't have been Kost," agreed the inspector. "He didn't have dinner up at the house, did he?"

"No," Mrs. Bradley replied. "His supper was served up to him on a tray, which was carried across to his hut by two maids taking it turn about. The maids were escorted by Joseph Herring, who bore a large stable lantern to light them upon their errand of mercy."

Bloxham sat up and looked at her in some astonishment.

"You've gone into the thing in style," he said, laughing.

"Oh, yes. I am very well informed upon all matters which turned out later to have no possible bearing upon the case," said Mrs. Bradley with her ghoul's laugh. "However—" She returned to the manuscript.

" '—and I switched it on. I explored every recess to make certain that the place was untenanted, and at last, satisfied, I returned to where I had left the bathchair; but it seemed to me that it would be easier to reconnoiter without it, so I left it where it was and ran noiselessly through the gate of the sports ground and over the grass. As I approached the wall of the sunk garden I slackened speed. The pit of my stomach felt cold. My throat was dry. My knees knocked together. Moistening my lips and ready to die with apprehension, I approached the gate. It was still unlocked. My nerve failed me. I turned and fled back to the gymnasium as though devils pursued me. I had seen the corpse once. I knew I should be sick if I saw it again.

" 'I reentered the gymnasium, dragged out the jumping-mats, and lay down on them. What I should do when morning came I did not know. I did not want to think about that. I hoped I should die during the hours of darkness. I did not die, and the harsh fiber of the mats worked through my suit and pricked my skin. I slid off them and lay down on the boarded floor. There was a shocking draft.

" 'Suddenly the hair rose on the back of my head. Someone was fumbling at the gymnasium door, which was still unlocked. The door opened and a woman came in, but hesitatingly because it was so dark, I suppose. I took heart, thinking it was probably one of the maids keeping an appointment with her young man. If I kept quiet neither of them would ever know I was there. I lay still in the darkness, trying not to breathe. To my amazement the woman shut the door behind her, grunted, and apparently, from the sounds, sat down on the floor with her back against the ribstalls. I heard a slight rustling sound now and again as she shifted her position for the sake of comfort, and perhaps five minutes went by. Then I heard another grunt, a

more pronounced rustling, and the flame of a match spurted up in the blackness. It lit up the woman's face. ... It was my sister.' "

"His sister?" exclaimed Bloxham.

"And his accomplice, apparently," said Mrs. Bradley. "He goes on to say:
" 'I knew my sister was a plucky girl. I had had ample proof of it—' "

"Yes, when she tackled him in Priscilla Yeomond's bedroom," said Bloxham. "He was very much impressed then by her pluck, I remember."

" '—and I determined to trust her with my frightful secret and see what she could suggest. Needless to say, I was amazed to see her—' "

"I bet he was. I wonder what she came to the gymnasium for?" chuckled Bloxham.

" '—and I called her by her name and said my own, distinctly, but very quietly. Then, when she had overcome her first sense of fright at being suddenly addressed by name out of the darkness, I crept near to her, and told her everything, including my abominable cowardice in leaving the body where it was. She laughed, and said that we must certainly recover it, and without delay, for in little more than an hour it would be daylight.

" 'We wheeled the bathchair round the cinder track once more and left it beside the gate of the sunk garden. Then she and I went in and knelt beside the unfinished goldfish pond and rolled back the heavy tarpaulin. I could feel the hard shape of the murdered man beneath my hands. My sleeve caught on a button of his coat, and, in attempting, with a jerk of terror, to get free, I moved him and fell forward on his stiff, cold body. My face touched his. ...

" 'It was so beastly dark. We shuddered, fumbling, but at last we raised him up and carried him between us to the waiting chair. My sister took his head. She said, "I'm wearing the most frightful waterproof. Nobody has seen me in it. If the head bleeds against it I can chuck it away, and no one need ever connect it with me." We did throw it away later. It is in the third pollard willow on the house side of the mere, pushed well down into the hollow trunk. At the time of writing no one has discovered it. We are not sure whether it is marked with blood.' "

"Might go and look for that. Obliging of him to give us a clue for nothing," said Bloxham, "although it's only corroborative evidence now."

" 'We had brought one of the thick gymnasium ropes with us,' " continued Mrs. Bradley, " 'and when we had propped the body in the bathchair as well as we were able—for he had gone rather stiff—we passed the rope as many times round him as it would go. We sawed it in two later with my sister's pocketknife and hid the pieces. Two days later I threw them into the rainwater butt outside the woodshed door. They have been found since, of course. The knife my sister also threw away, where I do not know, but we both judged it safer to be rid of it.' "

"That's funny," said Bloxham thoughtfully.

"Is it?" asked Mrs. Bradley, but not as though the remark had held any significance for her.

"Go on, please," said Bloxham, after a pause.

" 'We wheeled the bathchair to the lake, and laid the body on the ground. My sister said, "Will he float?" I did not know. I had an idea that dead bodies did float. I had an unpleasant recollection of the corpse of a dog I had seen in a canal. …

" 'She said, "How shall we get him out into the middle?"

" 'By the time she had worked out the answer and we had got the two clothes-lines from their hooks in the woodshed, the door of which we forced open with her pocketknife—that was before she threw it away, of course—' "

"Damn that rascal Herring!" said Bloxham explosively. "He didn't say a word to me about the door having been forced!"

"It doesn't make much difference," Mrs. Bradley answered soothingly, "because the description which follows here of how they tied the wrists of the corpse together and strung it up on the clotheslines which the flight of the javelin had carried across the lake from one willow tree to the other, and then of how they cut the line, when the corpse stopped at the knot in the middle—all this is so much like the idea which I sketched out for you some weeks ago that I can go on, if you like, to another part of the manuscript."

"I want to hear about the little mermaid," said Bloxham.

Mrs. Bradley obligingly turned over two pages of writing and ran her eye down a third.

"Here we are," she said.

" 'The body sank to the bottom, to our great joy. It was getting light enough to see things by this time. My sister said, "Can you get into your hut without waking the other occupant? Because, if so, you had better do so. I shall go back to the sunk garden, and pretend I'm out for a very early morning stroll if anyone sees me. Good-bye. See you at breakfast." ' "

"I'd never have thought it of Celia Brown-Jenkins," said Bloxham, laughing in spite of himself. "Still, I know she has plenty of nerve."

"Oh, plenty," Mrs. Bradley agreed enthusiastically

"Well, what about the little mermaid?" said the inspector. He knocked out and refilled his pipe.

"Oh, that?" Mrs. Bradley returned to the manuscript.

" 'It was further suggested by my sister that she should take the bathchair back to the shed, go next to the house to reconnoiter, and, it necessary, draw the fire of whoever discovered her. As she argued, the murdered man might not be missed until much later in the morning, and it was less suspicious in any case for her to be found wandering about at an unseemly hour than that I should be discovered doing so. "After all," said she in her logical way, "you are the murderer. I'm not."

" 'Thus we parted. I was to count a thousand slowly, and if by that time nothing had happened I was to stroll gently, and as though in rapt contemplation of the beauties of the morning, to my hut, and, if possible, to enter it undetected. If Yeomond awoke, however—' "

"Hah! Yeomond!" said Bloxham interestedly.

" '—I was to have been for a walk at dawn,' " Mrs. Bradley continued, without noticing the interruption. " 'My sister said, "After all, you murdered the man at about ten o'clock last night. Nobody ought to connect that with anything that happens at nearly five o'clock in the morning. Put a bold face on it and think about Caesar Borgia."

" 'I had just begun counting the ninth hundred when I saw her returning. In her arms she was holding one of the statues from the sunk garden. I could not decide which one it was until she came much nearer.

" ' "You know," she said, "we're very careless. We left that tarpaulin rolled back, and there are some very obvious bloodstains. Luckily the new cement had set quite hard and the body seems to have left no other impression. I thought I'd drown this, though. It is a terrible thing. Look at it!"

" 'It was the statue of the little mermaid. It had never appealed to me very much, but my sister seemed to regard it with such extreme aversion that to oblige her I helped her to put it in the middle of the lake just over the place where we had dumped the body. My sister then stripped off her clothes, leapt in, and fastened statue and corpse together. She dried herself on one of the towels that are kept in a laundry basket in the bathing-shed and resumed her garments. She then returned to the sunk garden and I to my hut. Very fortunately Yeomond is a sound sleeper. I removed my clothes and put on my pajamas. Then I looked over every inch of my garments for bloodstains, or other evidence of the night's work. There were none. I began to put on my trousers again with a good deal of unostentatious noise. It is not easy to make a good deal of unostentatious noise merely by getting into one's trousers, so I deliberately overbalanced and cannoned heavily against Yeomond's bed. This had the desired effect of waking him, and his immediate and indelible impression was of his roommate just getting up in the morning. I learned afterwards that my sister's ruse was also entirely successful. Nobody seemed to question a word she said.' "

"I say, they cut it rather fine," said Bloxham, as Mrs. Bradley put down the papers. "Why, I should think that just about the time they first left the gymnasium Amaris Cowes must have entered the grounds. They were lucky she didn't spot them, weren't they? Is that the end? I suppose he's signed it?"

"He confesses to the second murder, too," said Mrs. Bradley. Bloxham, impatient of listening, held out his hand for the papers.

"Does he, by Jove!" he exclaimed.

Mrs. Bradley relinquished her hold on the manuscript, and smiled like an

alligator that has enjoyed a satisfying meal.

"Perhaps you had better read the next part for yourself," she said. "He becomes rather scathing on the subject of the police. I fancy that he did not admire your methods."

Bloxham laughed.

"Can't say I was excited by 'em myself," he said. "But we seem to have got the goods now."

He read on, with his mouth puckered into a rueful smile and his brows knit.

"Oh, here's the second murder," he said. "Seems to have had a pretty hefty motive this time!"

"Yes," said Mrs. Bradley. "The whole thing was premeditated. He knew that Anthony had accompanied Kost to the lecture, and he knew enough of Kost's habits to be pretty certain that Anthony would come home alone."

"Interesting about the Roman swords," said Bloxham. "It seems that Anthony was the person who exchanged them and took the statue's sword to Colonel Digot's place in return for borrowing the real Roman *gladius*—"

"No. The model of a Roman *gladius,*" Mrs. Bradley interpolated. "Made of best steel, that dreadful weapon, and had edges like those of razors."

Bloxham read on with growing interest. "By Jove!" he exclaimed. "Do listen to this!"

Mrs. Bradley nodded, although she almost knew the entire confession by heart.

" 'From nine o'clock onwards I waited with growing impatience for the return of Anthony," read the inspector. " 'I had excused myself from table, for dinner that evening was unendurably protracted, and I stood on the terrace in the darkness waiting for the sound of his steps. He had to die. He had spoken his own doom three days before by accusing me of the murder of Jacob Hobson and citing my sister as my accomplice. He could not have known the truth of what he said. He had invented it. It was probably part of his ridiculous policy in attempting to scare us away from Longer. One with the bloodstained javelin and that rubbish. For all I knew, he was going to call the others in the house and accuse them and their sisters of participation in the crime also. My alarm came from the fact that in our own case the accusation happened to be true! Besides, I feared that sinister little old woman at the Digots. Long before she wrote to me I knew she knew. I would have killed her had I dared. She has been playing cat and mouse with me for weeks! I have seen it in those terrible black eyes—the eyes of a soulless bird of prey. I have seen it in her dreadful, mocking smile. I believe she is the devil.' "

"Your charms don't seem to have appealed to the champion cyclist," said Bloxham, laughing.

"Oh, very few young men really appreciate me," said Mrs. Bradley, grinning. "Their sisters usually prove to be far better judges of character than they are. Do go on. The whole literary style of the passage gains so much from your masculine interpretation of its beauties."

Bloxham looked at her suspiciously, but Mrs. Bradley's face was grave. He snorted, and continued:

" 'It was an awful mistake only to score the exact two hundred at the fair.' "

"What was that?" he demanded, looking up.

"Oh, darts," said Mrs. Bradley, waving her unsavory-looking hands. "Such a neat murder. Such a neat score. Just enough done to obtain the desired result in both cases. What the police would call"—she rolled her birdlike black eyes as though searching for the words—"er—corroborative evidence. But *do* go on. I am enjoying this so much!"

Bloxham cleared his throat.

" 'At last I heard him coming. I went out to the gate of the sunk garden to meet him. It was Anthony all right. And alone.

" ' "Hi, you!" I said, affecting to be overcome by wine.

" 'He stopped and shone his torch into my face.

" ' "Oh, it's you, Crippen, old duck," he said, giving me a slight push. I staggered as a drunken man might do, and clutched at him as though to save myself from falling.

" ' "Dear old fella," I said, clinging affectionately to his arm. "Dear old fella." And, still clinging to him, I led him towards the statue of the gladiator.

" ' "Betcha can't push that chap and make him hold your arm, dear old fella," I said, with a realistic hiccup.

" ' "You're nicely canned, boy," Anthony said, "And *because* you're nicely canned I'll show you something really interesting because you won't remember it in the morning."

" 'It was then that he reached up and unhitched the gladiator's sword.

" ' "Don't try and shave with it," he said, and he put in into my hands. It was heavy and keen. I stuck it into the heap of gravel the builders had left and held on to him more firmly. He himself had chosen the weapon for his death. Good. I would use it. I said to him:

" ' "Betcher can't pot his helmet with a stone from the other side of this heap of gravel." I lurched against him as I spoke.

" 'We both shone our torches on to the gravel and picked out two smooth large pebbles of good weight.

" ' "What do you bet, you mutt?" said Anthony. He was always hard up.

" ' "Five to one in fivers," I said. He insisted on writing it down and having me sign it.

" ' "Now, not a row," he said. "You first." I raised my stone as a man gets the weight into position before he puts it from him. Then I lowered it.

" ' "It's understood no chucking," I said, with another drunken hiccup. "Gentlemen don't throw. They put. Put and take."

" ' "Yes, not half," said Anthony. "You put and I'll take—twenty-five pounds, boy! Go on."

" 'I put the stone in my best manner, but of course in the darkness I missed my footing and stumbled in the middle of my movement. The shot went wide. Anthony used his torch freely to find out the limitations of our imaginary putting circle, and then took up his position.

" 'I took up mine. The *gladius* was now in my grasp. I had the torch in my other hand.

" 'There is a point in the action required for putting the shot when the athlete turns completely round, so that his feet are pointing in the opposite direction from that in which they started. It was this turn, and the moment of releasing the shot, that I was waiting for.

" 'At the first sound of movement, I switched on my torch. I must make no mistake. ... Have you ever seen a man put the shot? Anthony hurled his body on to the point of the keen-bladed *gladius* as I held it true. Nothing could save him. He did not even cry out. The stone flew wide. He would have lost the wager, anyway. I lost my own balance with the force of the impact, and for a minute or two we both lay still there— he the dead and I the living man.' "

Bloxham looked up, puzzled.

"But this puts the murder of Anthony too early," he said. "He wasn't killed until eleven forty-three."

Mrs. Bradley cackled.

"You remind me of the staff officer during the war who said the position of the front-line trenches was wrong because it did not agree with his map," she observed.

Bloxham grinned.

"I suppose I must read on to find the answer," he said, with his usual admirable good humor. He scanned the page, and then turned over."

"Ah, he goes straight on to make the point clear," he said, and continued to read aloud.

" 'My next problem was to hide the body. The courtesy of the landscape gardener's men in having dumped the gravel there a day or two before made the point easy of solution. There was even a spade to hand. Anthony, of course, had fallen across the heap, as I had planned he should. I made a shallow grave beside him very hastily, for time was precious, and to prove an alibi important. Then I placed my foot on his body, and after a tug or two drew out the sword and replaced it on the arm of the statue when I had cleaned it by wiping it on Anthony's clothing. Some blood probably flowed from the death-wound, but it must have soaked into the heap and been cov-

ered up by the fresh, unstained gravel which I shoveled in on top of the grave.

" 'Next I sought out my devoted sister and laid my case before her. Although suitably horrified at the thought of a second murder, she agreed that my personal safety probably depended upon the commission of the violent deed, and conceived what I believe to be the idea of a lifetime. She said, "Go with one of the others to his hut. Remain with him for the rest of the evening. Go on remaining with him. Make yourself as complete an alibi as you can, because at about a quarter to twelve tonight *Timon Anthony will come home!*"

" 'We discussed the plan for ten minutes longer. I then sought out Hilary Yeomond, and, after helping him remake his bed—the maids never turn the mattresses!—I invited him up to the house to play chess with me until the noises at the gate of the sunk garden proved that my sister had kept her word. We had previously arranged the business of setting fire to Yeomond's hut to cover ourselves if necessary.' "

Bloxham's mouth fell open. He put down the papers and gazed at Mrs. Bradley with a face that was almost ludicrous in its expression of shocked amazement.

"Setting fire to Yeomond's hut? But—but *that* was those Cowes!" he stated blankly.

Mrs. Bradley nodded.

CHAPTER XXI

Mrs. Bradley Takes the Bun

"BUT the confession wasn't signed," said Bloxham, "and he denied that he had written it. Still, we've got him tight enough, and he confessed all right to me when I'd arrested him. Funny he should have written that about the waterproof, though. We can't find it where he stated, but, even if we had, I see now why his sister was so certain nobody would connect it with her. *Of course* none of us had ever seen her in it! She's given us the slip, I'm thankful to say. Got away to South America."

"Thankful to say?" exclaimed the newly released Miss Caddick, opening her pale eyes wide.

"Yes, thankful to say," repeated Bloxham firmly. "That girl did nothing except try and keep her wretched brother out of taking the consequences of his crimes. I'm glad she got away with it. I still can't make out, though," he continued, turning to Mrs. Bradley—for the four of them, together with Clive and Celia Brown-Jenkins, Priscilla Yeomond and the Digot family, were at tea—"how you got to know enough about things to force that confession from him—"

"Which he denies having written," said Mrs. Bradley, with her eldritch chuckle.

"Yes, dear Mrs. Bradley," said Miss Caddick, tenderly stroking Mrs. Bradley's yellow and black jumper sleeve, "do tell us how you knew that Mr. Kost and I were not the wicked culprits."

Mrs. Bradley peered into her cup.

"A flight of arrows and a heart—no, two hearts," she remarked abstractedly. Kost and the erstwhile companion-secretary, who was now a lady of independent means, for old Mrs. Puddequet had obligingly unbelted the twenty-five thousand in a singularly sporting manner, exchanged loving glances and a gentle pressure of the foot beneath the chaperonage of the tea-table at which both were seated.

"Yes, you will recount to us, perhaps, your splendid methods," said Kost politely.

"My methods?" said Mrs. Bradley. "Well. I began by considering the most unusual feature of the case. That, of course, was the drowning of the little mermaid. After all, to have filled the corpse's pockets with stones would have served the murderer's purpose. Who would have chosen to sacrifice the

189

statue? It was a frightful piece of work, judged as art. Was there an artist among those concerned? There was. Amaris Cowes. The rest was easy, and only required to be put to the proof. The disturbances at one o'clock on that Saturday morning were part of the practical jokes played by Timon Anthony. The body could have been put into the lake more easily in the light of day, or, at any rate, in the half-light of dawn, than in darkness, or even in the moonlight. Well, Amaris Cowes turned up at the house about an hour before dawn. That was the first point on which I disagreed with the inspector"—she grinned at him—"for, although Amaris Cowes could not have been the murderer, she could have been, and in fact she was, the accomplice.

"Whom would she have consented to help in such a matter at such extremely short notice? I gathered from Margaret here that the three branches of the Puddequet tree were not even on ordinary nodding terms with one another. It must have been her brother, then, whom she helped.

"I could not convince the inspector about Amaris Cowes. I did try. As for Richard, his second alibi was really foolproof. The thing that I asked myself over and over again was where on earth Anthony could have been between the time Mr. Kost went into the public house and the time that awful noise went on outside the sunk garden. As I could think of nothing else, I concluded that Anthony had been killed much earlier than had been supposed by the police, and that the noise at the gate was a blind. You remember," she added, turning to Bloxham, "I demonstrated to you how it would have been possible for Amaris Cowes, immediately she heard her brother and Hilary Yeomond shouting from the terrace, to run round the house and get to Miss Caddick's bedroom door by using the back staircase."

Bloxham nodded.

"That brought me back to Richard Cowes again," said Mrs. Bradley briefly, "and the business of burning down Hilary Yeomond's hut."

"Did you know of the existence of the S.P.P.I.?" said Rex Digot. "I've found out that there really is such a society, but Richard Cowes is not the president of it. I suppose it was just his vanity which made him say in his confession that he was."

Mrs. Bradley grimaced horribly. Then she said:

"I suppose you all believe that that written confession was genuine?"

"Well, he's confessed the whole thing, verbally, to me since," said Bloxham.

"My dear lady!" exclaimed Colonel Digot. "Genuine! Why, just look into the facts for yourself!"

Mrs. Bradley laughed, and, reaching out a skinny claw, she seized a currant-bun from the cake-stand and regarded it with rapture.

"I *have* looked into them," she said, "and I came to the conclusion that, if somebody had to be hanged, it might as well be the real murderer and not our friend Kost. Therefore, at the midhour of night, when all the world was sleep-

ing, I took pen and paper and a good deal of thought, and wrote in my best copperplate the Confessions of Richard Cowes. After all, he himself told you in the little sitting room that day that he had committed both the murders, but you would not believe him!"

THE END

About the Rue Morgue Press

"Rue Morgue Press is the old-mystery lover's best friend, reprinting high quality books from the 1930s and '40s."
—*Ellery Queen's Mystery Magazine*

Since 1997, the Rue Morgue Press has reprinted scores of traditional mysteries, the kind of books that were the hallmark of the Golden Age of detective fiction. Authors reprinted or to be reprinted by the Rue Morgue include Catherine Aird, Delano Ames, H. C. Bailey, Morris Bishop, Nicholas Blake, Dorothy Bowers, Pamela Branch, Joanna Cannan, John Dickson Carr, Glyn Carr, Torrey Chanslor, Clyde B. Clason, Joan Coggin, Manning Coles, Lucy Cores, Frances Crane, Norbert Davis, Elizabeth Dean, Carter Dickson, Eilis Dillon, Michael Gilbert, Constance & Gwenyth Little, Marlys Millhiser, Gladys Mitchell, James Norman, Stuart Palmer, Craig Rice, Kelley Roos, Charlotte Murray Russell, Maureen Sarsfield, Margaret Scherf, Juanita Sheridan and Colin Watson..

To suggest titles or to receive a catalog of Rue Morgue Press books write 87 Lone Tree Lane, Lyons, Colorado 80540, telephone 800-699-6214, or check out our website, www.ruemorguepress.com, which lists complete descriptions of all of our titles, along with lengthy biographies of our writer

About Gladys Mitchell

Although some contemporary critics lumped Gladys Mitchell (1901-1983) with Agatha Christie and Dorothy L. Sayers as the "big three" of English women mystery writers, fewer than a third of her 67 books featuring Mrs. Bradley were published in the United States during her lifetime. But if she was not as well known on this side of the Atlantic as Sayers or Christie (or Ngaio Marsh, Margery Allingham, Patricia Wentworth, Josephine Tey, or Georgette Heyer for that matter), there was much in her prodigious output that has stood the test of tiime. In 1933 she became the 31st member of The Detection Club. In 1976, she was awarded the Crime Writers' Association's Silver Dagger.

During most of her writing career, Mitchell also taught English, history and games at various British public (here called private) schools. Her interest in athletics led to her membership in the British Olympic Association.

For more information on Mitchell and Mrs. Bradley please see Tom & Enid Schantz' introduction to The Rue Morgue Press edition of *Death at the Opera.*

Cast of Characters

Great-aunt Matilda Puddequet. A very rich, very ill-tempered, very old lady. She has decided that her grandnephews should compete athletically for an inheritance.

Godfrey Yeomond. Her n   than money.

Malpas Yeomond, Fran   **nd Hilary Yeomand.** Godfrey's four children, in   est.

Miss Myra Caddick. Mrs. Puddequet's   d companion, a pale, angular woman with romantic dreams. She has other expectations as well.

Clive Brown-Jenkins, the son of Godfrey's sister Mary, who is in competition with his own sons for Mrs. Puddequet's money.

Celia Brown-Jenkins. Clive's sister. Like Priscilla, she's just along for the ride.

Dick Cowes. Another cousin, also in competition for the inheritance.

Amaris Cowes. His sister, a Chelsea art student with bold bohemian ways.

Timon Anthony. Mrs. Puddequet's adopted grandson from a later marriage. Because he aspires to be an actor, he's naturally been written out of her will.

Joseph Herring. Known as the Scrounger, he is the old lady's churlish attendant.

Ludwig Kost. The trainer, a blond, stocky, handsome young athlete who has been hired to coach the grandnephews in various field sports.

Jacob Hobson. A loutish, abusive villager who comes to a bad end.

Janey Hobson. His wife, who doesn't mourn his passing.

Inspector Bloxham. He is perplexed at every turn of the investigation.

Mrs. Beatrice Lestrange Bradley. A noted psychoanalyst, who is visiting in the area and ends up guiding Bloxham's investigation.

The Digots. Her hosts. Their daughter **Margaret** is a friend of Priscilla Yeomond and their son **Rex** agrees to assist Mrs. Bradley in the investigation.

Mrs. Macbrae. Mrs. Puddequet's cook, every bit as irascible as her mistress.

Sir Bertram Palley. The Chief Constable.

Plus assorted servants, police officials, and villagers.